Advance Praise

"Set on a classic British estate just after World War I and brimming with local characters and high-bred horses, *All Men Glad and Wise* will have you turning pages until midnight and rooting for Harry Green, the precocious young groom investigating a murder. Yet author Laura Stevenson has created far more than a wonderfully old-fashioned whodunnit—think Agatha Christie meets *Remains of the Day*—skillfully weaving the social tumult and psychological damage of 'the war to end all wars,' exposing a corrupt regime's insidious classism and sexism, Stevenson illuminates an England in ragged transition. Stevenson's crisp, spare prose is effortless to read—like 4 o'clock tea, but steeped with pathos and humanity. I sincerely hope we'll be reading more of Harry Green's adventures."

–Melanie Finn, author of *The Underneath* and *The Hare*

"Laura Stevenson's *All Men Glad and Wise* is both a page-turning murder mystery and a fascinating glimpse into life in the Cotswolds area of England in the last century. Taking place when issues of class, background, and gender kept people 'in their place,' Stevenson's knowledge of horses—and horsemanship—add depth and interest to the story. The story begins in the spring of 1919, when England is recovering from the devastation of World War I and a global pandemic. The truth of young Harry's identity adds intrigue, while Harry's experience of grief and loss reverberates into our own time. A captivating read!"

—Liza Ketchum, author of *The Last Garden: A Memoir* and 17 books for children and young adults

"Laura Stevenson creates a protagonist whose story proves as fascinating in its unravelling as the intricately woven plot of this murder mystery. As you careen toward its immensely satisfying conclusion, you'll long to see Harry ride the magnificent horse Errant into a sequel to this 'ripping' tale."

–Janis Bellow-Freedman, professor of literature, Tufts University

"*All Men Glad and Wise* is a thoroughly engaging murder mystery set in the English countryside after World War I. It's also a moving exploration of issues we confront a century later. Encountering them in this earlier setting offers a surprising perspective. Stevenson gives us Harry, a stable lad, consummate rider, and self-appointed detective, who decides to unmask a murderer using their powers of observation and bold intelligence. The mystery is embedded in a time of terrible loss and chaotic change after the War, and the uneasiness of a society moving out of centuries of rigid class structure and economic immobility. We experience all this through the caring heart and eyes of Harry. As we do, the challenges and opportunities of changing technologies and fractures in longstanding class and gender roles take hold of us in a new way. Harry's tale reveals an unexpected past, but it also seems to pry the future open, even as it leaves questions unanswered. Harry is watched closely by several adults who offer the reader role models for the respect and support young people deserve as they face a world of unknowns. This book is a delight, opening us to the past and the present."

–Scudder Parker, author of *Safe as Lightning*

"Fourteen-year-old Harry Green knows horses. Trained under England's most gifted horseman in the years before the Great War, Harry's tenderness with both the animals and a visiting child on the once-grand estate of Willingford Hall is rooted in strength, wisdom, and grief, as well as love for family. Having discovered the steward of the Hall dead in the woods, Harry knows who to summon, and how to pay attention to the grudges and motives swirling through the estate. Harry's own secret, a matter of identity, can't be kept much longer. Scrutiny from the estate's men and women may force a revelation that will shift life's choices forever.

In Laura Stevenson's experienced hands, this historical mystery of drastic loss and change in a war-torn nation focuses intently on the painful growth that adolescence invites. Taking risks on and off horseback, Harry hunts the murderer in order to save Willingford Hall's workers and their rurally nurtured dignity from the invasion of a harsh new world. Harry's safety, the freedom of mourning families, and at last the survival of Willingford Hall itself depend on reading the horses and the humans with an accuracy grown from loyalty and love."

–Beth Kanell, author of *The Long Shadow*, *This Ardent Flame*, and four other mysteries and novels about Vermont's past

"*All Men Glad and Wise* is a delightful book for all readers who enjoy a very good story, beautifully told. Set in Oxfordshire, England after the first World War, the book offers an intriguing mystery full of twists and turns, a poignant account of coming of age in another era, and a glimpse into a lost world. Stevenson details with sensitivity and insight a time and place where horses and horsemanship were critically important to daily life, and where bad characters and evil actions could prove to be as challenging to a young person as the perils and complexities of growing up. Highly recommended!"

–Reeve Lindbergh, author of *Two Lives* and *Under A Wing*

All Men Glad and Wise

All Men Glad and Wise

A Mystery

Laura C. Stevenson

Rootstock Publishing
Montpelier, VT

First Printing: April 2022

All Men Glad and Wises, Copyright © 2022 Laura Stevenson

Release Date: April 19, 2022

Hardcover ISBN: 978-1-57869-080-0
Softcover ISBN: 978-1-57869-079-4
eBook ISBN: 978-1-57869-087-9

Library of Congress Control Number: 2021917274

Published by Rootstock Publishing
an imprint of Multicultural Media, Inc.
27 Main Street, Suite 6
Montpelier, VT 05602 USA

www.rootstockpublishing.com

info@rootstockpublishing.com

Interior and cover design by Eddie Vincent, ENC Graphic Services
(ed.vincent@encirclepub.com)

Cover art credit: Shutterstock

Printed in the USA

For permissions or to schedule an author interview, contact the author at:
lstevemarlboro@gmail.com.

To Arthur And Lynda Copeland
And The Friendship Of A Lifetime

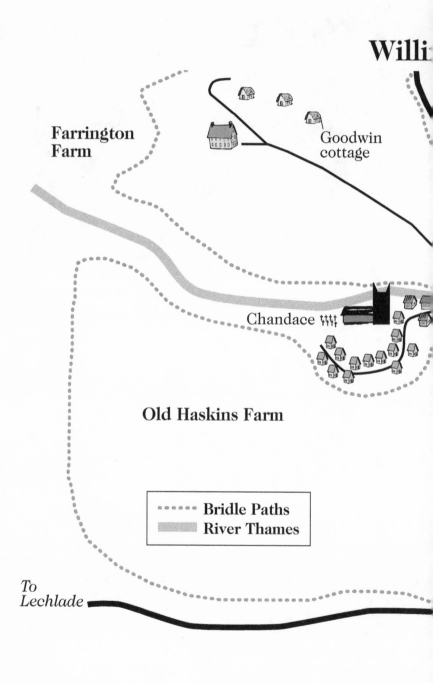

l Hall

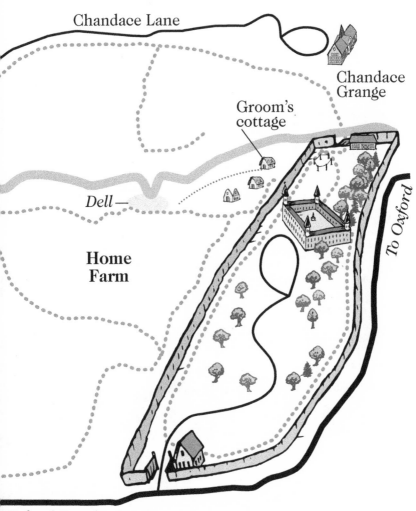

Chandace Grange Farm

Chandace Lane

Chandace
Grange

Groom's
cottage

Dell —

**Home
Farm**

To Oxford

Oxford Road

Cast of Characters

At Willingford Hall, 1919, Oxfordshire, England
Sir Thomas Chandace Willingford, ninth baronet, b. 1864
Hugh Chandace Willingford, his son, d. 1917
Administrative staff:
John Vanter, steward
Edmund Lovejoy, a friend of Hugh's in the Signals Corp during WWI, and newly appointed agent
Stable:
Harry Green, stable lad and narrator
Edward Green, head groom and Harry's father
Edith Haddon Green, Harry's "Mum," d. 1918
Household Servants:
Mrs. Baggum, housekeeper
Mr. Parks, butler
Mrs. Middleton, cook
Polly and Mary, housemaids
Agatha, scullery maid

At Sir Thomas Chandace Willingford's Estate, 2000 acres
The Home Farm, directly under Sir Thomas's supervision
The Farrington Farm, leased to Farmer Robert Farrington
Chandace Grange, leased at no cost to John Vanter as part of his steward salary
The Haskins Farm of 500 acres, sold to Henry Norton after Armistice, 1918, being developed

Laborers

Barth Goodwin, plowman for Home Farm, father of ten children

Nellie, d. 1904 and five other daughters; Henry, Charles and Will, all d. 1917

Jimmy, 10 years old

Mrs. Goodwin, Barth Goodwin's wife and mother of ten

Joey Rushdale, retired Haskins Farm plowman, now Sir Thomas's mechanic and chauffeur

In Chandace Village

Dr. Joseph Baines and his wife Lucinda

Lady Sylvia St. John, daughter of the Earl of Atherton, guest of the Baineses

Lord Sandford, whose title is a recent one, called Sandy by his friends

Reverend Herbert Williams, pastor of St. Barnabas church

Richard Williams, Reverend Williams' son and WWI veteran

Mr. Johnson, owner and proprietor of The Chandace Arms

In Town

Henry Norton, wealthy brewer

Emily Norton, his wife

Cyril Norton, their young son

Geoff Hutchins, Norton's chauffeur

John Dunster, Norton's secretary/agent

The navvies, laborers clearing the Haskins Farm for Norton's new bungalows

The navvy minders, who keep them in line

Chief Police Officer Edward Morgan

Officer Tim Jenkins, once Hugh's secretary, a 1917 amputee

Mr. Davis, coroner

Earth might be fair, and all men glad and wise.
Age after age their tragic empires rise,
Built while they dream, and in that dreaming weep,
Would man but wake from out his haunted sleep,
Earth might be fair and all men glad and wise.

Clifford Bax, "Turn Back, O Man," 1916

Chapter 1

The steward of Willingford Hall was murdered in the Dell on 12 March 1919. I found his body because I'd been thrown by a horse.

It's difficult to say which event was more unlikely.

To begin with, Willingford Hall was the last place in Oxfordshire one would expect to find a steward murdered in a wood. The estate had seen no violence since the 1640's, when Howard Willingford, a wool merchant, had joined King Charles's cavalry against the Roundheads—a service for which he was made a baronet and married to the daughter of the Earl of Chandace after the Restoration sorted everything out.

Subsequently, generations of Chandace-Willingfords had served the Crown by sending their sons and horses overseas to hold off Louis XIV, Napoleon, and the Kaiser, but Willingford Hall itself had straddled the peaceful upper Thames with nothing but an occasional ale-soaked scuffle at The Chandace Arms to lend its days variety.

As for my fall—I was taught to ride by Hugh Chandace-Willingford, England's most gifted horseman, which means I had grown up learning to move with a horse, anticipate its feelings, and school it so tactfully that it wouldn't resist my demands. Consequently, by the time I was ten, the other stable lads began to say not just "The horse doesn't live that can throw Hugh Chandace-Willingford," but "The horse doesn't live that can throw Harry Green." Hugh and my father, Willingford Hall's Head Groom, were pleased, but they knew as well as I did that no horse had thrown me chiefly because I'd never let a situation develop that would give it an occasion to.

Unfortunately, this particular situation had been beyond my control.

*　*　*

I was returning to the Hall along the bridle path from Chandace village, where I'd just delivered a note from Sir Thomas, the current baronet, to his friend Reverend Williams. I was riding Errant, Hugh's magnificent gray, and as we trotted between the newly blooming hedgerows, I was laughing at him, because he snorted ferociously every time we passed lambs and watched with satisfaction as they skittered away, their little tails twitching.

When we reached the Dell, his ears shot forward and, not seeing anything, I looked up the rise towards the Hall. A boy had just climbed the stile where the footpath crossed the track. As he paused to watch us, I saw he was Jimmy Goodwin, whose dearest wish was to become a stable lad like me.

Showing off is, of course, despicable, but I could feel Errant's muscles gather themselves expectantly, and there seemed no reason not to touch him with my heel. He broke into a collected canter, asking but not demanding to go faster, and just as I was reveling in his power and grace, he suddenly slid to a halt, reared, and spun into the hedgerow. Tearing away, he bucked furiously, as if some monster had dropped onto his neck.

A flash of color in the wood made him rear and spin once more, causing me a fatal moment of imbalance, and when he crashed back down and bucked, I pitched over his ears.

I struggled to my feet, groggily dodging his trampling hooves as well as I could, but my head spun so fast that I was near falling again, when Jimmy, who could run like a hare, appeared by my side and tore the reins from my hand.

"Ush, ush," he said softly, following Errant's frantic plunging up the track. "K'mathee, k'mathee."

Errant paused, shaking, and one ear swiveled forward. Slowly, Jimmy stepped towards him, his right hand outstretched. Glancing again towards the wood, the horse reared and struck out. Jimmy merely moved to the side and kept crooning, "K'mathee, k'mathee."

The phrase was one Jimmy's father used with the great, solemn work horses that worked Willingford Hall's Home Farm, and its familiarity, along with Jimmy's gentle voice and steady hand, gradually had an effect. Errant came to a halt, and after a last fearful look towards the wood, he dropped his head.

I limped towards them stiffly. "In good time," I croaked. "Thank you."

Jimmy's thin face was filled with worry. "You're bleeding, Harry!"

The warm trickle down my temple told me he was right, but it was easily wiped away with my hand, and though my steps were shaky, I knew there was nothing to worry about. "I'm well enough," I said. "But if Errant is hurt ... ! Did you see anything?"

"I was too far off," he said. "But see there." He pointed to Errant's sweating neck. I looked and saw a still-swelling welt that couldn't possibly have been caused by an insect. Only his heavy mane had kept whatever had caused it from leaving an open wound.

I looked at it in horror. "What ... ? How ... ?"

"Someone must've flang a stone at him. There's lumps like that when lads toss rocks to make the calves run."

"A stone!" I looked from the soft woodland soil to the smooth surface of the bridle path and the early cow parsley at its edge. Not a stone in sight—no, wait! Twenty feet away, I saw something lying amongst Errant's trampling tracks. I limped back and picked it up: a stone some three inches long, an inch thick, and completely smooth. I held it out to Jimmy, who had followed.

He had to look quickly, because the way Errant was staring into the wood threatened another outburst, but it took only a glance to see that whoever had thrown it had brought it from the river. "Criminal!" he said angrily. "Wish we could've catched him."

I looked at Errant's listening ears. "Maybe we still can!" I said, and in spite of my sore head and hip, I darted into the wood.

Behind me, Jimmy's warning shout made me hesitate, but just as I was about to turn around, I saw a heap of clothes lying a few paces ahead. Tweeds. A gentleman's country cap. I tiptoed forward through the eerie silence, ready to run if somebody appeared, until I stood beside it.

It wasn't a heap. It was a man, but it couldn't be the man who had thrown the stone at Errant. He was lying on his side, the back of his head smashed in by something much heavier than a three-inch rock. I crouched down painfully and felt for his pulse to see if there was any chance of life. There wasn't.

Chapter 2

I stood up, shaking. Not shocked by death—the Spanish Influenza had hardened most of us to that. Shocked by *who* was dead: a man I'd hated, heart and soul.

"God forgive me," I whispered as flies began to settle on his familiar, contorted face. I stared at the empty eyes, remembering all the times I'd thought how I'd celebrate if something terrible happened to him. But surely, I hadn't wished for . . . Surely even if I had, that couldn't have caused . . . I shook the thoughts out of my aching head and limped back to the track where Jimmy was anxiously walking Errant back and forth.

"Mr. Vanter is lying in the wood," I said as calmly as I could. "He's dead."

Jimmy's pale face went several shades lighter. "Dead! For certain?"

Somehow, I couldn't bring myself to say yes. "See for yourself," I answered, taking Errant's reins.

Jimmy disappeared into the wood. I listened as his light step hurried forward, slowed, hesitated, stopped, and then ran back, bringing him to the track with terror in his eyes. "He's murdered!"

I nodded.

He ran a hand through his cowlicky hair. "What are we to do, Harry? Fetch Sir Thomas?"

"No," I said. "We need the police, and that means finding somebody with a telephone. If you can run to the stable and help my father with the feeding, tell him I'll be late. I'll ride back to

Chandace and ask Dr. Baines to call them."

"Police!" Jimmy's eyes widened. "The police on Sir Thomas's lond!"

"Sir Thomas is a magistrate. One of the things magistrates do is work with the police," I said, hoping I was right. "My father will tell Sir Thomas once the horses are fed. So. Will you go?"

He nodded. Then, after watching me painfully reach up to ease Errant's reins back over his head, he offered me a leg up. I accepted the necessity with shame, for my skill at vaulting on was the talk of the estate. As Jimmy ran back up the hill, I turned Errant the way we had come. He trotted obediently, but uneasily and with no more snorting at lambs.

Dr. Baines and his wife lived in one of the pretty houses near St. Barnabas Church. As we turned into the lane, I saw that their motor was gone and there was no smoke coming from their chimney. I pulled Errant up, trying to think what I should do. Reverend Williams was not a possibility; the organ music that floated through the quiet air told me that he was conducting evensong, and though Richard, his son, was sure to be home, he'd lived shut up in his room since he'd come home from France.

The only other telephone in the village was at The Chandace Arms. I was reluctantly turning Errant towards it when I heard a motor leave the North Road. As it rounded the corner, I saw with great relief that it was carrying Dr. and Mrs. Baines and a lady I had never seen before. The doctor stopped beside me, and the two ladies leapt out, leaving him to put the motor in its place.

"Harry!" said Mrs. Baines. "What on earth has happened to you?"

"Mr. Vanter has been . . ." I paused over the dreadful word, recalling that some ladies fainted at news like mine. "Mr. Vanter has been hurt. I found him in Willingford Dell. If you could please telephone the police, I think they should come."

The two ladies looked at each other, and the one that I didn't know said, "If there was an accident in Willingford Dell, shouldn't Sir Thomas be called first?"

Mrs. Baines smiled as she moved lightly towards the gate. "Willingford Hall has no telephone," she explained over her shoulder. "Sir Thomas won't hear of it—Joseph, come quickly!"

Dr. Baines hurried into the lane, taking off his driving gloves. "What is it? Why, Harry! You're in a bad way! Let me look at that gash!"

"It's nothing, sir," I said. "Just a scratch."

He insisted, however, that I dismount and sit on the wall. To my surprise, the lady I didn't know took Errant's reins with a practiced hand and walked him up and down the lane.

"Look," she said, as they returned to the spot where Dr. Baines was still investigating my aching head. "This glorious horse has been struck, too."

"Someone threw a stone at him," I said. "It frightened him, but it won't leave a mark. The important thing is that Mr. Vanter has been hit on the back of the head in Willingford Dell, and if you would please telephone the police . . ."

"I just telephoned them, Harry," said Mrs. Baines, hurrying out with a bowl of warm water, a cloth, and a bottle of Mercurochrome. "They'll come immediately."

"They can't get to the Dell in their motor," I said. "Perhaps I should show—"

"—there's no difficulty," said Mrs. Baines. "Officer Jenkins said he knows where the Dell is and how to get there."

"And I'll go myself," said Dr. Baines, expertly cleaning my forehead. "If Vanter has a head wound, he'll need immediate attention."

"I think, sir . . ." I glanced at the ladies, but they showed no sign of fainting. "I believe he is beyond attention."

The doctor started. "He's dead?"

"Yes, sir."

"Dead—and you and your horse are injured? You haven't told us all that happened, Harry!"

I told them, swallowing my annoyance at their relief that Jimmy could confirm my story. There was no mistaking their concern. As Dr. Baines dabbed Mercurochrome on my forehead, he glanced at his wife. "Can you come with me in the motor and leave me by the footpath to the Dell?" he said. "Even if there is nothing to be done, the police will need a medical opinion for the coroner." He turned to me. "There, Harry—you're fit to ride home, I think."

"Certainly, sir."

"Game lad. Tell your father to let you rest a little, if it's possible. The police will want to talk to you this evening."

"Yes, sir." I paused before turning to tighten Errant's girth, which the lady had loosened. "Will they be talking to Jimmy Goodwin, too, sir?"

"Yes," he said, frowning. "Somebody should warn him. Will he be at the stable?"

I glanced at the St. Barnabas clock. "They should have finished feeding by now. He may have started home. It's four miles to walk since Mr. Vanter evicted them."

Dr. Baines pursed his lips. "I hope a good many men saw Barth Goodwin and his horses in the fields this afternoon," he said grimly.

"Don't think such thoughts!" said his wife indignantly. "Mr. Lovejoy says there's hardly a man on Sir Thomas's land who *doesn't* wish John Vanter ill. As for Jimmy, Lady Sylvia and I will find him after we let you off." Turning to her friend, she added, "The Goodwins have had more than their share of trouble—the eviction worsened Mrs. Goodwin's case of influenza, and the family lost three sons at Passchendaele. "

"Were the sons in Hugh's regiment?" asked the lady.

"The cream of it, to hear Richard talk," said Mrs. Baines. She sighed. "Today must have been a terrible reminder of all those village lads for a boy of . . . how old is Jimmy now, Harry?"

"Nearly eleven, ma'am."

"And you, Harry?"

"Coming up fifteen, ma'am." That was stretching it; I'd turned fourteen in December.

"Fifteen counts as a man grown these days," remarked the doctor as he boosted me into the saddle. As he watched me settle Errant, his professional expression changed into a careworn smile. "Bless you, lad—and take the high road. We need no more accidents in the Dell."

I almost argued, for the lorry traffic to and from the building site of the new bungalows planned for the Hawkins Farm had so hardened the high road that it risked injuring a horse's legs to ride on it at more than a walk. But I was grateful for his kindness, so I nodded, touched my sore forehead to the three of them, and rode Errant slowly home.

*   *   *

Willingford Hall's stable was one of the finest in Oxfordshire. It wasn't so grand as Blenheim's, of course, but anybody who knew anything about stables remarked on the quality of the Amsterdam clinkers on its floor, its hardwood mangers, and its splendid harness room. The original stable had been built in the eighteenth century. Half its twenty stalls were loose boxes; the rest were roomy straight stalls along a vaulted arcade with ornate plastered ceilings. When the Hall was brought up to modern standards at the time of the Diamond Jubilee, it had been given what Hugh had called invention's greatest gift to stables: electric light.

As for the horses, they were the best England could offer, and after Hugh returned from his Grand Tour with two Viennese brood mares and a passion for haute école, he'd planned to cross our English horses with the best in Europe. Between those horses and Hugh's skills, we—the stable, that is—had become a center for a new school of English riding, and we were never without visitors. My father had an assistant groom and five lads beneath him, not counting me, and they all expected to serve in the best stables in the midlands. Everybody knew the care we gave our horses was beyond compare.

I tried not to think of that as I turned Errant into the courtyard, but I couldn't forget how much had been lost. Not the stable itself, of course. It was still immaculately kept, and the care we gave our horses was still up to my father's exacting standard. But the horses—the brood mares, the carriage horses, Sir Thomas's hunters, Hugh's Irish Thoroughbred, the pony on which I had learned to ride, the useful cob to which I had been promoted, the Clydesdale team that worked the Home Farm, and the well-schooled hacks Sir Thomas and Hugh kept for their guests—had all been requisitioned in 1914 and sent to France. Not one of them had come home to us.

We were supposed to take comfort in the knowledge that they'd died for England and duty, like Hugh's regiment, but the knowledge often deserted me when I passed the silent, empty stalls under the silent, empty loft where the stable lads had slept. And felt Hugh's absence, everywhere, everywhere.

There were only five horses living in the midst of all that silence. Two of them had been colts in 1914—Errant and Sebilla, out of the Viennese mares. Two—Pip and Squeak, the Home Farm team—rightfully belonged to Barth Goodwin and were staying with us only because of Mr. Vanter's unjust eviction. The fifth was Atlas, a cart horse my father had found starving in a barn after its master died of influenza. My father still hoped Sir Thomas would replace the carriage horses, but I doubted it. He'd kept Hugh's motor (a Lanchester, he called it), and after he'd sold the Haskins Farm, he'd engaged Joey Rushdale, who'd been its plowman, to be his chauffeur.

Sir Thomas hadn't ridden since Hugh died. People said it was because he'd been so ill with influenza, but he'd been mending for several weeks and hadn't so much as set a foot in the stable that he'd once visited each morning.

As I rode into the courtyard, the great clock struck the quarter hour, and glancing at it, I saw that by the time I had put Errant up, dinner in the servants' hall would have ended. Perhaps, I thought, wearily sliding to the ground, my father would tell Mrs. Middleton I had been held up, and she would save me a bite or two.

"As for you," I told Errant, stroking his face as he rubbed his head affectionately against my shoulder, "I'm about to make you the best mash I know. You're a hero."

"You can water him first," said my father's voice. "You've brought him in cool."

I turned to him in surprise. "I thought you'd be at dinner."

"At dinner, eh? When Jimmy Goodwin's brought word that a horse and lad will be late coming in because they've been hurt in the Dell where the steward's been murdered?"

Even if the question had required an answer, surprise would have made me wordless. For instead of immediately looking Errant over, my father inspected me, from the gash on my forehead to the dirty spot on my breeches. "You had quite a fall," he said.

"I'm sorry, sir. I got unbalanced, and—"

"—No disgrace, Harry. Jimmy said it was a miracle you kept your seat as long as you did. He'd never seen a horse in such a panic. I've seen superb riders go off at times like that."

"Truly?" I said, with silent thanks to Jimmy.

"Truly," he answered. "Thanks to the good Lord, you've come away with nothing worse than bruises."

He stepped closer to Errant. "Now, as for this fellow." Parting Errant's mane gently, he whistled when he saw the size of the welt. "No wonder he panicked! Why, Jimmy said it was just a matter of a stone!"

"I found nothing else," I said, drawing the stone from my pouch. "It was lying on the track, but see? It came from the river."

He turned it over in his hand, his thick eyebrows coming together. "Did Errant shy before he was hit?"

"No, sir. He was cantering, and then he ... just exploded."

"Remind me: do the branches from those old oaks in the Dell overhang the track?"

"No, sir. The wood begins ten paces away, and the branches are still mostly bare."

"Ten paces. And you saw nothing?"

"I thought I saw something flash when Errant was bucking, but it might only have been a bird."

"Odds it was the villain running off, knowing you'd be distracted." He looked at the stone again. "What puzzles me is that, to raise a welt like that, the stone had to have been thrown very hard indeed. He must have been as close as he was vicious. And what did you do but run into the wood to catch him, young fool!"

"I was angry about Errant, sir."

"You never considered that a monster who would stone a horse and lad would think nothing of killing you?"

"Not until afterwards, sir, or I would never have let Jimmy go in to look." I glanced at him and caught something close to a smile. "But there seemed to be no danger, sir. Not a sound. Just Mr. Vanter, lying with his head coshed—"

"—no need to go into it. Jimmy told me. The Lord pardon me, but if it weren't such a terrible thing, I'd have trouble feeling regret. As it is . . ." He shook his head. "I'm glad you're safe home, Harry. I'll water this horse and put a cold cloth on that welt, if he'll let me, while you make him a mash. Then we'll see what Mrs. Middleton will give us in return for the news she's surely waiting to hear. I had to tell Parks why I needed to talk to Sir Thomas, so the whole servants' hall is no doubt abuzz."

"It'll be more abuzz soon. Dr. Baines said the police will want to talk to me."

"I'm sure they will," he said, leading Errant to the fountain. "All the more reason to eat before they come."

*   *   *

Sir Thomas had never resumed eating a formal dinner after his long illness. He satisfied himself, though not Mrs. Middleton or Mr. Parks, with a substantial tea in his library and nothing thereafter except a little brandy before he retired. There was, accordingly, a lull in the kitchen after the servants had eaten dinner, and when my father and I entered, Mrs. Middleton was sitting at the long table with a cup of tea in the company of Mr. Parks and Mrs. Baggum, the housekeeper. Not surprisingly, given the circumstances, the two housemaids, Mary and Polly, managed to find business in the kitchen within minutes of our arrival, and Agatha, whom I knew from the village school, looked out from the scullery.

Mr. Parks kept his usual butler's countenance, but the women exclaimed over my forehead—as well they might, for, as the dim mirror in the groom's quarters had shown me, my gash now stared out of an unsightly black and blue lump.

"Merciful heavens, look at you! —What a fall you've had! —It's a mercy you weren't killed, too! —Such a terrible thing for you to see! —Didn't I always say John Vanter would get his just de—"

"—Come, come," said Mr. Parks, interrupting the last comment. "Your talk will do the lad much less good than Mrs. Middleton's rhubarb custard pie."

"Rhubarb pie!" I breathed. There had been no fresh fruit, except a few oranges not good enough for Sir Thomas's table, since Christmas.

My enthusiasm made them laugh, and soon my father and I had sat down to mutton stew, tea and bread, with half a pie sitting not far away. My father's grace was longer than usual, and though I knew I should be thankful to my Maker, my thoughts slid to Jimmy, who had only bread, dripping, and thrice-boiled tea to brace him for his visit from the police.

The rhubarb custard pie was a rare treat, not only because of the rhubarb, but because Mrs. Middleton had been generous with the sugar in its custard. I would probably have eaten all that was left after my father served himself, but just as I finished what I'd hoped was only my first piece, we heard a crunch of tires on the sweep.

Mr. Parks hurried upstairs, and my father rose to his feet. "That will be the police," he said, scrutinizing me amidst the sensation caused by his words. "Wipe your mouth, lad, and straighten your jacket. It's important the police find all in order here."

I obeyed him, wishing—not for the first time—that the suit of livery I'd received at Christmas still covered my wrists, or that the growth that had made me lengthen my stirrups a hole had been accompanied by grace of movement.

It seemed a long time before Mr. Parks came back and said that Sir Thomas, Police Chief Morgan, and Deputy Jenkins would see me in the library. My father and I stepped forward together, but Mr. Parks raised a hand. "I'm sorry, Green," he said. "They wish to see only the lad."

The look I threw my father caught a flash of indignation and concern, but it quickly disappeared behind a mask of acquiescence. "Go ahead, Harry," he said. "Remember, think before you speak, and don't let their questions rattle you."

"Yes, sir," I said. And I followed Mr. Parks up the stairs.

Chapter 3

I had only a hazy idea of what lay beyond the green baize door at the top of the stairs, because though I'd worked in the shadow of Willingford Hall's great house all my life, I'd known only the stable and the Head Groom's cottage. Mum had made the cottage pretty and homey, and since Hugh was much fonder of my parents than he was of Sir Thomas—"my Victorian father," he'd called him— he'd used our cottage as his horsemanship base. Of course, Hugh had dined and slept at the Hall when he wasn't at Oxford or Vienna.

Since we ate at home, I'd hardly seen the servants' hall until Hugh and Mum died and my father had requested a move to the assistant groom's empty quarters, across the courtyard from the steward's office. But even after we'd started eating with the house servants, I'd never had occasion to go into Sir Thomas's part of the house.

While I'd known the servants' quarters were different from the Upstairs, I hadn't realized *how* different until that evening, when I followed Mr. Parks through the grand rooms that led to the library. Even though I was worried about seeing the police, I kept wanting to stop and look up through the dusk at the distant ceilings, or to peer at the shadowed paintings on the walls, or simply to stare at the elegant sofas, chairs, and tables that I passed.

I didn't do those things, of course, but *not* doing them distracted me so much that I had to remember myself quickly when Mr. Parks opened a door three times my height and said, "Harry Green, Sir Thomas."

I stepped into the room, blinking in the electric light and awed by the sight before me. "Library" to me meant the small collection of books Reverend Williams had assembled for the use of St. Barnabas's parishioners. Here, shelves of books with handsome bindings rose from the carpet on the floor to the ornate plaster ceiling thirty feet up, with a catwalk running along three walls so the volumes in the higher shelves could be reached. I was still staring at them when a nudge from Mr. Parks reminded me to bow.

I complied quickly, but when I stood straight again, I could hardly hide my surprise, for if I hadn't known that the gentleman sitting before the marble fireplace had to be Sir Thomas Chandace-Willingford, I wouldn't have recognized him. During the years I'd held his horse, he'd been a strict, imposing man; now he was somehow smaller, with shoulders bent forward. His face, which I remembered tanned by hours on horseback, had lost its color, and his hair, which had once been as dark as Hugh's, had gone gray. Only his eyes seemed familiar, and even they gave me pause, for he looked at me with confusion.

"*This* is Harry Green?" he asked Mr. Parks incredulously.

"Yes, sir," said Mr. Parks. "He has shot up since you've seen him last."

"Of course." Sir Thomas coughed several times and turned to the policemen who sat facing his chair. "Forgive me," he said. "My memory still plays me false now and again."

He nodded to Mr. Parks, who withdrew; then he beckoned to me. "Harry," he said, regaining the official voice I associated with him, "Officers Morgan and Jenkins have come to question you about your experience this afternoon. I am here not just as your employer but as the local Justice of the Peace. We need to know what you have seen. Your testimony is of utmost importance. I trust you are aware of that."

"I am, sir," I said. I turned to include the officers in my answer. The pudgy older one was unfamiliar to me, but I recognized the younger one as Tim Jenkins, who had served as Hugh's secretary before they'd both left for the Front. He was changed, too, his face much thinner and his right leg extended unnaturally before him. But he gave me a small smile before Officer Morgan demanded that I tell them what had happened.

When I'd told the tale in the servants' hall, I'd given it some dramatic flair, but Officer Morgan's dour scrutiny warned me to offer only a flat narrative, pausing now and then so Officer Jenkins, who was writing down everything I said, could keep up. "Then," I finished, "I sent Jimmy to the stables to ask my father to tell Sir Thomas, and I rode to Dr. Baines's house and asked him to telephone you."

"You acted with great presence of mind," said Sir Thomas, glancing at the others, and Officer Jenkins nodded in agreement.

Officer Morgan looked at me steadily. "You say you fell from your horse," he said. "Is the nasty gash on your forehead the result of that fall, or of . . . some other accident?"

"The fall, sir," I said in surprise.

"And in spite of that gash, you dashed into the wood and found Bailiff Vanter?"

"Yes, sir."

"And you are quite sure that Bailiff Vanter was dead when you found him?"

Don't let their questions rattle you, I told myself as I saw what he was implying. "Yes, sir."

"Tell me why you are sure."

"I felt for his pulse, sir. And there was none."

"I see." He leaned forward. "Now tell me. When you felt for Vanter's pulse, was his arm warm or cold?"

The question, I realized, was what Sir Thomas would call "of utmost importance," and as I strove to remember, I inwardly kicked myself for not having noticed something so essential. "So far as I recall, sir, his arm was cool to my touch, but not the cold of death."

Officer Morgan raised his eyebrows. "You're familiar with the cold of death?"

"Yes, sir. My mother died of influenza a year ago."

Sir Thomas lifted a hand, and Officer Jenkins stirred uncomfortably.

Seeing that, Officer Morgan sat back in his chair, but he kept both eyes on me. "Then you would say that Bailiff Vanter was murdered a very short time before you found him?"

"Yes, sir."

"Perhaps even after your horse threw you?"

Again, I resented his implication, but I answered him levelly. "I couldn't say, sir."

"You wouldn't even venture a guess?"

"No, sir," I said firmly. "I don't know how much time elapsed between my fall and my hurrying into the wood. And I don't know how long it takes a body to cool."

Officer Jenkins came very near to smiling, but Officer Morgan went on. "You said there was no sound when you found Vanter's body. Are you sure you heard no footsteps?"

"Absolutely, sir. I was listening very carefully because a few minutes before, Errant had become nervous again, and I thought he might have heard something."

"Ah. And what does the silence imply?"

"That whoever it was had left, sir."

"Not that he was hiding somewhere near you?"

"I think not, sir. I believe he threw the stone to distract me, and then escaped." Remembering my father's concerned face, I added, "I suspect that if the murderer had seen me find the body, he wouldn't have let me leave the Dell."

"Good God!" murmured Sir Thomas.

"Quite possibly," said Office Morgan. "Now, you're a perceptive lad. Tell me: how could he have left the Dell without being seen by you, Jimmy, and your horse?"

"By the river, sir. He'd come from there. The stone that hit Errant was rounded and smoothed."

"Was it?" he said. "That confirms our own observations. Your testimony has been very useful, and I am sure Jimmy Goodwin will support it. —Sir Thomas, can you tell us where to find the boy? There was no roof on the cottage where Jenkins expected his family to live."

I waited for Sir Thomas to answer, but as he looked questioningly at me, I said, "They live on the far side of the river, now, sir. Farmer Farrington has leased them another cottage."

Officer Jenkins frowned. "Goodwin no longer works on the Home Farm?"

"Oh, he still does," I said. "But—"

"—I'm the one who has to answer to this," said Sir Thomas. "And while I'd prefer not to tell the tale, it has considerable bearing on the case at hand." He paused, and Officer Morgan signaled Officer Jenkins to take notes. "In September of '17, Vanter advised me that he was about to relieve Barth Goodwin of his duties as plowman on the Home Farm and evict him from his cottage."

"On what grounds?" asked Officer Morgan as Sir Thomas paused to cough.

"According to Vanter, Goodwin's records of the Home Farm harvest contained errors that kept me from receiving adequate compensation for its corn." He sighed. "I had always thought Goodwin to be an honest man, and I knew Hugh was close to his family. It happened that Hugh was due to come home on leave, so I told Vanter to hold off until we had talked to Goodwin.

"Vanter was displeased, and when Hugh and I met with Goodwin, we saw why. Goodwin's so-called 'errors' suggested that Vanter was keeping a substantial portion of the income from the Home Farm corn for himself. Nothing could be proved in the time Hugh had, so he did his best to make peace between them. But just before he left, he suggested that I should replace Vanter with a bright young Signals chap he'd met at the Front, a London-trained accountant who would make me an honest steward."

Sir Thomas coughed again and looked bleakly across the room. "Dismissing a steward is a huge undertaking. It generally involves legal action, and in this case, it was complicated by a tenancy agreement:

Vanter had free lease of Chandace Grange as part of his payment. I thus decided to put off the unpleasant process until Hugh's next leave . . . only to be overwhelmed by Hugh's death and my illness.

"During those months, Vanter dismissed Goodwin, evicted him, and tore the roof off the cottage in which his family had lived for twenty years. Goodwin's wife was seriously ill with influenza at the time. The eviction so greatly slowed her recovery that she has been unable to work for the last year, thus depriving the family of much-needed income. Fortunately, Farmer Farrington had engaged Goodwin, so he was not destitute. As soon as I was fit to conduct business again, Ned Green told me of this injustice, and I re-engaged Goodwin for the Home Farm. Until my circumstances permit me to replace his cottage roof, however, he has to come here from a considerable distance."

"And so," said Office Morgan, "Barth Goodwin has a grudge against John Vanter."

I shivered, recalling that Dr. Baines had made much the same observation, but before Sir Thomas could reply, footsteps approached the door and Mr. Parks opened it.

"I'm sorry to disturb you, Sir Thomas," he said. "But Mr. Lovejoy wishes to see you. He says the matter is urgent."

Sir Thomas looked at the two policemen. "Lovejoy is the Signals chap Hugh wished me to hire as my steward. He has been in my employ for six weeks, his instructions being to audit Vanter's handling of my affairs. Perhaps you would find his testimony valuable. Yes? Very well." He coughed several times. "Show him in, Parks."

As the man behind Mr. Parks stepped into the room, I realized I'd seen him talking to Mr. Vanter occasionally, but without particularly noticing him. There was, in fact, not much noticeable about him: he was about Hugh's age, short and wiry, with mouse-brown hair and a face that was intelligent but not good-looking. His eyes took in the two policemen, but as he straightened out of a brief bow, he addressed Sir Thomas. "Good evening," he said. "I see you already know what I had come to discuss."

"Yes," said Sir Thomas. "This lad found Vanter in the Dell."

"So Baines told me, when I returned to Chandace," said Mr. Lovejoy.

"When was that?" asked Officer Morgan.

"The St. Barnabas clock was chiming half past six when I stopped by Baines's house."

"Where had you been?" asked Officer Morgan.

"Running," said Mr. Lovejoy, a little defensively.

"From what?"

Officer Jenkins laughed. "Not *from what*, sir," he said. "*Where to*, if he's a runner."

"Ah, of course," said Officer Morgan, without smiling. "Where to, then?"

"I don't know, exactly," said Mr. Lovejoy. "Instead of my usual run to Lechlade, I ran east to the point where the towpath jumps the river at a lock."

"That's a better run than Lechlade," remarked Officer Jenkins conversationally. "Good water birds, and hardly a soul in sight at this time of year. Hugh and I used to allow it two hours—from here, of course. It would be twenty minutes longer from Chandace."

Mr. Lovejoy nodded, his eyes meeting Officer Jenkins's with instant kinship, but Officer Morgan merely said, "So you were gone for two hours, twenty minutes?"

"Closer to three," said Mr. Lovejoy. "I had to do an errand for Baines along the way— and paid for it by running the last quarter hour in near dark."

"I see," said Officer Morgan, glancing at Officer Jenkins to be sure he had taken the information down. "Now, Sir Thomas says he has asked you to audit the accounts of John Vanter. Can you tell us a little about your discoveries?"

Mr. Lovejoy looked uncertainly at Sir Thomas.

"Don't hesitate on my account," said Sir Thomas brusquely. "I've already told the officers about my failure to dismiss Vanter after his mistreatment of Goodwin. And have a chair, man! You've some sixteen miles behind you, not to mention cycling here."

Mr. Lovejoy sat in a straight chair whose position allowed him to face all three men.

"Vanter's accounts begin in 1911, when Sir Thomas engaged him to deal with the new taxes that Lloyd George's People's Budget had added to the ones already bankrupting his fellow landowners. Under Hugh's supervision, his accounts were impeccable, and superficially they continued to be so after Hugh went overseas.

"But oddly enough, I found that those impeccable records showed Willingford Hall losing a great deal of money on corn during the War, when harvests were good and prices were the highest they'd been for years. Vanter told Sir Thomas it was a matter of the new taxes, but I thought of the way he'd treated Goodwin, so I talked at some length with Farmer Farrington and Joey Rushdale, who'd been plowman on the Hawkins farm.

"They showed me their own records which, like Goodwin's, proved Vanter was skimming off a substantial part of Sir Thomas's net income from both rents and agricultural profits, apparently taking it in cash before writing anything in the books. And they were much relieved that Sir Thomas was having the matter investigated. They had wished to speak up, but they had been intimidated by Vanter's retaliation against Goodwin."

"So, embezzlement," said Officer Morgan. "How much did he take?"

"About a third of the total," said Mr. Lovejoy. "A 'loss' so serious that during his illness, Sir Thomas allowed Vanter to arrange the sale of the Hawkins Farm to Henry Norton of Norton's Brewery."

The two officers exchanged enlightened glances. Though the sale of the Hawkins Farm was old news, the reason for it was still a subject of speculation in every pub and manor house between Cheltenham and Oxford.

"Vanter initially assured Sir Thomas that Norton would build himself a fine house on the Hawkins Farm but make no other changes. At the last moment, however, he removed the stipulation from the contract—"

"—and my punishment for failing to catch the subterfuge," interrupted Sir Thomas, "is having to watch the farm be torn apart by the gang of navvies Norton brought here from some railway cutting, and knowing I will soon have to watch a crew of slipshod builders throw together a hundred bungalows—each of which Norton will doubtless sell at double the price he paid for the whole. I need hardly tell you that his investment will permanently alter Chandace and its surroundings."

He coughed several times, then continued. "The prospect of that alteration so distressed Dr. Barnes and Reverend Williams that they begged me to hire Lovejoy to look into my affairs. And it's well that I complied, for only last week, Vanter came to see me with a long tale about my diminishing income, which he finished by making me an offer for the Farrington Farm."

"The Farrington Farm!" said Officer Jenkins. "I'd heard that Farrington wanted to make an offer himself!"

"He did make an offer," said Mr. Lovejoy. "But Vanter refused to pass it on, telling him Sir Thomas would want considerably more than what he could afford. At least, that's what Farrington said last Saturday night."

"You heard him say this?" asked Officer Morgan.

"Yes. At The Chandace Arms, where I'm lodged."

"Did you tell him Vanter had made an offer?"

"Yes. Not, of course, in front of his mates. I waited until he'd started home."

"What was his response?"

"As you would imagine, he was angry."

"Angry enough to murder the man who'd deceived him?"

Mr. Lovejoy smiled sardonically. "Fortunately for us all, it's possible to wish a man to the Devil without performing the introduction."

"Of course," said Officer Morgan. "But as you and Sir Thomas have told us, both Goodwin and Farrington had substantial motives for performing that introduction."

"No more reason than Sir Thomas or myself."

"Ah. So *you* disliked Vanter?"

"It's difficult to like a smooth-faced fellow who's rapaciously dishonest."

Officer Jenkins nodded emphatically, but Officer Morgan merely said, "You must have talked with Vanter several times. What was his manner? Courteous? Belligerent?"

"Courteous to the point of fawning at first; then defensive, and finally—well, not to put too fine a point on it, he ordered me out of his office this afternoon."

"Great heaven!" said Sir Thomas. "You should have told me, Lovejoy."

"I wanted to cool my temper first," said Mr. Lovejoy. "That's why I went for a run."

"A wise choice," said Officer Morgan.

Left to myself, I would have mistrusted Morgan's tone, but the others seemed not to mark it, and in any case, it was covered as Sir Thomas's mantel clock stuck nine.

The two officers rose to their feet. "Thank you very much for your time, gentlemen," said Officer Morgan. "I'm sure you will understand when I ask you to remain in Chandace and its environs until the inquest, and perhaps beyond."

"Of course," said Sir Thomas, ringing for Mr. Parks. "And tell the coroner—Davis, is it? —that if he needs my testimony at the inquest, I'll be happy to comply."

"Thank you," said Officer Morgan stiffly. "We value your cooperation."

Mr. Parks appeared (rather more quickly than I would have expected, given the distance from the butler's pantry), and the four of us were shown out.

As we passed through the grand rooms, their emptiness now dimly lit, the two officers were questioning Mr. Lovejoy about the quickest route to the Goodwins' cottage. I longed to ask them to wait until morning, for Jimmy and his father rose at four o'clock in order to walk to Willingford Hall and prepare the horses for work that began at six, but they gave me no chance to do so.

Chapter 4

I'd expected my father to be waiting for me in the servants' hall, but Mr. Parks said he had gone back to our quarters. As I crossed the courtyard, I realized the murder had spooked me: instead of acting as a beacon, the light from our window created weird highlights on the cobblestones and threatening shadows in the side passages. When an owl hooted, I nearly broke into a run. Fortunately, I managed not to burst through the door, for when I stepped in, I saw my father had fallen asleep on the settle.

A year ago, I would have awakened him and told him all about the interview . . . actually, no. A year ago, he would have been pacing up and down, firing questions so fast that I could scarcely answer them. Now when I looked at his sleeping face, I saw lines and graying hair that told of all the worry and sorrow he'd fought off in the past months. I paused on the mat, half wondering why I hadn't seen them before, half fearing that he would awaken and realize that I'd seen them at all. A snore assured me there was little chance of the latter, so having slipped off my boots, I tiptoed across the flagged floor, exchanged my livery for my ageing nightshirt, and sat heavily on my cot.

The straw mattress rustled invitingly, and my sore forehead and hip urged me to lie down, but my father's weary face had made me realize that he had long known what I had learned only tonight: that Willingford Hall was in a perilous state. I'd noticed changes, of course. Besides five horses in the stable instead of twenty, there were seven servants, including us, at dinner instead of fourteen; one gardener and a boy, Jimmy, instead of five.

Before tonight, though, I'd thought of these changes as merely temporary, assuming that with the War over, things would return to normal. Now, as I looked around our barren room, I realized with a shock that "normal" might very well be a Willingford Hall as lost to me as Hugh and the village men who had followed him to the Front.

Shivering, I realized Hugh had foreseen it five years ago, when we'd ridden through the estate for the last time before the army collected the horses, a few days before he'd left for the Front himself. "This is the end of everything," he'd told my father. "The end of estates, the end of the privileged few who live off the labors of the many, and the end of wealth that's based on the sweat of man and beast. "Peace has kept the whole wretched system alive long beyond its years; it can't survive a war. The landlords who own England are done for— and we *should* be done for. Cromwell saw that in 1650!"

He urged his mare into a canter up the rise. At the top he drew up, silently taking in the neatly squared-off fields of corn and sheep, the wood, the blue ribbon of the Thames. Finally, he looked back at us, shaking his head. "If only it weren't so damned beautiful."

My father had dismissed the moment as a fleeting expression of the socialistic politics that had made Hugh forbid everybody on his father's estate to call him "Master Hugh," "Mr. Chandace-Willingford," or even "sir." But that morning's passion hadn't been fleeting. He'd come home on leave advocating social equality more strongly than he had before. There had been a rumor at The Chandace Arms that he'd said Willingford Hall's four farms should each be divided into holdings of fifty to one hundred acres and sold to their tenants.

Though people had laughed and said even Hugh wouldn't be that crazy, the word "sold" had lingered in the air. And now, with Hugh dead and the baronetcy coming to an end, the Haskins Farm already gone, and financial difficulties as serious as tonight's discussion suggested, Sir Thomas had little reason to keep his struggling estate intact.

Or keep it at all.

I wrapped my blanket about me, though the room was no colder than usual. What would happen to us if Sir Thomas sold Willingford Hall altogether? My father had come to Willingford stable five years before the Queen's first Jubilee, starting as a lad of thirteen; his devotion to horses had brought him to the position of Head Groom before he turned thirty. He'd early identified and fostered Hugh's talents as a horseman, and, after the turn of the century, he'd joined Hugh in making the stable what it had become.

Distinguished service like that should have brought him honor. But even before the War, great estate owners had started exchanging their carriages for motors, and now mere gentlemen like Dr. Baines—even the police—had made motor travel part of their lives. If Sir Thomas sold the estate, what hope was there of finding another gentleman who would engage a 55-year-old groom?

As for me . . . I gripped my blanket more tightly as I looked at a future made unpredictable by a single, simple fact. Willingford Hall knew me as Harry the stable lad, but my true name was Harriet, and I was not a lad at all.

As Mum had explained my peculiar upbringing, she had lost five babies before she had me, so the whole estate had celebrated my successful arrival. But by the time good news had reached Sir Thomas, it had somehow acquired the assumption that I was a boy. Delighted, Sir Thomas had immediately sent a telegram to Hugh, who was studying haute école in Paris, and within hours, Hugh had cabled enthusiastic congratulations "to the parents of Willingford Stable's future Head Groom." Hearing this, my parents had hesitantly decided to let the assumption stand. My father had been particularly reluctant, but Mum had convinced him that if I were generally accepted as a boy, I would be able to prove myself as a horseman and perhaps even earn the groom's position in a way that would be impossible if I were known to be a girl.

The story had been so much a part of my life that I'd accepted the decision as normal—in part because its benefits were so obvious. I'd been introduced to the saddle (not a side saddle) before I could walk, and I'd spent hours in the stable while I was still in toddler's dresses.

Other advantages appeared once I was breeched. Instead of studying domestic arts with the girls at the village school, I'd learned history and mathematics with the boys. Instead of facing a dull, indoor life in domestic service, I'd looked forward to joining Hugh in making Willingford Hall the home of the finest stable in England. For years, in short, I'd been more than content to be the lad everybody assumed I was . . . until recent physical changes had made it increasingly difficult to keep up the subterfuge.

To be fair, I hadn't been *intended* to keep it up. Mum had promised that we would reveal my identity on my fourteenth birthday, and both she and my father assured me that Hugh would still welcome me as a future groom. I had never doubted that he would; I'd grown up hearing him argue that women deserved all the rights, positions, and privileges that were currently assumed to belong only to men.

I also knew that Hugh had returned my parents' many kindnesses to him by being kind to me. In addition to teaching me to ride, he'd taken me to Reverend Williams's library, lent me thrilling books of his own, and taught me mathematical games to occupy my mind as I performed my routine tasks.

But by the time my all-important fourteenth birthday had come, Mum and Hugh had died, and I knew without even asking that given the perilous condition of the estate, my father didn't dare take up my case with Sir Thomas. To admit that I was a girl would be to reveal that the Head Groom in whom Sir Thomas placed complete trust had been deceiving him for over fourteen years. The revelation wouldn't necessarily result in my father's dismissal, but it would certainly hurt Sir Thomas's pride—and as the whole manor knew, Sir Thomas's actions were unpredictable when his pride was wounded. The real danger, however, was that if Sir Thomas thought that my father's deception qualified years of otherwise faultless service, he would say so in any references the sale of Willingford Hall would require him to write to Father's prospective employers.

And yet, how could I go on as I had? I was tall and strong, and fortunately not what Hugh's gentleman friends had called "well endowed." But unlike the boys who had left school when I did, I had no signs of facial hair, and while I had trained my voice into its lowest registers, it was never going to break. Soon, the truth would emerge—and what would happen then? Without Mum, who could perhaps have helped me find some sort of position if Sir Thomas sold Willingford Hall, I had nobody to turn to.

Unless . . .

I sat up straight. I'd found Mr. Vanter's body and got Dr. Baines to call the police. Sir Thomas had said I'd acted with great presence of mind. Officer Morgan had said I was perceptive, something Hugh had always said about me, too. What if I *used* the presence of mind and perceptiveness they'd noticed to find out who had killed Mr. Vanter, while the police were still casting around for leads? Wouldn't that prove I was worth people's notice?

It might. No, it *would!* I'd make bloody well certain that it did. And then instead of being merely a girl with no experience in the kinds of service open to girls, I'd be Somebody. A girl who had foiled "the whole wretched system" that Hugh had deplored and whose brain and bravery had given her some say in her future. A girl worthy of Hugh's respect.

The clock in the courtyard, which had been chiming the quarter hours while I was reflecting, struck ten. Knowing that the next day would begin at five o'clock, I lay back, but I was so excited by my thoughts that I was sure I'd never sleep.

Chapter 5

My father shook me awake out of such thrilling dreams of sleuthing that they still hovered around me as I stumbled across the courtyard. The familiar chorus of nickers brought me to myself, and we had all the horses fed by the time Jimmy and his father appeared through the sun-lit morning mist.

Jimmy's sleepiness was visible from a distance; Goodwin's fatigue was so deeply ingrained in his face and movements that I could barely recall the cheerful man he'd been before the War. Yet their first concern on entering the barn was for me, Jimmy exclaiming at the spread of my bruise, and Goodwin taking my face between his enormous hands and examining my forehead.

"It's no fine sight, but it'll come right aater a bit," he said, smiling. "And Errant?"

"Come look," said Father. "He still has a lump, but it's not hot."

They walked to Errant's box, my father stocky and bustling, Goodwin tall, stooped and long-striding. Jimmy took the opportunity to whisper, "We had the police last night."

"What did they say?"

His eyebrows drew together. "They asked Dad where he'd been, who'd seen him—as if *anybody* couldn't tell them he'd *never* do something like that!"

"They did that to me, too," I said. "But they were just compiling evidence. I tried not to take it amiss."

"Dad took it greatly amiss," he said. "And Mum . . . I can't away with the way she cried after they were gone." He doubled his fists. "As if she hadn't more than her share of troubles already."

I nodded sadly, wishing I had been able to see Mrs. Goodwin lately. When the Goodwins had lived down the row from the Head Groom's cottage, she'd been an older version of Jimmy's beautiful and energetic sisters. But the loss of Jimmy's three brothers had left her pale and weary even before she'd suffered so much from influenza and the eviction. "Tell her the police must ask in order to be sure," I told Jimmy. "As soon as they talk to all the people who saw your father plowing yesterday, that will end it."

"Jimmy!" Goodwin's voice filled the stable, though it wasn't angry. "Come, fetch the horses out, lad! The day won't wait for us."

Jimmy started to move away, but I seized his shoulder and slipped him a chunk of bread and cheese I'd saved for him. He stowed it quickly in his tattered jacket and scurried off, embarrassed but too hungry to turn down an extra bite.

I shook my head, wishing he could eat an early breakfast in the servants' hall, but when I'd suggested the possibility to Mrs. Baggum, she'd refused outright and given me an earful as well. It seemed that Jimmy's eldest sister Nellie had been a junior parlor maid in the Hall, but she'd disgraced the household by getting into trouble. Mrs. Baggum, not content with sending her packing, had decided she couldn't trust any of the five younger Goodwin girls to serve at the Hall, and she had also managed to avoid all four boys.

Of course, I understood that dismissing a maid for misconduct was one of a housekeeper's duties, but I couldn't help thinking that neither Nellie's sisters nor Jimmy, who hadn't even been born yet, should have been penalized for Nellie's disgrace. To say so would have incensed Mrs. Baggum, so I'd heard out her indignation in silence. But someday, I told myself as I fetched the brushes, someday, after I'd solved the murder and become Somebody, I was going to fight injustice directly, as Hugh had, instead of raiding the larder.

The clock was striking six when Goodwin drove his great horses off to the fields and Jimmy hurried to the kitchen garden, where he'd pull weeds for an hour before starting the two-mile walk to school. I waved to them both; then I mucked the stalls, dumped the manure, brushed the floors, and wiped the windows clear of spider webs, a job my father insisted be done daily, to save work in the long run.

After breakfast, there were only bridles and saddles to clean before I could begin exercising the horses, and as I soaped and oiled the leather, I was looking forward to schooling Atlas, the half-draft carthorse. He had recovered from his understandable surprise at being ridden rather than driven, and he was becoming supple in a way that would have pleased Hugh, who had often argued that every horse, regardless of breeding or work, could benefit from basic dressage training.

While I was in the midst of these pleasant thoughts, I heard a motor approach the Hall and stop at the entrance. I knew better than to peek out and see who it was, but my thoughts slid from horses to the police, and from there to planning a visit to the Dell to look for evidence they surely had missed, because, as Mum had said again and again, "Men never notice things."

Two quarter hours later, the motor drove away, and I turned my attention back to the bridle that had somehow become idle in my hand. As I shamefacedly pieced it together, my father hurried through the door of the harness room. "Harry, Sir Thomas wishes to see you in the library."

"Whatever for?"

"Are you questioning Sir Thomas's wishes?" he said, raising his eyebrows ominously.

"No, sir."

"Good. Be sure to change your boots before you go."

"Yes, sir. Should I wear livery?"

He looked at me from head to foot. "No. Your shirt is clean. But comb your hair."

I changed out of my mucking boots into riding boots, did what

I could for my hair with a mane-and-tail comb, and hurried to the servants' hall, where Mr. Parks was waiting.

"Do you know what it is?" I asked as we climbed the stairs.

"I know only that Dr. Baines came to talk to Sir Thomas, and that he has now left."

We walked again through the deserted, elegant rooms, and in the morning light I saw a portrait of Hugh over the drawing room mantel. It must have been painted when he was little older than I, for his face was still boy-like, and he was holding a horse I didn't recognize. Even half-grown, he'd been strikingly handsome, with gray eyes that were somehow both gentle and rebellious. I blinked the mist out of my own eyes and hurried after Mr. Parks, arriving at the gigantic library door as he announced me.

Sir Thomas was sitting at his desk, a large book opened flat before him. He nodded as Mr. Parks closed the door, but he didn't acknowledge my bow, so I remained where I was, gazing at the beautifully shelved books while he ran his pen up and down columns of figures. After one or two minutes, his clock chimed, making him look up and cough.

"Ah, Harry," he said. "Come here, lad. I have something to tell you."

I walked across the considerable space that separated the door from his desk and stood on its far side, but he pointed to the delicate chair that stood next to it. I sat down gingerly, suddenly aware that my trousers were patched at the knee and that my shirt was made of thick cotton. At least their coarseness kept them from revealing my sex.

"The bruise around your gash is truly impressive," he remarked. "Is it painful?"

"Not very, sir."

"That's what Baines told me you would say," he said. "He visited me earlier this morning, and among other things, he asked me to send you to his house at teatime this afternoon so he can be sure no infection has started. You are to arrive there at four o'clock."

I managed not to ask why Dr. Baines hadn't crossed the courtyard and examined me in the stable. "Yes, sir. Will that be all, sir?"

"Not quite. Dr. Baines told me two other things. First, there will be an inquest at The Chandace Arms tomorrow morning at eleven, at which you will be required to testify under oath."

An inquest! I'd be able to hear all the testimony and make deductions of my own! "Yes, sir."

"The second thing—and I rather think it explains Dr. Baines's desire for your presence this afternoon—is that his examination of Vanter's body revealed that the man had been hit two times: once on the side of the head, resulting in temporary unconsciousness, and once, probably as he lay on the ground, on the back of the head with a cosh of some sort." He coughed several times before adding, "Harry, look at me."

I looked up, and his eyes, so like Hugh's, burned into mine. "Now," he said, "without looking away, can you assure me that the second blow was not given by you?"

His face told me there was something behind his question other than doubt. Puzzled, but reminding myself that I might soon be Somebody, I met his gaze levelly. "I can, sir."

He nodded. "So I thought. But the question may be asked of you again at the inquest tomorrow. Be prepared to answer it with the same directness you answered me."

"Yes, sir."

"And if Mr. Davis, the coroner, inquires into your feelings about Mr. Vanter, it would be circumspect of you to say merely that you respected him as the Hall's steward."

I raised my eyebrows. "Did you not say I will be under oath, sir?"

"I did indeed. But that doesn't mean you must incriminate yourself unnecessarily."

I considered. "Perhaps, sir, I could say I had had few direct dealings with Mr. Vanter. That would at least be true."

He came close to smiling. "That will do very well. Now, I am about to write a note for you to take to Dr. Baines. While I am so engaged, you may look over the books you were scanning so eagerly." He pointed directly behind me. "Start there."

I rose and moved to the bookshelves to which I'd been dismissed, smarting as I realized that Sir Thomas must have decided to test both my truthfulness and my mettle before the inquest. It was possible that he had done so in order to protect me, but I was stung by his lack of faith in me.

For some moments, my irritation obscured my appreciation of the books before me, but gradually, the gilded titles on the rich leather bindings took recognizable shape: an ornate small series of plays by William Shakespeare, followed by uniform sets of Anthony Trollope, Charles Dickens, George Eliot, Elizabeth Gaskell, Wilkie Collins, Edward Bulwer Lytton.

A few shelves over, I saw sets of more recent authors—Stevenson, Kipling, Barrie, Shaw, Doyle, Hope—some of whose works I had read at Hugh's suggestion and enjoyed a great deal. On higher shelves, I caught sight of names I didn't recognize: Hume, Berkeley, Locke, Newton. Finally, as I gazed up to the great tomes above the catwalk, I was struck both by what I didn't know and what I did—the latter, that a few of the bindings were beginning to crack and fray.

"You are frowning." Sir Thomas's voice made me jump. "You disapprove?"

"No, sir. I was just . . ." I broke off, realizing my thoughts had been above my place.

"Come, come. What were you *just* . . . ?"

His face, as I turned so I could see it, was as peremptory as usual, but also curious, so I took the liberty of saying, "I was just thinking, as any stable lad would, that the leather on many of the bindings needs attention."

He glanced up. "Some of the books up there are over three centuries old."

"All the more reason they should be preserved, sir."

His eyes came back to me. "You believe in preservation, eh?"

"They are beautiful books, sir."

"That does not quite answer the question I asked." His tone made me quiver.

"I was trying to keep to the subject at hand, sir."

"So you were," he said, with a smile that brought me great relief. "Very well. The subject at hand is the books on the second tier, whose bindings, in my father's day, were carefully preserved by a librarian. Ask Parks and Mrs. Baggum what preservative he might have used, endeavor to find some, and come here next Tuesday morning at eleven to engage in preservation."

I thanked heaven for *my* preservation. "Yes, sir." I waited for a dismissal, but he'd suddenly looked out the window, coughing. Following his glance, I saw my father cantering Sebilla along the bridle path that ran behind the house. As they disappeared, he turned back to me. "Is that one of Hugh's Viennese colts?"

"Yes, sir."

"The stallion or the gelding?"

"The gelding, sir. His name is Sebilla."

Sir Thomas tapped his fingers together. "Baines tells me that Vanter's tragedy will make it necessary for me to be more . . . present in the parish than I have been for some time. I have asked Rushdale to prepare the Lanchester to go out this afternoon, but it confines me to the high roads. Can you recommend one of the Austrians to me as a steady mount?"

"They are both young, sir," I said hesitantly. "And though they aren't skittish, they're full of spirit—"

"—and thus likely to kick up their heels during the first hour out," he said, adding sadly, "I used to enjoy that. But at present, I will have to motor."

A thought flashed into my mind. "There's Atlas, sir."

He raised his eyebrows. "Who might that be?"

"He's the horse my father found starving in a dead man's barn last winter. He's not highly bred, but good feed and light work have made him quite handsome, and he's as steady as any man could wish. My father and I often use him when we do errands, because if you knot his reins, he'll stand for up to an hour without being tied."

"Will he, indeed?" said Sir Thomas. "Well, perhaps some morning I will come to the stable and see for myself." He rang for Mr. Parks and went back to his desk, and I went back to the stable with good news to give my father when he returned.

Chapter 6

That afternoon, my father and I agreed that I shouldn't ride Errant to Chandace. The track past the Dell was one we used often, and it would be a great nuisance if, by riding Errant there when yesterday's panic was still fresh in his mind, I encouraged him to develop a permanent fear of the spot. Furthermore, he became impatient if he had to stand for more than a minute, and that would create difficulties if Dr. Baines wanted to talk to me for any length of time. Accordingly, I groomed Atlas and set off.

As we approached the Dell, I slowed to a walk and began to collect evidence. The distance of the old oaks from the track was ten paces, just as I'd told my father. Although their branches extended a considerable way from their massive trunks, they were still bare, so they couldn't have hidden the movement involved in throwing a stone, which Errant surely would have seen. I halted Atlas at the place where Errant's chaotic hoof-prints still marked up the track and peered into the shadows.

Two blows. I could see why Dr. Baines and Sir Thomas had been concerned. Mr. Vanter's body had been perhaps twenty paces past the first oaks. I hadn't seen it until I was almost upon it. But would the murderer, coming from the river, have known it couldn't be seen from the track? If he'd heard hoof-beats after he'd stunned Mr. Vanter, wasn't it possible that he'd panicked, run towards the sound, thrown the stone, then bunked, leaving Mr. Vanter for me to murder?

To think otherwise was to suppose that both blows had been given before hearing Errant—in which case, why bother to throw the stone before escaping? Alternately, one had to suppose that in the space of a very few minutes, the murderer had knocked Mr. Vanter senseless, run twenty paces, thrown a stone with great force without being seen, run back, coshed his victim, and slipped away so quickly that there was not a sound to be heard when I rushed into the wood.

I frowned, considering these two unlikely alternatives and trying to imagine a third. I wished I dared ride into the wood, but that would make me arrive at Dr. Baines's house after Sir Thomas's appointed hour. Consequently, I rode on at Atlas's tireless trot, alternately thinking of the murder and wondering what Dr. Baines could possibly have to say to me.

We arrived with Atlas cool, having walked the last half mile, just as the great clock on St. Barnabas's tower started to chime the hour. To my surprise, the Baineses and Lady Sylvia were already at their gate, grouped around a large motor with a stocky young chauffeur in front and a fair-haired gentleman, a fragile lady, and a restless little boy in the back.

I drew up, quickly running my eye over the group. The lady in the motor was wearing a pelisse and the kind of afternoon dress I'd learned to associate with ladies before the War—a great contrast to Mrs. Baines's rose-colored frock, which fell only to the top of her ankles, or Lady Sylvia's perfectly-fitting blue dress, whose hem floated around her calves.

The gentleman was impeccably dressed, but the material of his coat was not as fine as Sir Thomas's, and he wore it with none of Hugh's careless ease. By the time I'd dismounted and bowed to the whole party, I felt fairly confident the people in the motor were not the Baines's guests, but simply acquaintances who had stopped by on their way to some other destination.

Dr. Baines greeted me with a laugh. "It's comforting to know that despite war and pestilence, everything at Willingford Hall still runs according to the clock," he said.

The man looked at me with seeing eyes for the first time. "You are one of Sir Thomas's servants, eh?"

"His stable lad, sir."

His reply was forestalled by his son, who tugged on Dr. Baines's sleeve. "Is the servant here about the big bruise on his forehead?"

"Cyril!" said his mother, making him sit down.

"He is, as a matter of fact," said Dr. Baines. "It and the gash in its center come from the lad's connection with yesterday's tragedy."

The big man smiled. "What tragedy can possibly have affected this lovely village?"

"Good heavens!" said Lady Sylvia. "Lechlade must be further off than I think, if you haven't yet heard of Mr. Vanter's accident."

"Accident?" The man's eyebrows drew together; his wife gasped; Cyril and the chauffeur leaned forward with rapt attention.

"Yes," said Dr. Baines. "Harry, here, found him lying in the Dell, cudgeled by some marauder."

"I trust he's recovering well," said the man, his face full of concern.

"I'm afraid not," said Dr. Baines. "There will be an inquest tomorrow."

A small sound made us look at the lady, who had turned deathly pale and slumped back, just as I'd expected Mrs. Baines and Lady Sylvia to do the evening before. The two women hurried to her side of the motor, Lady Sylvia drawing smelling salts from some pocket hidden in her frock. "Here, Emily," she said, with no hint of impatience. "One whiff and you'll be yourself again."

I was wondering at Lady Sylvia's use of the lady's Christian name when Cyril leaned dangerously far out of the motor's open window. "Did he cudgel you, too?" he asked me eagerly.

"No," I said. And hoping to avoid the next question, I asked his father, "Would Cyril like a ride on this horse?"

The man nodded, fighting his evident annoyance at his wife's reaction, but Cyril drew back indignantly as I offered to lift him the rest of the way out the window. "That's *Master* Cyril to you," he said.

Dr. Baines looked up sharply from the lady, who by then was coming to her senses, but Cyril's father laughed in a way that told me to smile and say, "Indeed it is, Master Cyril. Would you like to ride Atlas, here?"

"Can I make him gallop?"

"No. A boy can't ride a horse at a gallop until he has learned to ride him at a walk." Seeing him pout, I added, "But walking is the first step to galloping later on."

He considered for a few seconds; then he held out his arms. I lifted him into the saddle, and my concerns about urging feet and flapping hands were immediately quelled. Obviously intimidated by the size of the creature beneath him, the boy grabbed for the mane and even gave his father a worried look.

"Excellent," I said to reassure them both. "The first thing a true horseman feels is respect for the power of his horse. Now, Master Cyril, sit up straight—very good. Here we go."

Atlas, bless him, walked with supreme care, and little by little, Cyril sat straighter and began to move with him. "Excellent," I said. "You have a natural seat."

He looked at me with such vulnerable happiness that I suddenly liked him. "Do I really?"

"You do indeed. If you were to keep riding, in a year, you could ride anywhere you wanted on a horse like this."

"Like Sir Lancelot and Sir Galahad?"

I smiled. "Like Sir Lancelot and Sir Galahad when they were boys. You can't become a knight until you're . . . say, sixteen. In the meantime, you practice and practice."

"Is that what they did?"

"Absolutely. You don't read about it in the stories because everybody takes it for granted."

We finished our circle and drew up by the motor, where the others, excepting Cyril's father and Dr. Baines, who were talking earnestly, watched us with interest. I lifted the boy down, and he grinned hugely.

"That was ripping!" he said, and seeing that his mother had recovered, he began to tell her about the whole adventure.

As I backed Atlas away from the motor, Lady Sylvia gave me a most unladylike smile and wink. "Well done, Harry."

My reply was covered by the man's slightly raised voice. "Lovejoy, you say? Will he be at the inquest tomorrow? Excellent. Perhaps I will come myself if my business allows. Thank you very much, Baines. Good afternoon, ladies." He bowed slightly. "You are gems in a perfect foil—All right, Hutchins."

Dr. Baines drew a breath or two as the enormous motor negotiated the corner past St. Barnabas. "Well," he said finally, "rumors about Norton's business sense seem to be true. Others may speculate on the murderer's identity or blindly accuse the navvies without realizing that they work in fear of their minders—but no sooner does Norton hear of Vanter's death than he considers making Sir Thomas an offer on Chandace Grange."

"He'd do better to pay more attention to his wife," said Mrs. Baines.

Lady Sylvia shrugged. "He paid enough attention to stop his motor when she recognized 'Lady Sylvia,'" she said sardonically. "It was undoubtedly the possibility of such recognitions that made him give her permission to join the volunteer ladies at the Hospital. If, of course, he remembers giving it— Here, Harry, let me hold that handsome horse of yours while Dr. Baines examines you."

"Thank you, my lady," I said. "But he'll stand by himself."

"Goodness!" said Dr. Baines. "How did he learn such a trick?"

"He was a cart-horse, sir."

"Really?" Lady Sylvia eyed him critically. "Well, he may have pulled a cart, and his mother before him, but I'd say his father broke into the common."

It was an old horseman's joke, but I found myself blushing to hear it from a lady's mouth. Seeing that, she laughed, not unkindly. "I beg your pardon," she said. "My standards of conduct have been lowered by my years at the Front."

"The Front?" I said in bewilderment.

"Lady Sylvia and I both served as nurses in France," explained Mrs. Baines, adding, with an affectionate glance at her tall husband, "That's where Joseph and I met."

"Let me look at the lad's head before we begin conversation," said Dr. Baines. "Come into my surgery, Harry."

I knotted Atlas's reins, patted him, and followed the doctor into the house.

"Before you begin, sir," I said as he opened the surgery door, "Sir Thomas has sent you a note." I drew it out of the interior pocket of my jacket. "I apologize for not giving it to you earlier, but I didn't want to interrupt your conversation with Mr. Norton."

He took the letter but looked at me instead of opening it. "You know Norton?"

"No, sir. You mentioned his name after he left. It's familiar to everyone at the Hall because of the bungalows and the Hawkins farm."

"I see," he said, giving me a sharp glance. "Well, sit there while I look this over."

I sat obediently, my eyes roving around the room. It was filled with instruments vaguely familiar to me from the farrier's bag, all neatly laid out. In the corner nearest the window, I recognized a microscope from pictures I'd seen in the parish library's meager supply of medical books. I longed to look at it—and into it—but I knew I couldn't ask.

Behind me, paper rustled as Dr. Baines laid down Sir Thomas's note. Soon he'd crossed the room, examined the gash carefully, and gently touched it with more mercurochrome. "I'm sorry it stings," he said, as I winced. "But it prevents infection. The gash is healing well, and the bruise will soon fade. I doubt you'll even have a scar."

"Thank you, sir."

He looked at me seriously. "You're fortunate to have gotten off so lightly. It was a brutal murder, and Sir Thomas told me this morning that Vanter's body was still warm when you discovered it."

"I'm not certain, sir. I didn't think to notice at the time, and my memory may have been faulty."

He shook his head. "If he had been cold—or in a state of rigor mortis—you would have noticed."

I nodded, shivering as I thought of the soundless wood. "May I ask a question, sir?"

"Of course."

"Is it possible that Mr. Vanter was knocked out in one place, carried to the Dell, and murdered there?"

He started. "Why do you ask?"

"When I was riding here, sir, I began to wonder how Mr. Vanter had gotten to the Dell."

"The police assumed he and his assailant arrived together, by boat."

"Yes, sir. But it seems odd that Mr. Vanter would have taken a boat to the Dell when it's less than a mile from the steward's office in the Hall on the footpath that crosses the track."

His eyebrows shot up. "I hadn't known that. Interesting. But is it not, as you put it, odd that Vanter would have gone to the Dell at all?"

"That's why I asked if he could have been injured elsewhere, sir."

"It's an excellent question," he said, looking thoughtful. "I'll telephone Davis. I had assumed that the two blows were given within a few minutes of each other, but I'd like to look again." He followed my anxious glance out the window and smiled as he saw Atlas politely accepting a treat from Lady Sylvia. "Go save your horse from being spoiled," he said.

"Thank you, sir," I said, "My father will be expecting me."

"Truly?" he said. "I think the ladies had hoped to talk with you. Well, take it up with them." He turned to the telephone, and I left.

The ladies did want to talk, but I refused with the polite phrases my parents had taught me to use when declining excessive favor. Seeing me adamant, Lady Sylvia hurried inside, promising to bring me a few biscuits to eat on the way back, but Mrs. Baines remained, drawing her shawl about her as she watched me tighten Atlas's girth.

"Reverend Williams and his son have been telling us about your talents in school," she said.

"That's kind of them," I said, "But I left school last December, when I turned fourteen, as permitted by law."

"So they said. But Harry—" She looked at me earnestly. "You must know that schooling doesn't necessarily end when the state ceases to require it."

"I do know, ma'am."

"Do you also know that Sir Thomas and Hugh set aside a substantial sum of money to support boys whose families worked for Willingford Hall if they wanted to go on to the Lechlade School?"

"Yes, ma'am." I eyed the front door, desperately wishing Lady Sylvia would return.

"And do you know Tim Jenkins and Charlie Goodwin—that's Jimmy's eldest brother—received such scholarships?"

"Yes, ma'am. Their families were extremely proud of them."

"As your father would be proud of you if you were to obtain such a scholarship," she said pointedly.

Lady Sylvia hurried out, a small package in her hand. "I would have given you a larger one," she said, "but I remembered you had to put it in your jacket." She handed it to me, looking from one of us to the other as I slipped it in its place. "Have I interrupted something?"

"Not at all, my lady," I said, vaulting on. "Thank you very much for the biscuits. I regret that my duties call me away."

I touched my forehead to them and rode off quickly. They were very kind, and I knew that a word from either of them to Sir Thomas would bring an offer of a scholarship. Books, mathematics, and microscopes hovered temptingly before my eyes as Atlas and I trotted along the track, but if Sir Thomas offered me a scholarship, honesty would compel my father to reveal that I was a girl, leading to chaos in which the withdrawal of the scholarship would be the least of my worries. But if I could solve the murder and become Somebody, perhaps schooling like that would be possible, enabling me to become

. . . well, who knew?

I urged Atlas into a canter, planning to listen closely at the inquest so that I could figure out how Mr. Vanter had gotten to the Dell, and who had met him there.

Chapter 7

The Chandace Arms stood a few hundred paces downriver from St. Barnabas, with which it shared a faithful congregation. As Mr. Johnson, The Arms' proprietor, was eager to tell anybody who asked, river shipping had brought it steady business in the years before the railroads, and later, its reputation for cheer and comfort had attracted many carriages the short way north from the Oxford Road.

It was still popular in the summer, because pleasure boaters could pull up to its dock and enjoy a pint before going on, but its old carriage house had recently been rebuilt as a shelter for motors, a fact so distressing to my father that he insisted on walking to the inquest. That was no small matter, as we were both dressed in full livery that included riding boots ill-suited to journeys on foot, but my observation that cycling would be faster and more comfortable met with a look that froze my words in the air between us.

We arrived to find the village in a state I had previously seen only when casualty figures had been announced. Every plowman, ditcher, hedger, sower, and carpenter on the estate seemed to have taken the morning off, and the village wives had quit their laundry tubs and poultry to join them. As we neared The Arms, I saw Goodwin leaning down to talk to Farmer Farrington, like a Percheron sharing confidences with a pony. Closer to the door, Reverend Williams was talking earnestly to Dr. and Mrs. Baines, Lady Sylvia and Mr. Lovejoy, all of them looking about in a manner that suggested they were waiting for someone.

The sound of a motor parted the crowd, and Hugh's Lanchester inched forward under Rushdale's careful guidance. When it reached the courtyard, Sir Thomas stepped out, smiling at the warm greetings of his tenants, and doffing his cap to the ladies. My father jogged my elbow, and I started to follow him, only to be startled by a klaxon horn. Turning, I saw Hutchins maneuvering Mr. Norton's enormous motor through the crowd on the bridge, forcing some villagers to climb on its pediments. They didn't object; rumor had it that Mr. Norton had sent two hogsheads of free ale to The Arms for everyone to drink when the inquest was over.

As the St. Barnabas clock struck eleven, the other witnesses and I were ushered into the front of The Arms' largest room, in which benches and chairs from the rest of the building had been placed. Those not testifying, including my father, were forced to find what places they could, and within minutes the room was packed with people, many of whom were standing. A few of them graciously opened the windows so people who couldn't get in at all would remain informed.

If Mr. Davis, the coroner, found the press of a crowd unusual or distracting, he gave no sign of it. Small and sleek, with whiskers that gave his face the cautious, sharp-eyed expression of a river rat, he talked to all of us who were testifying in a friendly manner, introduced us to the four men on the jury, and unnecessarily explained the meaning of testifying under oath. That done, he began the inquest by calling Dr. Baines forward from his seat next to me, swearing him in, and asking him to describe the results of his medical examination.

Dr. Baines gave the description in technical language that puzzled us all, but no matter—by now, the basic facts were common knowledge. Having heard it, Mr. Davis asked, "You say there were two blows, the first far less severe than the second. Can you tell us if the blows came close together in time or were separated by, say, an hour or more?"

Dr. Baines's eyes flickered to mine. "I'm afraid I can't, though I know that an answer one way or another would be of great help to the case. If he could be proved to have been unconscious for a half hour before he was murdered, that would open the possibility that he was stunned in one place and brought to the Dell to be finished off."

Aware of the murmur his words had occasioned, he glanced around the room. "But having examined the body carefully, I am convinced that the first blow was not of sufficient force to incapacitate the victim for longer than a few minutes at best. I've therefore concluded that the murderer, having stunned Mr. Vanter with the first blow, realized that the weapon he'd used was inadequate and inflicted the second blow with a cosh or some other weapon that provided leverage."

"You are saying, then, that the blows were given with different implements?"

"Exactly."

"Would you say it was likely that the second blow was given by a different person from the one who gave the first?"

"There is always that possibility, but I would say it was the work of a single man."

"Would you agree that the murder was not an act of impulse that sprang from a verbal or physical disagreement, but one in which both the place and the weapons had been carefully planned?"

"The place, probably. The weapons, certainly."

"One more question, though it does not touch your professional competence: can you speculate on the murder's possible motive?"

Dr. Baines hesitated. "I really can't, except to assure you that it was not robbery. As the police can confirm, Vanter's wallet and watch were untouched."

"Thank you. You may step down—Harry Green?"

Mr. Davis swore me in, and as I faced the village, I forced myself not to look as frightened as I felt. Mr. Davis, however, introduced me to the jury as "the plucky lad who found the body," and allowed me to tell my story without asking any of the suspicious questions Officer Morgan had asked in Sir Thomas's library.

His questions to Jimmy, who was next, were of the same kind. As

Jimmy returned to his seat, Mr. Davis's eyes met mine, and it occurred to me he'd deliberately led the jury to believe in our innocence— which meant, among other things, that his questions weren't as neutral as I'd unthinkingly assumed. That was an essential lesson to learn if I wished to solve the case myself . . . but Officer Jenkins had been called to the stand.

As he limped forward, I felt a stab of sadness that my anxiety had made me ignore when I'd seen him two days earlier. The summer before the War began, he'd been seventeen, and he'd done so brilliantly at the Lechlade School that Hugh and Sir Thomas were working to get him admitted to Oxford, while allowing him to support himself as Hugh's secretary. Then, hope and confidence had been visible in his every step.

Now, though he'd been decorated for bravery and especially commended for his service as a sniper, his prosthetic leg made him walk clumsily, and his face had the drawn look of somebody in perpetual pain. His intelligence, however, remained, and as he testified, I made a mental note to find out whether Officer Morgan, who had business that prevented his attending, sufficiently appreciated his capable subordinate.

Mr. Davis began by asking him to corroborate the time, the place, the weapons, and the lapse of time between the murder and the police inquiry. He then asked, "Do you agree, on the basis of your investigation, and with Dr. Baines's testimony, that the murder was committed only in the Dell?"

"I do. Officer Morgan's investigation of the river landing place in the Dell proved that it is so short that a skiff cannot be brought in parallel to the bank. Thus an unconscious man would have to be carried out over the bow, a task probably requiring two assailants; the ground around the landing place showed too little disturbance for that to be a possibility."

"Was there sufficient disturbance to suggest that Mr. Vanter and his assailant arrived in the Dell together, by boat?"

"Officer Morgan said not. Furthermore, given the Dell's proximity to Willingford Hall, it would seem more likely that Mr. Vanter walked to the Dell to meet the assailant, who arrived by boat."

"Is there any evidence that would support your theory?"

"We hope there will be. Officer Morgan is trying to arrange for dogs to come this afternoon before the rain that threatens."

"Excellent. Now, in a more general way, can you explain to the jury how and where Mr. Vanter spent his days in Sir Thomas's employ?"

"Evicting cottagers!" muttered a voice in the crowd.

"Tearing off roofs!" hissed another.

Mr. Davis whirled around. "This inquest exists for the purpose of discovering the cause of John Vanter's death. Those of you who wish to express an opinion of the man himself should do so elsewhere."

Silence. Mr. Davis nodded at Officer Jenkins.

"Mr. Vanter worked from the steward's office in the service wing of Willingford Hall," said Officer Jenkins. "Except on market days, he spent most of his mornings in that office, attending to financial matters. He spent his afternoons overseeing work on the estate's various farms."

"And how did he get about?"

"In his early days, on horseback, but in 1913, he purchased a motor, which he sometimes used to drive to the Hall from his home at Chandace Grange."

"Only sometimes?"

Officer Jenkins smiled. "Willingford Hall's farms are laid out to be reached on foot or on horseback. Bridle paths encircle the whole estate and cut across it at key points, the two most important being the bridge in Chandace village where the bridle path merges with the North Road to cross the river and, roughly a mile and a half downstream, the wooden foot and horse bridge that connects Chandace Grange and Willingford Hall. By the wooden bridge, the Hall is barely a half-mile from the Grange, which is why Sir Thomas's grandfather had it built.

"By motor, however, it is necessary to drive over a mile west from the Grange to the North Road, a mile and a half south through Chandace village to the Oxford Road, two miles east on the Oxford Road, and finally half a mile north through the park: roughly three-and-a-half sides of a square, and a total of between six and seven miles."

Mr. Davis smiled. "You surmise that Mr. Vanter often came to the Hall on foot?"

"It's not a matter of surmise. Mr. Parks, Sir Thomas's butler, has told us that Mr. Vanter rarely motored to the Hall more than one day a week, even in inclement weather. Last Wednesday was not one of those days. That evening, we found Mr. Vanter's motor in its shed at Chandace Grange."

Mr. Davis thanked Officer Jenkins and released him to his seat. I smiled to myself, for Mr. Parks had discreetly not revealed that Mr. Vanter *cycled* to the Hall. The issue of cycles on bridle paths was a delicate one. Hugh had forbidden them, reserving bridle paths for horses alone, and until his death the order had been respected. But during Sir Thomas's illness, Mr. Vanter had bought an expensive cycle and used it for his rounds, and gradually, estate workers with much humbler cycles had begun to use them too. Mr. Parks, a cyclist himself on his days off, had clearly thought it would be wise to avoid the whole issue, since Sir Thomas had not lifted the ban. Well, at least that was one thing I knew that the police didn't.

Goodwin testified next, and Mr. Davis turned from questions concerning Mr. Vanter's habits to those investigating possible motives for his murder. After briefly summarizing Mr. Vanter's injustices to the Goodwins for the jury, he remarked, "Given this record, Goodwin, it would seem you had ample reason to hate Mr. Vanter."

"Little reason to love him, surely."

"Did you wish to retaliate against him?

Goodwin looked thoughtful. "Like telling Hugh and Sir Thomas the truth about his stealing corn money and skimming to top off of the rent money?"

"More than that. Thoughts of revenge."

Goodwin's slow smile spread across his face. "Dueling's not for the likes of me."

People behind me tittered.

"So," said Mr. Davis, "you never wished him ill?"

"We're told to turn t'other cheek," said Goodwin simply. "I had faith that Sir Thomas would deal with his shenanigans. Which he did, over time." He smiled again. "You don't plow a field in an aaternoon."

Mr. Davis looked at him with a kind of respect. "The police and Dr. Baines agree that the murder took place sometime between three and four o'clock in the afternoon last Wednesday. Can you tell us where you were at that time?"

Goodwin said he'd been plowing the field closest to the Oxford Road, working with a plowboy (he pointed) and chatting with two hedgers (he pointed again) when he rested his team. All three stood up to confirm Goodwin's words.

Mr. Davis thanked them, asked them to sit down, and turned back to Goodwin. "Do you own a boat, Goodwin?"

I heard stirrings and whisperings behind me, and Goodwin looked taken aback. But after a second's pause, he grinned and said, "And what would I do with a boat? Slippery creetur'd throw me into the river and drown me like a kitten!" Amidst general laughter, his face sobered. "My lads had a skiff, years past, but they sold it in '14, so they could get to the Front, bless 'em."

The room went suddenly silent, and Mr. Davis let him go.

The atmosphere changed when Farmer Farrington was sworn in, which was no surprise. He was little and bent over, with a grim face and an evil tongue. His farm, which he'd leased from Sir Thomas after years of working as a hedger and a skilled mender of tools, was prosperous. He treated his workers fairly, but possibly excepting Goodwin, he had no friends. As Hugh had put it, Farrington was like a good horse soured by overwork; he could be trusted to do his job honestly and well, but you had to be wary of his teeth and his heels.

How much of this Mr. Davis knew I couldn't say, but his face was carefully neutral. "Let's begin," he said to Farrington, "with your whereabouts on Wednesday last, between three and four o'clock in the afternoon."

Farmer Farrington's eyes shifted back and forth across the room. "I've no recollection of the time, but that aaternoon I wur working on my skiff."

"Where?" asked Mr. Davis as a ripple of interest crossed the audience.

"By the river."

The audience chuckled.

"Farmer Farrington, I am going to have to ask you to be a little more explicit. Where exactly were you working?"

"I wur working where the end of the Farm meets the river," he said. "There's no dock because of the tow path, but come spring, I moor my skiff alongside the path, where there's a little spot of shallows."

"Were you working by yourself or with others?"

"A boy help me put her in the water, but aater that I sent him off and rowed a bit."

"How far did you go?"

"Upriver to the lock, then back."

"Are you a good oarsman, Farmer Farrington?"

"Fair."

"How long would it take you to row to Willingford Dell?"

Farmer Farrington half rose. "Now, see here! Don't put lies in my mouth!"

"I was merely seeking information, Farmer Farrington," said Mr. Davis smoothly. "I am not an oarsman myself, and I would like to know how long it would take one to travel from your spot of shallows to the Dell. That is all."

Farmer Farrington shrugged. "Quarter hour, unless there's fools on the river for larks."

"Thank you. Now, on another subject—did you have any dealings with Mr. Vanter earlier this week?"

Farmer Farrington nodded with a scowl. "Here at The Arms, Saturday last."

"On business?"

"Vanter was always on business. With men, anyway. With women, well . . ." He grinned unpleasantly.

The audience chuckled.

Mr. Davis silenced them, then said, "Did you discuss your plans to buy the Farrington Farm with him?"

Farmer Farrington gave Mr. Lovejoy a sour glance as surprised whispers circulated the room. "You told them, eh?"

Mr. Lovejoy nodded and was about to speak, but Mr. Davis held up a hand.

"All in good time, " he said. Turning to Farmer Farrington, he said, "Did Vanter discourage you?"

"Said he couldn't waste Sir Thomas's time with an offer that low. So I started home—then *he* told me Vanter'd made an offer lower than mine!" He pointed at Mr. Lovejoy.

The growl that rippled through the room suggested that the story had not been common knowledge.

"When you found out, how did you feel?"

"How'd *you* have felt?"

"Did you wish him harm?"

"Wished him in hell. Hope he's burning now."

The shiver that went around the room mixed with muttered agreement.

"After last Saturday night, did you have anything to do with Mr. Vanter again?"

Farmer Farrington hesitated, then said, "Is it likely I would aater that?"

Mr. Davis thanked him and swore in Mr. Lovejoy.

As he did so, I felt a warmth of good will behind me that couldn't be explained merely by Mr. Lovejoy's knowing Hugh from the Front; generally, Hugh's friends had passed unremarked, once caps had been tipped. Clearly Mr. Lovejoy's conversations with Sir Thomas's tenants and workers had convinced them that at last somebody was willing to take their part—the murmurs and whispers that circulated as he described Mr. Vanter's embezzlement were full of delighted triumph.

As Mr. Lovejoy finished his testimony, Mr. Davis remarked, "Can you tell us more about Mr. Vanter's motives? His increasingly risky subterfuges seem to be almost—"

"—a gamble," said Mr. Lovejoy, nodding. "The end was not, or not only, the fortune he was accruing. It was the thrill of betting against the odds, seeing how long a winning streak could endure. An obsession."

"I assume you didn't allow your interest in the case to prevent you from confronting Mr. Vanter with his 'obsession.'"

"No. I disclosed my findings to him last Wednesday, sometime close to one o'clock."

A ripple of surprised murmurs went through the room.

Mr. Davis's face changed. "Ah. And what was his reaction?"

"Absolute refusal to believe I had found him out. He began by saying I couldn't possibly have found evidence of any wrongdoing. He threatened to take me to court for slandering him. He insisted that Sir Thomas would never believe me."

"That must have been very trying."

"Oh, yes," said Mr. Lovejoy. "But it was also fascinating in its way, because he didn't even try to refute any of my points. No rational argument whatsoever. Again, like an addict confronted with his addiction, he simply got more and more furious, raising his voice—"

"—Raising his voice? This interview took place Wednesday in Mr. Vanter's office, which, as Officer Jenkins has told us, is in the service wing of Willingford Hall. Was Mr. Vanter's raised voice heard by anybody at the Hall?"

"I doubt it. By the time his voice was raised, the servants were eating their mid-day meal; the servants' hall is a substantial distance from Mr. Vanter's office, and his door was shut. Fortunately, I might add. Because he said that if I made my accusations public, he'd reveal a disgraceful secret that he'd learned about Hugh in the course of his work."

"Mr. Vanter threatened to denigrate the character of Hugh Chandace-Willingford?" asked Mr. Davis, incredulous as a growl circulated the room. "How?"

"I must beg you not to press me. To repeat slander is to give it life."

As Mr. Davis paused thoughtfully, I bit my lower lip, for I knew what form the slander had taken. Mr. Vanter's 'confidential' voice sniggered in my ears. *He surely favors you, lad—good thing you're so accommodating. Always was one for lads, our Hugh.* And with that voice there had been the eyes that roved over me, the insinuating arm around my shoulder . . .

Mr. Davis broke into my reluctant reverie by asking, "What did you do in response to Mr. Vanter's threat?"

"I called him a liar, a cheat, a blackmailer . . ." Mr. Lovejoy sighed. "Probably some other things, too. Before I was well finished, he stood up—he'd been sitting at his desk—and ordered me out of his office."

"Can you tell us what time that was?"

"The clock in the courtyard was chiming three quarters when I got on my cycle."

Mr. Davis raised an eyebrow. "Your cycle? You didn't go to Sir Thomas straight away with news of the quarrel?"

"No. The threat of blackmail had upset me, and I wanted to think how to proceed."

"Where did you go?"

"To The Chandace Arms, where I bought a mug of ale and a plowman's lunch. I ate them by the river, even though it was chilly. As I was finishing, my friend Baines pulled up to the bank in a skiff. I told him about the quarrel, and he sensibly suggested that before seeing Sir Thomas, I should organize my thoughts—and cool my temper—by taking a run."

"And did you take that run?"

"Yes."

"Straight away?"

Mr. Lovejoy hesitated, looking at Dr. Baines. "I did Baines a favor first."

"Which was . . . ?"

"He'd been out rowing in the Willingford Hall skiff, to which Sir Thomas has given him access. As we were talking, Mr. Johnson hurried out to tell him one of the hedgers had cut himself badly and needed a doctor as soon as possible—maybe even a lift to the hospital. So Baines asked me if I would row the skiff back to the boathouse, a mere twenty minutes, he said, then run downriver for a change of scenery." Mr. Lovejoy smiled wryly. "Of course, I agreed."

"What time was this?"

"Three o'clock, or thereabouts."

"And did you return the skiff to Sir Thomas's boathouse straight away?"

"I changed into running clothes first, but essentially, yes. As I pushed off, the clock was striking the quarter."

A little murmur went around the room.

"Remind the jury—is Sir Thomas's boathouse upriver or downriver from here?"

"Downriver."

"Can you tell us what time you reached the boat house?"

"I'm afraid not. To say I'm no oarsman is to put it mildly. I'd only rowed once before, so I took the precaution of leaving my pocket watch in my room in case I splashed."

"Very wise. Were you in danger of running into other boats?"

"Fortunately, mine was the only boat in sight—then, and when I ran along the towpath as well. When I've run the other way, upriver to town, I've occasionally seen skiffs on the water and dog walkers or fishermen on the path. But as Officer Jenkins remarked when we first discussed my run at the Hall, a downriver runner has the river to himself before Eastertide."

"And when did you return?"

"Half past six, perhaps a little later. It was almost dark when I stopped by Baines's house to return the boathouse key. He told me about the murder, and I was appalled. I changed at The Arms and cycled to the Hall, where I told Sir Thomas and the police about my quarrel with Vanter and about my run."

"You were appalled, you say. Were you appalled by the murder, or by the fact that nobody had seen you between the hours of three and half past six?"

"Initially, by the murder. It was only when I was talking to Sir Thomas and the police that I realized I might be in a difficult position. I confess, that made me leave out the matter of the skiff, since they did not ask me about it directly." He sighed. "But here, having sworn to tell the whole truth, I feel obliged to do so."

Mr. Davis nodded. "Thank you. You may step down—Sir Thomas?"

A murmur went through the room as Sir Thomas stepped up to be sworn in, for the many people who had not seen him since Hugh's funeral were as shocked by his ashen appearance as I had been on Wednesday night.

Mr. Davis treated him with great respect, expressing sympathy for the loss of his son— sympathy which, as that son would have instantly noticed, he had not extended to Goodwin. He began with questions clearly designed to preserve Sir Thomas's dignity: the size of the estate; 1500 acres, formerly 2000; the number of farms, three, formerly four; the years it had been held in the family: since the thirteenth century.

That done, Davis asked, "Your son also had great faith in Mr. Lovejoy's abilities as an agent, is that true?"

Sir Thomas coughed several times before he nodded.

"And due to your loss and unfortunate illness, you needed an agent you could trust to fulfill your wishes?"

"Yes."

"Now, as I understand it from Mr. Lovejoy's testimony, one effect of Mr. Vanter's embezzlement was the loss of one of your farms in a sale that wouldn't have been necessary if you had received income due to you. Did that news make you angry at Mr. Vanter?"

"Yes. But also, at myself. Lovejoy's figures made it clear to me—as his testimony must have made it clear to everybody present—the extent to which my estate has suffered from my negligence."

Dr. Baines stirred uncomfortably in his chair, looking with concern at Sir Thomas's defeated face. I was worried, too, but mainly because I suddenly saw the direction in which Mr. Davis's questions were moving.

"Were you planning to use those figures to terminate Mr. Vanter's employment?"

"Of course."

"Mr. Lovejoy's testimony suggests that he would not have gone without a fight. Did you expect the kind of blackmail Mr. Lovejoy has described?"

"I have known other landowners to be blackmailed by stewards they have let go. I have learned, in the past weeks, how far Mr. Vanter could sink. So, while I did not expect blackmail of any specific kind, I'm not entirely surprised."

"Even barring blackmail, did you expect a lengthy legal case?"

"We hoped not, but it seemed well to be prepared."

"Such a case can become extremely expensive."

Sir Thomas nodded, coughing.

"Given the threat of that expense, given the extent of the disservice Mr. Vanter had done to you, and—most of all—given an agent who for both personal and professional reasons disliked Mr. Vanter and had an obligation to please you, would it be surprising if you were tempted to ask that agent to ... solve the problem more expeditiously?"

The room was perfectly silent as Sir Thomas looked at him. After a full five seconds, he said, "It might not be surprising to *you*, Mr.

Davis. But it would greatly surprise many other people here to think *any* gentleman of honor would ask a loyal agent to commit murder to save him from legal expense."

A murmur of approval went through the audience, and Dr. Baines muttered, "Well said."

"In other words," said Mr. Davis smoothly, "you can assure the jury that despite your serious grievance and your local power, you had nothing to do with Mr. Vanter's murder?"

"I can assure the jury that despite my many failings, I have not fallen that far."

"Thank you, Sir Thomas. You may step down."

Amidst the whispered conversations that accompanied Sir Thomas's descent, Mr. Davis informed the assembly that the jury would now withdraw to consider the evidence presented, and that those testifying were free to leave the room but should stay on the premises until the verdict was given. He and the jurymen left by a side door.

The hall erupted in noise and movement as people hurried to the courtyard, where Mr. Norton's rumored ale was in fact flowing freely. Dr. Baines touched my shoulder as we stood up. "Fetch Sir Thomas a pint, lad."

I nodded and worked my way through the crowd, aided by my livery, which made people realize I was not there for myself. After a brief wait, I secured two pints (one for my father) and took them back, a far easier trip, for the hall was now almost empty.

As I expected, Mr. Lovejoy, Dr. and Mrs. Baines, Lady Sylvia, and Reverend Williams were clustered around Sir Thomas, with my father, Goodwin and Jimmy behind them. As I had not expected, Mr. Norton was with them. "Farrington, definitely," he was saying as I gave Sir Thomas his pint. "No alibi, a skiff, a good oarsman—and did you see him hesitate at the last question? Not yes or no. Equivocation. A slippery man."

My father was frowning as he took the other pint from me, but he said nothing, for Mr. Lovejoy was speaking.

"That's true, now that you mention it," he said thoughtfully. "Though I wouldn't have thought him dangerous. He was angry Saturday night. In fact, and this is just between us, of course, he said Vanter was going to find himself coshed some dark night—"

"—Well, there you have it!" said Mr. Norton.

"Not necessarily. In the first place, talk is different from action. In the second, try to imagine the action. Vanter was nearly six feet tall and well built; Farrington, if he were to stand up straight, is under five and a half and thin as a lathe."

"Hence the necessity of two blows," said Mr. Norton. Looking around at the dubious faces, he shrugged. "Well, we shall see what the jury thinks—Come, Harry, let's see how many pints we can contrive to bring our friends." He started towards the door, and, after receiving a nod from Sir Thomas, I went with him.

"I like to see a lad who brings his father a pint as well as his master," he said, smiling as we stepped into the hall. "I hope Cyril will do the same for me some day." He held up six fingers to Mr. Johnson. I did a quick count and said, "Isn't it seven, sir?"

"Is it? Lovejoy, Lady Sylvia, two Baineses, Reverend Williams, myself . . ."

"And Goodwin, sir."

"Ah. I see Hugh made you a socialist. Seven it is." He caught Mr. Johnson's eye and held up seven fingers.

"Now," he continued, "about sons. Ever since you gave Cyril a ride on that black horse of yours, he has been after me night and day to get him a pony. I am perfectly willing to do so, but I know that at that age a boy's fancies turn easily from one wish to another. Would it be possible for you to give him a few lessons on your gentle giant, so he can see if he really likes it?"

The pints were ready, which gave me time to think. By the time we started back I had my answer prepared. "That might be possible, sir, and very pleasant for me, as I think Master Cyril is talented. But the arrangements would have to be made with Sir Thomas and my father."

He raised an eyebrow. "No sidelining, eh?"

"No what, sir?"

"Sidelining—making a little money on the side of your regular work. Many a lad has made his way upwards by engaging in it."

"The horses aren't mine, sir."

He chuckled. "So they aren't. Very well, I shall consult with your superiors and hope that something can be arranged—Here we are, my friends: ladies first." He passed three pints to the ladies, reserving the fourth for himself while I served the men.

Goodwin took a pull on his and passed it to Jimmy for a sip, grinning appreciatively. "That's no small beer," he said.

"Indeed it isn't," said Mr. Norton. "It's our finest ale. And I'm pleased to say The Arms has recently agreed to keep it on tap."

"That's good to know," said Mr. Lovejoy. "It's excellent. Well done, Norton."

As they drank and chatted, I mulled over the testimonies we'd heard. What seemed peculiar was that so little evidence had turned up. Whoever the murderer was, he'd been either very lucky or extremely clever, or both. And if I were going to become Somebody, I was going to have to be the same.

I was separated from my thoughts by the sound of a gong. It was apparently the signal that the court was going to reconvene, for Officer Jenkins limped hurriedly in with Farmer Farrington and guided the rest of us to our seats.

Mr. Norton strode out, miraculously carrying ten empty mugs, as the crowd flocked in, smelling strongly of ale but in a solemn mood. I saw Dr. Baines exchange a worried glance with Mr. Lovejoy.

The room became perfectly quiet as the four jurymen entered through the side door. Standing before us, Mr. Davis said, "The jury has declared the death of John Vanter to be one of murder with malice aforethought by person or persons unknown. It demands, however, that pending further investigation, two men must swear solemnly not to leave the Willingford Hall estate for any purpose, and to present themselves in person to Officers Morgan or Jenkins each day. Failure to do so will result in imprisonment."

He paused.

"The two men are Robert Farrington, farmer; and Edmund Lovejoy, Willingford Hall Agent. Court is adjourned."

Chapter 8

The exclamations that followed the assembly out of The Arms were cut short by rain that, having threatened all day, finally started to fall. The villagers scuttled back to their houses; the laborers turned up their collars, pulled down their caps and started off to the fields. Thinking resignedly of the amount of time it was going to take our livery to dry, I stepped out the door, only to be stopped by Lady Sylvia, who alone of those present had had the foresight to bring an umbrella.

"Harry!" she called. "You and your father aren't going to walk, are you?"

"I'm afraid we are, my lady," I said, trying to smile.

"That's ridiculous. Let me see what I can arrange."

I glanced at my father, who smiled and asked, "Who is the lady?"

"She's Lady Sylvia something, visiting Dr. and Mrs. Baines." Ashamed of not knowing more, I added, "I think she's a rider. She knows horses, in any case."

"Does she, now?" My father looked approvingly at her purposeful stride. "If she's a friend of the Baineses, she's probably a quality lady who became a nurse at the Front."

I nodded, admiring the way she hurried past Officer Jenkins and turned back to face him rather than call to him, which would have made him turn on the slippery cobblestones. After they'd spoken a few words, she started back to us, but she had to jump out of the way as an enormous motor roared out of the courtyard and drew up with a muddy splash.

Behind me, I heard a muttered curse, and Mr. Norton pushed past my father and me.

"Dammit, Hutchins," he said as he stepped into the back seat. "Don't you know a lady when you see one?"

Hutchins started to mumble an excuse, but Lady Sylvia smiled and walked towards the motor. "It's entirely my fault for walking in the midst of things," she said, smiling as Mr. Norton lowered his window. "And in fact, I'm grateful to Hutchins for giving me an opportunity to thank your lovely wife for being so helpful in the hospital Wednesday afternoon. Her shock at Mr. Vanter's death made me forget to mention her help when we saw you yesterday. It was her first time volunteering, and many ladies are overwhelmed by the circumstances, but she worked long and hard. It was nearly five o'clock when she finally consented to go."

"The hospital, you say?" Mr. Norton's face was the picture of incredulity. "Wednesday afternoon? Surely not! She said nothing about it."

Lady Sylvia looked at him levelly. "Perhaps you came home so full of the events of your day that you forgot to ask her about hers."

"Quite possibly, quite possibly," said Mr. Norton with a weak smile. "I have much to learn in that regard. In any case, I will ask her this evening and pass along your kind words. All right, Hutchins. Slowly."

Lady Sylvia caught my eye as they drew off. "You're wondering how a lady who fainted when she heard of a murder managed so well in a hospital, aren't you, Harry?"

I had been wondering precisely that, but I hesitated to admit I'd been listening.

"Oh, come!" she said, laughing. "Of course you are! Well, you've caught me in a polite fiction. Emily Norton was in fact very timid at the hospital, often had to sit down, and was deeply disturbed by what she saw. But she stayed. She tried to work. Mrs. Baines and

I are hoping the fiction will become reality, as it has done with so many other sheltered ladies, and that she will join us again."

I smiled, because like Hugh, she was talking to me as if I were a person, not a servant.

But before I could speak, Officer Jenkins drove up in the police motor, and she said, "Heavens! I got so involved in Mrs. Norton that I forgot to tell you Officer Jenkins has offered you and your father a ride back to the stable!"

"Oh!" I said, delighted. "Thank you! Father—"

"—I heard," he said. "We are extremely grateful, my lady. And to you, too, Officer Jenkins."

We scrambled in, and Lady Sylvia waved as we drove off.

"She's a real lady," said my father.

"In every sense of the word," said Officer Jenkins. "She's the daughter of the Earl of Atherton."

"Atherton," muttered my father. "Atherton. Has a fine stable just north of London. His sons rode here with Hugh once or twice. Excellent over fences, as I recall."

"Not anymore," said Officer Jenkins grimly. "They both went down at the Somme. The estate, its debts, and its stable followed after. War, requisition, death, bankruptcy . . . a familiar story. So is Lady Sylvia's for that matter. She was—is—a beauty, and there was a pervasive rumor that she was going to be married off to Lord Sandford's son to pay off the famous Atherton mortgages."

"Lord Sandford indeed!" snorted my father. "He's no kind of a lord—just an inventor chap who got a title for some sort of scientific work. Doesn't own an acre."

"I don't know about the acre," said Officer Jenkins, "but he is—was, rather—he died last year—involved with the wireless communication that was so helpful to our Navy in the War. You can argue that service like that deserves rewarding."

My father's frown made me see that distraction was necessary. "What about Sandford's son and Lady Sylvia?" I asked.

"Nothing came of it. He left for the States—his mother is American—just before the War, and after it started, Lady Sylvia jumped at the chance to become a nurse. A fine one. I should know. She was one of the ones who kept me alive after . . . well, after."

"Oh! So, you knew her!"

"Yes, and the Baineses, too, though they weren't married back then. It seems a long time ago." He sighed and turned onto the Oxford Road, peering through the little clear fan his wiper left in his windscreen. "I'm glad I could spare you a walk in this, but it will make it impossible to use the dogs Morgan has been trying to call in."

"Officer Jenkins . . ." I began, but he cut me off.

"Tim. Address me as you addressed Hugh, Harry. It's the same politics."

I smiled, pleased, but the interruption had given me time to think better of telling him that Mr. Vanter had probably cycled to the Dell. Instead, I asked, "Can you tell us what you think of the verdict?"

"I can tell you that it was the one I expected, given two men with no alibi and access to skiffs at the time of the murder."

I frowned. "But there's no proof that either one of them did it. Just that they might have been there but most likely weren't."

He turned at the gate house and stopped to show his badge to the gatekeeper, who ran out in the rain. "It's called circumstantial evidence," he said as the gates swung open. "And you're right. It's different from proof, which is why they were asked to stay on the estate, not jailed, while we do more investigation."

"I suppose it's wise to keep an eye on them," said my father. "But I admit I have difficulty believing either of them would commit murder."

Tim shook his head. "I used to think I could tell who would commit murder and who wouldn't. But in my line of work, you learn a great deal about the dark side of people."

"I can see Farmer Farrington's dark side," I said. "But Mr. Lovejoy seems—"

"—Harry," he said, "every man who's been to the Front has a dark side. There are *no* exceptions."

His tone silenced me, but I knew—just *knew*, the way I knew how a horse would react to a rustle in the bushes—that the inquest had made suspects of innocent men, implying that the only choice was which one of them had done it. Surely, I could do better than that. *Think!* whispered Hugh's voice in my ear. *Listen. Watch. Until you can do that, you'll never be a horseman. Or anything else.*

Tim pulled up as near to the stable as he could, and my father hurried off to check the horses. I was about to follow, when Tim said, "Harry, not being able to use the dogs is going to greatly complicate our inquiry. Is there *anything* besides a gut feeling that makes you doubt that either Lovejoy or Farmington is guilty?"

"No," I confessed. "Not really."

"Well," he said, smiling, "I remember how sharp Hugh always said you were, so I hope I can count on you to tell me if you come across any useful information."

"Of course you can!" I said over my shoulder as I dashed to the stable.

My conscience reproached me for the rest of the day. Tim wasn't just "the police." He was Hugh's friend, whom I'd always liked, and instead of helping him, I hadn't told him about Mr. Vanter's cycling. Nor had I suggested that if Mr. Vanter had gone to the Dell on his cycle, it might still be there, presumably hidden someplace. Most importantly, I hadn't told him that I was going to go to the Dell and search for it.

Chapter 9

I'd hoped to get to the Dell on Saturday, but the morning's rain made it necessary to exercise the horses in the afternoon, so I had no time free. Sunday, however, was by Hugh's decree a day in which the horses were turned out in the paddock and allowed to *be* horses, and thus a day of rest for my father and me. After church, that is.

The Willingford Hall servants attended St. Barnabas every Sunday morning, a custom that dated back to the thirteenth century, when the Willingford family had thanked the Lord for their success in the wool trade by building the largest parish church in the area, with a handsome tower and deep-toned stained-glass windows. Usually, I went willingly. Now that I'd left school, Sunday was the only day on which I could talk to my friends—including Jimmy, whose lovely voice had earned him a place in the choir. I also liked Reverend Williams's sermons, which, as Hugh had once pointed out, came from a mind and soul very different from the ones I met with the rest of the week.

Today, however, I was so involved in my ideas about Mr. Vanter's cycle that I hardly heard the sermon, and when, at the end of the service, my father joined in the general conversation in the churchyard, I could hardly hide my impatience.

As I looked around the crowd, I was surprised to see Lady Sylvia, Mr. Lovejoy, and the Baineses, who rarely went to church, talking to Reverend Williams's son Richard, who rarely went anywhere. He'd been invalided out after the Somme, and although there was nothing visibly wrong with him, he was so frightened by loud noises that a backfiring motor would make him curl up with his arms over his head, shaking and sobbing. Hugh, who'd been his classmate at Eton and Oxford, had tried to convince him that the reaction was the result of trauma, not cowardice, but since Hugh's death, shame had kept him mainly inside the Rectory. I was in the middle of noting how pale and sad he looked next to the others, when he caught sight of me and beckoned.

"Harry!" he said, in something of his old voice as I joined him. "Good God, can it be that long since I've seen you? You must've grown a foot."

I looked down at my boots and shook my head. "No, sir—I still have only two."

"Still sharp, I see," he said, smiling as the others laughed. "In spite of that colossal bruise. What are you doing, now that your schooling's ended, besides getting your head banged up and finding corpses?"

Afraid that the conversation might lead to more talk of scholarships, I answered quickly. "Working horses, sir."

"No 'sir,' please," he said. "Hugh would be appalled. Say, Lady Sylvia says you were hurt riding that superb gray of his . . . Err, Error—"

"—Errant," I said, laughing. "He has nothing to do with error, except when I make one."

"Well, next time you and he search for the Grail in Chandace, stop at the Rectory. I missed him on Wednesday, but I'd love to see him." He smiled. "And you."

"I gather *I've* missed something here," said Mr. Lovejoy. "The only horse I've seen Harry ride is a black. When do you work Errant, Harry?"

"Usually first thing after breakfast: half an hour in the manège, and an hour and a half on the bridle paths."

"Well, I'll stop by the manège tomorrow, then, if the weather is decent," said Mr. Lovejoy. "I'll be spending a great deal of time at the Hall, it seems, since Davis won't even allow me to do errands in town. Good thing I got that oxalic acid for you last Monday, or you'd have nothing to clean your boot tops."

"I'm much obliged," I said, with a wry face that made him chuckle. I hated cleaning boot tops. It was a tedious job made miserable by my father's fear of the cleanser, which he reiterated weekly had the same chemistry as rhubarb leaves and was even more poisonous. Why he was so sure I would take a sip, I'd never known.

"Are you really confined to Chandace and the Hall?" Richard asked Mr. Lovejoy.

"They say they'll jail me if I so much as step over the boundary," said Mr. Lovejoy. "Can't blame them, legally speaking. No alibi, and that wretched skiff."

Dr. Baines shook his head. "That's your penalty for honesty."

Mr. Lovejoy shrugged. "Better to say it at the inquest than to have it come up in a later inquiry. At least the police know I'm not trying to hide anything."

"Meanwhile, you're nearly as cloistered as I am," joked Richard— then looked up anxiously as a motor started up somewhere in the lane. I saw concern in the faces of his friends and, though sorrowing for Richard, I took advantage of their distraction to move towards Reverend Williams, who was talking with my father. Afraid that they might be discussing my need for continued education, I felt obliged to point out that Mr. Parks and Mrs. Middleton had already left, and we should hurry home to dinner.

We were, in fact, just in time, and we ate quickly, for Mr. Parks and Polly were to serve Sir Thomas as soon as we had finished. After dinner, my father went back to our quarters, where he would spend the afternoon dozing over his Bible and the only other book I'd ever seen him read, *The Guide to Service: The Groom*. He had, by now, given up any hope that I would spend my one free afternoon similarly occupied, so he made no comment when I changed into my workday clothes and slipped off.

I had originally planned to ride my cycle, but as I'd finished my second piece of rhubarb pie it had occurred to me that walking would be less conspicuous and more flexible. Thus, I set out for the Dell on foot, buoyed by a sense of adventure that generally came my way only in books like *Coral Island* and *The Thirty-Nine Steps*. I took the footpath that Mr. Vanter would have taken, carefully looking for tire tracks. There were none, which, while no surprise after Friday and Saturday's rain, discouraged me until I remembered Hugh's dictum that the absence of evidence should never be confused with proof.

When I climbed the stile on which I'd seen Jimmy and looked down the bridle path to the Dell, I was annoyed to find that my heart was beating fast. I ignored it, however, and got to work by standing under the oaks nearest the path and throwing a few pebbles I'd picked out of the manège. Granted, I was not a strong thrower—my father's attention to my dart game had emphasized accuracy rather than distance—but I could easily manage a ten-pace toss.

What I *couldn't* manage was a fling of such force that it would raise a welt the size of the one still visible on Errant's neck. I tried from several different spots, but the throw was simply impossible for anybody but a man far taller than I, and of overwhelming strength. That description fit neither one of the two suspects. The observation made me feel superior until I realized I had no better idea to propose. Patience, I told myself. *Watch. Think.*

I stepped into the trees, following a sad swath of bluebells that had been crushed by the police and Dr. Baines. They were most crushed in the little clearing where I'd found Mr. Vanter, and as I reached the spot, I stopped, uneasily remembering the silence that had surrounded me when I felt for his pulse. There was no such silence now. Birds flew here and there; a squirrel scolded from the oak nearest me; and after I'd stood still for a minute, a rabbit ventured out and gazed at me with interest but no fear.

Perhaps the silence had been in my imagination. No, I *knew* it hadn't. Admittedly, it could have been caused by the way I blundered into the clearing myself, but it seemed more likely to have been caused by the murder and the hasty flight to which I probably owed my . . . I shivered.

Now, I heard not only friendly woodland noises, but the steady murmur of the river. Walking towards it, I noticed that there were no bluebells, damaged or otherwise, under my feet once I'd taken a few steps, for a faint path ran beneath the outreaching branches of an ancient beech. It led to a narrow inlet half filled with rushes, but as I reached its bank, I saw that trampling footsteps and the rain had created mud that concealed any evidence that a skiff had been landed. In fact . . .

I stopped at the edge of the mud, frowning. As Tim had said, there was no room for a skiff to come against the bank broadside. But as he had *not* said, the water was so shallow that the bow of a skiff couldn't have approached the bank closely enough to be drawn up at all. How could a man of Tim's intelligence miss something that obvious?

Out on the river, something splashed quietly and glided. Oars?

I shook my head, chiding my over-active imagination. It was nothing.

No, not nothing. A stroke. A pause. A stroke. Backwater. Two ducks thundered up from the rushes closest to me.

I turned and ran to the only place that offered cover—the beech. After swinging myself into it, I climbed as quietly as I could and stretched myself along the highest of its thick branches.

Below me and slightly downstream from the path, a skiff was moving slowly through the reeds in the inlet. Its occupant was looking over his shoulder frequently, and from my perch, I could see what he sought: a crude dock that extended from the inlet's side. All his movements were furtive, and when a river rat slipped into the water near his skiff, he startled visibly. However wary, though, he knew what he was doing.

Within a minute, he had pulled his skiff expertly against the dock, tied it to a pier, and stepped ashore. And though his cap was pulled down over his face, his stance and his walk told me instantly who he was: Farmer Farrington.

Terrified that he might look up through the still-bare branches, I hardly dared to breathe, but as he stepped off the dock onto the slippery bank, he had eyes only for the muddy ground around the supposed landing place, careful, as I had been—God be praised—to stay at its edge. He examined it closely for quite some time, then muttered something and started into the Dell on the path under my tree.

I was tempted to climb down and follow him, but fortunately I didn't, for he soon returned, this time walking faster. After one more look at the muddy ground, he hurried to the dock and examined a rope that was tied around the end pier. He stepped back without touching it, untied his skiff—and hesitated, looking at something in the reeds. Suddenly, he laughed. "Bloody fools!" Shaking his head, he stepped into his skiff, pushed himself off, and rowed silently back to the river.

After waiting for perhaps a quarter hour, I climbed down and crept to the dock myself, unnerved by every whisper of the reeds. Following Farmer Farrington's careful steps, I walked to its end. Close up, I could see that the rope he'd looked at was partly wound around the pile farthest out. It had evidently been thrown off hastily, for half its length had slid into the water, and only a few days ago, as even somebody as inexperienced as I could see from its lack of slime.

But it wasn't the rope I stared at. It was the sight that had made Farmer Farrington laugh: a nearly submerged wheel two feet from the end of the dock. Reaching out, I moved it a little, but a couple of pulls showed me I could get no leverage. I unwound the rope from the pile and, having fixed it around the wheel with a knot that would have made Hugh scoff, I stood up and pulled with all my strength.

The wheel rose slowly at first, then came loose with a sucking sound and a sudden ease that nearly tipped me into the water. Once I'd recovered my balance, I pulled it to the dock, hand over hand. Soon it lay before me, covered with mud and broken reeds: the expensive cycle Mr. Vanter had wheeled into the old carriage house of Willingford Stable every morning.

My first sensation was pride in my successful sleuthing. Within minutes, however, my pleasure was overshadowed by the realization that I knew nothing Farmer Farrington did not. The more I thought about it, the more I suspected that he'd found exactly what he was looking for: evidence that the police, *bloody fools*, had missed. Which meant that *he* knew what had happened in the Dell.

Chapter 10

I got home without meeting anybody on the footpath, and I'd brushed the mud off my trousers so well that my father took no notice of it. But whenever I closed my eyes Sunday night, I dreamed about cycles that rose muddily from the river, or skiffs that appeared out of nowhere and spotted me on the secret dock. Farmer Farrington's laugh woke me a dozen times, the last so thoroughly that I heard the wretched courtyard clock mark most of the quarter hours after three in the morning.

As the chimes marched relentlessly on, the scornful laugh gradually mingled with Dr. Baines's serious voice: *You're fortunate to have gotten off so lightly.* I buried my head under my pillow, only to dream that as I leaned over Mr. Vanter's corpse, I heard footsteps creeping towards me through the trees. The clock chimed half past five, and I got up, shaking.

Jimmy and his father reached the stable shortly before six, and we'd just led the team out for currying when we heard a motor drive up the sweep. At that hour, perhaps only a gunshot could have been more shocking, but after an interchange of surprised looks, my father and Goodwin continued with their work as if nothing had happened, so Jimmy and I had to do the same. Whoever it was didn't go to the front entrance; the footsteps in the courtyard were approaching the stable. I felt my breath come faster as I realized they were slightly uneven. Clearly, somebody had found the place I'd hidden the cycle . . .

"Good morning to you all," said a pleasant voice.

My father spun around with a gasp. In the days before the War, Hugh had always come to the stable at first light and greeted the bustling grooms with exactly those words. And though I had already recognized Tim's footsteps, I, too, felt a surge of wonder as I saw the tall, slim figure silhouetted in the doorway against the early morning mist.

Goodwin, his vision undisturbed by phantoms, saw only a policeman. "Morning," he said, touching his forehead with suspicious courtesy.

Tim included us all in his smile, but he spoke to Goodwin. "I'm sorry to interrupt you," he said, "but I wanted to be sure of finding you and didn't know where you would be working today. It's about Vanter, of course. A new piece of evidence has come to light . . ."

I could scarcely make myself move the brush.

". . . about Farmer Farrington. Officer Morgan said, 'Go talk to Green and Goodwin. Maybe you'll find out more about it.'"

Goodwin made an acknowledging grunt; my father turned to Jimmy and me. "You lads fetch the harnesses."

We left, but with one mutual glance, we quietly gathered the harnesses and tiptoed back within earshot.

" . . . know that things overheard are not always accurate," Tim was saying. "Still, though Joey Rushdale's getting on, I'd say he was reliable, wouldn't you?"

"No man better," said my father. "I should know, our cottages being in the same row for twenty years. As for getting on, he may not be up to heavy work these days, but he's the only man on the estate that can keep Sir Thomas's Lanchester running."

"A fair genius with machinery, he is," agreed Goodwin. "I've thought to have my lad work for him. A job for new times, might be."

Jimmy and I stared at each other in appalled silence.

"I'm glad to hear all this," said Tim. "All right—Monday last, Rushdale was at The Chandace Arms playing darts with Farrington and some others. Farrington won, and he kept all his winnings instead of standing the others to a pitcher."

Goodwin and my father made disapproving noises.

"Shocking, I know," said Tim. "But what's important was the reason he gave. According to Rushdale, he said he was going to save every shilling to buy his farm, because he'd fixed things so Vanter could never deal behind his back again."

"Monday last?" asked Goodwin. "With Mr. Lovejoy telling him aboot the farm only Saturday?"

"So Rushdale says. And as you say, he's a man of—"

"—It's not Rushdale I'm worrit aboot," said Goodwin. "It's Farmer Farrington."

"Yes?" An edge of interest sharpened Tim's voice.

"Begging Mr. Davis's pardon, Farmer Farrington's not a mon to murder. More like to burn a hay rick, start rumors. You take my meaning?"

"I do indeed."

"Then, too, he's not a mon to win a wager without collecting.'"

My father laughed. "I should say not!"

"True," said Tim. "But so far as I know there was no . . ." His voice trailed off in a way that made me think Goodwin had put up a hand.

"Sunday a week past," he said, "I saw Farmer Farrington aater church. He wur so sore at Vanter, he swore he'd make it so the mon would never see money to buy farms again. Knew how to do it, too." There was a little pause. "Well, crossing Vanter wur a fearful risk, so I wagered him a pint he dasn't do aught except talk. Joking, you know."

"Of course, joking," said Tim as Goodwin paused again.

"But if Rushdale's telling true, Farmer Farmington'd gone and done sommat by the very next night."

"That does sound odd," said my father thoughtfully.

"Not so odd as passing on a free pint."

"Hm," said Tim. "How often do you see Farmer Farrington?"

"This time of year, not so often, what with planting."

"So it's possible he simply didn't see you Tuesday and Wednesday, and then heard about the murder and decided it'd be wiser not to call attention to that pint."

"That's so," acknowledged Goodwin.

"Still, as you say, it's odd," said Tim. "I'll go talk to him. He may—"

"—Talk to a policemon?" scoffed Goodwin. "Not he! Terrible sore he is, being kept from market. But there's darts at The Arms tomorrow evening. Let me take sommat for the pint and do some listening."

"Well," said Tim. "Morgan won't like the delay, but you'll probably learn more than we ever would. Just so you tell me—Say, the lads have been a long time with that harness."

"Oh, we're right here, sir," said Jimmy, before I could shush him.

Since there was no alternative, we stepped forward. Goodwin gave Jimmy a look that boded him no good, but Tim just laughed and helped us harness the team.

After Jimmy and Goodwin left, I took a deep breath and stopped Tim as my father started in to breakfast. "I need to talk to you. It's important."

He looked at me keenly. "Now?"

"It will take a little time," I said, "and I don't want anybody else to know until you say it's all right."

"Ah," he said, his eyes lighting up. "You'll be working Errant for two hours this morning, is that right?"

I blinked. "How did you know?"

"I have to confirm Lovejoy's presence on the estate every morning. He told me to meet him here because he wants to watch you ride. After that, can you arrange your timing so that you get to Chandace Grange in a little over an hour after you leave the manège?"

I nodded, carefully not asking in words or expression what took him to the Grange.

"Fine. I will arrange *my* timing so I can meet you there. Meanwhile, your father is looking impatient. Hurry along!"

I hurried, wondering how my sudden decision to trust Tim

with my discoveries would affect my desire to become Somebody. During breakfast, however, those thoughts gradually gave 'way to my awareness that I was about to ride Errant in front of somebody other than my father. Granted, Tim would be there on duty, and Mr. Lovejoy was chiefly interested in Hugh's horse, not in my horsemanship. But as Hugh had said, riding for an audience required the ability to concentrate on one's relationship with a horse instead of one's relationship with people it was important to please or impress. That was a difficult assignment, and I'd had no occasion to work on it for over a year.

All in all, I was a little nervous as I led Errant into the manège where Tim and Mr. Lovejoy waited expectantly. Errant, however, appreciated their open admiration of his beauty, and from the moment I vaulted on, he behaved faultlessly. Walk. Halt. Turn on the forehand. Walk. Sitting trot. Circle left. Halt. Rising trot. Circle right. He was so perfectly in hand that I soon moved on to extensions at the trot, which he had mastered only recently, then back to a sitting trot with a few shoulders-in and serpentines. With those successes behind us, I ventured a canter, prepared for his usual Monday-morning buck; but he went into it perfectly and performed circles on each lead with collection that thrilled me. Everything around us—the stable, the weather, the watchers—was lost to us both as we did one movement after another, and when we finally trotted down the center, halted, and saluted, I was startled by the applause and bravos from the ringside.

Turning, I saw that our audience had increased. My father's presence could have been anticipated, but he was standing next to Sir Thomas and an impeccably-dressed man—perhaps a member of the Council. I walked Errant towards them on a long rein, elated but not quite sure what to say.

My father made it easy for me by instructing me to take Errant out on the bridle paths immediately, so he would feel rewarded for his discipline and collection. I left, as ordered, but to my delight I heard Sir Thomas say, "If he's brilliant at this age, think what he'll be in a few years!" It was wonderful to know that somebody besides myself thought Errant's brilliance was extraordinary.

I had decided to follow the chain of bridle paths that surrounded the estate, since the ride took approximately the time that needed to pass before I met Tim. So, with Errant in high spirits, we set out, and in a few minutes, we'd reached the pretty row of cottages that had once been home. As we drew nearer, Joey Rushdale hurried out his door, carrying a toolbox. I waved and drew rein—but only after we'd halted by his gate did I see his face.

"Rushdale!" I said. "Are you all right?"

He broke into his nearly toothless smile. "Bully," he said. "It's just that seeing you on that horse gave me a turn. Thought you wur Hugh come back."

"I had a turn like that this morning when Officer Jenkins stopped by the barn. Seems we're seeing Hugh everywhere."

"Shows he's watching over us, and a good thing, too, with murder aboot." He smiled again, but his eyes were serious. "Surely it was him seeing to it you've got nothing more than that bruise. Speaking of trouble, you're not heading towards the Hawkins farm, are you?"

"The bridle paths are still open to the Hall's horses," I said. "Sir Thomas told my father it's part of the contract. And the navvies are no trouble if you leave them alone."

"Be sure you do, then," he said. "They're a rough lot. I offered Tim Jenkins it might be one of them as done Mr. Vanter in, but he says not likely. They got three minders—*there's* men not to cross!— watching them and hauling them in and out with lorries."

"Lorries!"

He nodded. "The minders told me, coz not one of them knows aught aboot fixing a lorry when there's trouble with it. See, Mr. Norton had the navvies tear down the cottages where they could've slept fine, coz he knew even his minders couldn't have kept them in at night. So, he beds them down in town, with their minders to watch them, and hauls them here before dawn. They're near done, though. The building'll be work for a better lot."

He sighed. "A hundred housen, and if you can credit what you hear at The Arms, not a mon in them'll work where he lives. Seems Mr. Norton expects them to own motors—flivvers, most likely—so they can travel to town and back every day."

"They may not *all* need motors. I've heard Mr. Norton is asking the Council to get a motorbus to come and go from Lechlade to Oxford. Evenings, too. That would mean we could go to the pictures!"

Rushdale nodded. "He's a coming mon, is Mr. Norton. Looks ahead, sees the new world you're growing into. Think of yourself, fifty years on. You won't even know this place, with roads, busses, motors, housen all aboot."

Fifty years on. 1969. Myself, sixty-four. The dream of an evening at the pictures faded into a vision of motors and lorries roaring through the now-silent farmland. The rooks in a nearby oak cawed in Hugh's voice: *The landlords who own England are done for—and we* should *be done for.*

Rushdale put his hand on my knee. "You're thinking you like it the way it is, eh, lad?"

I hadn't been, but when I looked at the daffodils in the cottage gardens, the warm Cotswold stone of the cottages themselves, the familiar footpath to the stable, I nodded.

"So do I," he said. "But your mum, she lost five babies before you, coz she couldn't pay for the care grand folks would've got for them. And this row of housen ends in empty walls instead of the cottage where the Goodwins and their fine brood kept us all lively, coz there's no law to stop a steward from taking a tenant's roof off. And nobody dared tell Sir Thomas that Vanter was cheating us all, for fear he'd do to us what he'd done to Goodwin. Your world'll be a better one for us on the bottom of the heap, Harry. You mark my words." He chuckled as Errant pawed the path. "You'd best get on."

"Seems so," I said, smiling. "It's good to see you." As Errant and I passed the walls and staring windows of the cottage that had been the Goodwins', I remembered I'd meant to ask Rushdale about Farmer Farrington and the dart game, in case he'd be more forthcoming with me than he'd been with Tim. But he'd already disappeared down the path.

We rode on at a rising trot, which, together with a few canters, took us through the Home Farm to the old Hawkins Farm. Half a mile past the gate, Errant suddenly neighed, and as we rounded a curve, we came upon a group of navvies in ragged clothes digging out the hedgerows that had separated the fields from the bridle path. I drew rein, reluctant to ride through them, but the work extended only a few hundred paces, and if we were going to get to Chandace Grange at the hour Tim expected us, this was the only possible route. So we walked on—or rather, pranced on, for Errant was putting on airs and graces for the benefit of the overworked, starved horses that were hauling the prickly branches to a nearby pile. The navvies made what room for us they could, and though none of them returned my nods or my thanks, their hardened faces were at least neutral.

We were almost in the clear when one driver rolled his cart up far too fast, wrenched his horses to a halt, and jumped down almost at Errant's feet. "Wot a fancy lad!" he said, leering. "Decked out soft and sweet as a gel. Shame t'let 'im pass w'out a kiss, wot?"

Had he seen? Was it so obvious? I looked desperately at the others, but though a few of them murmured, most of them merely stopped work and looked on with interest. As Errant was sidling anxiously, I urged him forward, but the driver's arm shot out and grabbed his reins just below the bit.

Errant half-reared and struck out so fast that I didn't realize what he'd done until I saw the man lying on the ground. Horrified, I urged Errant back on the track, but instead of obeying me, he reared over the navvy, who yelled and rolled to the side. I shifted my weight to prevent our doing terrible damage, but it wasn't until I'd driven Errant ten paces past the hedgerow work that I dared halt and look back to see if the navvy was badly hurt.

He wasn't. He'd been yanked to his feet by a man in muddy boots and an ill-fitting tweed coat.

"You're better off than you deserve," said the man, shoving the limping navvy towards his cart. "And a good thing, too, as you'll be looking for other work tomorrow."

He turned to the others, who were energetically digging up the hedge. "You know the rules. Good behavior, hard work—that's all Mr. Norton asks of you. Step out of line, and you're out a job." His tone changed as I collected my reins. "As for you, lad . . ."

Errant stood uneasily but obediently as the man walked towards us. In spite of his clothes, I judged him to be a horseman, both by the appraising glance he gave Errant and by his tactful approach. "My apologies for your scare," he said, in an accent I couldn't quite place. "Smith's used to the nags that work for him, not a horse like this. As for his insults, I'll ask Mr. Norton to send Sir Thomas a note. These men . . ." He shrugged.

Something in his otherwise handsome face made me say, "They've been no trouble when I've passed them before, sir. And the others were civil enough today."

"They might not have been if I hadn't happened to come inspect their work," he said tersely. "I hope Smith hasn't done damage to Sir Thomas's stud."

"Oh no, sir."

"There's all kinds of damage." Stepping forward, he reached out a practiced hand. Errant sidled away uneasily and laid back his ears. "Ah. Has he done that before?"

"No, sir," I said, distressed.

He stepped a little closer, and Errant sniffed his outstretched hand through flared nostrils. For several seconds, neither of them moved; then Errant dropped his head and the man stroked his neck. "That's better, m'lad." He looked up at me. "Is this the horse that found Vanter?"

"In a manner of speaking, sir."

"From Vienna, is he?"

"His dam and sire were, sir. But he was foaled at Willingford Hall."

"A real beauty, and always treated like the prize he is, I'm sure. Give him a little time, and he'll have forgotten all this. Faster than you or I, I'd wager—You're Harry Green, are you not?"

"Yes, sir," I said, disconcerted by the appraising look that shifted from Errant to me.

"Well, Harry, ride on, and be sure Mr. Norton and Sir Thomas will hear of this."

"Thank you, sir." I touched my forehead and moved Errant off at a trot.

I was some time recovering from the encounter, but just as the man had said, Errant was himself again by the time we'd crossed the Chandace Bridge and followed the bridle path that ran parallel to the long drive to Chandace Grange. Gradually, I relaxed, too, for the Grange, sloping gently towards the Thames, was the most beautiful of the Hall's farms. Traditionally, it had been the home of the baronet's heir before he came into the title, but since Sir Thomas had been only eighteen when his father died, it had been leased to Willingford Hall's steward, and continued to be even when Hugh came of age, for, having no family of his own, he'd had no use for it.

A half mile from the house, I slowed Errant to a walk, so he would be cool when I talked with Tim. At first, he put up some token resistance, for despite twelve miles, he was as fresh as he'd been when we began. Soon, however, he contented himself with looking about us with such interest that I realized my fear of meeting Mr. Vanter had kept me from exercising the horses anywhere near his farm. Even now, riding here made me so uneasy that Errant began to jig.

Ridiculous. I was here to tell Tim what I had discovered, offer to help him further, and trust his good will to help make me Somebody.

As it turned out, the big house was being emptied into lorries, not carts. The scene was so unfamiliar that Errant, who passed motors without a glance, shied and pranced until I walked him up to a lorry and made him see it was only a cart with a motor in front. It took only a few minutes to settle him down, and soon we reached Tim, who had been waiting for us on the portico.

He limped down the stone steps and gestured towards the back of the house. "Let's go to the stable, where it's quieter," he said. "Your father said Errant becomes impatient with standing."

I almost protested, but after Tim threw an eloquent glance towards the movers, I followed him without a murmur.

"You needn't use the stall if you don't want," he said in a low voice as we reached the stable. "I know only a few of the men Davis engaged, and I want to be sure what you say is for my ears alone. So—what have you discovered?"

"Mr. Vanter's cycle," I said. "Sunk in the reeds next to a dock hidden in the Dell."

"What a find!" said Tim, with unconcealed admiration. "Brave lad!"

"Hardly," I said laconically. And I told him about the beech and my terrified observation of Farmer Farrington's tour of the Dell.

"Well," Tim said drily after I'd finished, "the first thing you've proved is that the police are indeed bloody fools. On Wednesday, when we decided to examine the riverbank, Officer Morgan made me stay with Dr. Baines and Vanter's body, on account of my game leg. I was fool enough to repeat his conclusions at the inquest—*knowing* he's a town-bred man with no knowledge of boats—rather than risk a charge of insubordination by returning later for another look." He sighed. "Fortunately, you're not a bloody fool, so we now know that it was possible to moor a skiff in the Dell."

"Don't we know more than that?" I asked. "I thought we knew that Mr. Vanter moored a skiff there and was cycling down to use it."

"I wish we did, but all you've *proved* is that there's a dock in the Dell, and that Farmer Farrington is familiar with it. What makes you think that Vanter hid a skiff there?"

"There was a rope on one pile and the marks of another on a

second. And I thought Farmer Farrington expected . . ." I looked at Tim's skeptical face. "Oh, I see. The murderer could have temporarily tied up *his* skiff at the dock, and Farmer Farrington could have been confirming a suspicion . . . Come to think of it, why would Mr. Vanter moor a skiff in the Dell, rather than in the Willingford Hall boathouse?"

"Clever lad. That's exactly what we need to find out."

"You know," I said thoughtfully, "there was a blazing row about the boathouse when Hugh was home the last time. I don't know what it was all about, but I could ask Mr. Parks. He's in charge of the keys to the outbuildings."

"Excellent!" said Tim. "Now, about Farrington: we know he had a wager with Goodwin about stopping Vanter . . ." He paused and grinned. "I'm assuming that you lads heard everything this morning."

"Yes," I admitted, patting Errant as he began to step about restlessly.

"How do you think that fits in with what you saw yesterday in the Dell?"

He was really asking me, not just posing a question he'd answered for himself, and his respect made me think carefully. "I suppose you *could* say that when Farmer Farrington made the wager, he meant to stop Vanter by murdering him, that he did it, and then came back to look at what he'd done."

"You don't sound convinced."

"I'm not. His being in the Dell doesn't make him a murderer any more than my being there makes me one. And if he *knew* what happened, why take the chance of coming back?"

"You're saying that he'd thought one thing had happened, and my testimony at the inquest implied that something different had happened, so he'd come to see for himself."

I nodded, stroking Errant again as he sidestepped. "Will you arrest him?"

"I can't tell you, Harry. Even though you've been so helpful."

"All right," I said, hurt. "But if you did arrest him, that would be too bad, because by Wednesday, Goodwin could have talked to him, and I would have talked to Mr. Parks about the boathouse. So we'd have a lot more evidence."

"I take your point," he said gloomily. "But waiting two days to tell Morgan is as much as my job's worth." Then, looking at Errant's erect ears, he whispered, "Excuse me," and strode to the door.

I heard a scuffle of feet, and a young man in a dark green jacket dashed towards the house.

"Curse my game leg," muttered Tim, limping back in as the man in green disappeared into the house's back door. "You didn't happen to recognize him, did you?"

"No," I said slowly. "Though something about him was familiar . . . Crikey! Is somebody spying on the investigation?"

"It's more likely that one of the men Mr. Davis engaged to inventory Vanter's effects for probate is looking for news to pass to his mates," he said. "The whole tale is ripe for local gossip, Vanter being so unpopular. I'll look over Davis's men as soon as we're finished here. But first, there's something I want to tell you. This morning Lovejoy told me what Vanter had said about Hugh that had made him so angry. It, er, concerned you."

"I wager I know what it was," I said grimly. "He accused . . . no, he *never* accused; he insinuated. So, he probably told Mr. Lovejoy that Hugh had praised my riding, then added something like, *Always one for the lads, our Hugh. Nothing like a boy's fair face.*"

Tim stared at me. "Those are almost exactly the words Lovejoy said he'd used! Good God! Did Vanter say such things to you? About his employer and yours?"

I nodded. "It began right after Hugh stopped him from dismissing Goodwin, so I ignored it, thinking it was just the kind of spite he was famous for. When I thought about it later, though, I realized he was hoping I'd blush, or flair up, so he'd have 'evidence' that would allow him to blackmail Hugh and Sir Thomas if they dismissed him."

"The hound! Did he keep saying those things to you?"

"No, he stopped," I said flatly. There was no need to tell him how Mr. Vanter had started looking at me last spring after he'd returned from London on some errand. How he'd finally cornered me in the harness room, leering as he mentioned 'lads' fair faces.'

—How he'd gripped my shoulder painfully with one hand and moved the other towards the buttons on my trousers.

—How he'd jumped away in alarm as my father's hurried footsteps had neared the door.

—How I'd bolted into the courtyard, leaving the two of them face to face.

I would never share that shame with Tim, but the combination of shock and compassion in his face made me feel I could trust him with the doubt that had grown out of it.

"I was angry about being used to blackmail Hugh," I said, struggling to express what I'd hardly even dared to think. "But what really hurt was the implication that it was wrong for Hugh to . . . to like me." I looked up at him, willing my eyes not to water. "It still bothers me, because Hugh meant a great deal to me."

"Of course he did," said Tim gently. "And true affection is never wrong." He paused a minute, then added, "There was something . . . unusual . . . about Hugh's attachment to you. Other people who loved Hugh—and there were many of us—occasionally remarked on it, but never quite understood, at least not until this morning."

He smiled and patted Errant. "Harry, watching you ride is seeing Hugh all over again. Men with backgrounds like Lovejoy's and mine don't become horsemen, but even we could see that you have the perfect coordination with a horse that makes a superlative rider. The gentleman Sir Thomas brought out with him to watch was deeply impressed."

I blushed. "It was Errant. He's a wonder."

"Maybe, but you bring out the wonder in him. Hugh clearly recognized your gift from your earliest days in the saddle and knew enough to treasure it. And you." He looked at me earnestly. "So you must *never* let Vanter's corruption twist the way Hugh cherished you into something it wasn't."

I played with Errant's mane, unable to speak.

"All right," he said after a moment. "I must go quickly and impound that cycle-- behind the beech, you say—and talk to Morgan. Meanwhile, if you learn anything about the boathouse, let me know." He smiled. "I'm grateful for your help, Harry."

If he was grateful, I was . . . well, I had difficulty finding a word for what I was as Errant and I started back through the wood to Willingford Stable. Grateful, certainly, for Tim's respect and praise. But beyond that, I had unfamiliar feelings that mingled inappropriately with my lad's haircut and livery. I was so preoccupied with them that I was taken completely by surprise when, as we approached the wooden bridge between the Grange and the Hall, Errant stopped, his nostrils flaring.

Snapped out of my reveries, I listened. Looking in the direction of Errant's quivering ears, I heard a rustling that might be footsteps, then silence—except Errant's snorting. Gradually, his breathing quieted, but it was some minutes before I could get him to go on, and several more before I stopped looking through the trees myself. Because I was almost, but not quite, sure I'd seen someone in dark green slip behind a massive oak.

Chapter 11

I returned to the stable to find my father grooming Sebilla. As I'd expected, he was a little short with me for being twenty minutes behindhand, but Errant was cool, which he accepted as a self-evident explanation of my tardiness. Relieved of the necessity of lying, I put Errant up, still shaken by the rustle in the woods.

I was brought back to myself only as I found Father waiting for me at the stable door. "Sir Thomas will call for Atlas tomorrow morning at nine," he said. "He has asked that you and Sebilla accompany him when he visits the Farrington farm and the Rectory."

I was about to express excitement when I realized that Father was hurt at not having been asked to accompany Sir Thomas himself. Thinking quickly, I said, "May I guess that you introduced him to Atlas after I left this morning, sir?"

"It was easily done. The gentleman with him was interested in the stable and its history, so I could introduce the horses as a matter of course." He added with satisfaction, "The gentleman was much impressed with the way the stable was kept. Sir Thomas was pleased, and that's when he asked us to make Atlas and Sebilla ready tomorrow morning."

"Brilliant!" I said. "I'll wager you'll soon have Sir Thomas here every day."

"God willing," he said. His face relaxed a little, and in a few minutes, he brought Atlas out and started grooming him to a shine. "You'd better brush your white breeches," he said over his shoulder.

"They got a little spotted after the inquest."

They'd got more than that; Mr. Norton's motor had splashed them when Hutchins had pulled it up, and I hadn't yet brushed off the mud. I went to our quarters to work on them, but soon I realized that the spots contained oil as well as dirt, thus requiring more than brushing. Good, I thought suddenly. I would have to enlist support Inside, and I might run into Mr. Parks.

Fortune favored me. Mr. Parks was there, and since he'd been a valet before he became a butler, he knew exactly what to do for my breeches, even offering to oversee the project. That would not have been true in years past; but now one felt that time hung a little heavily on his hands.

"Mr. Parks," I said, rubbing the cleanser he'd provided into the spots, "does anybody use the boathouse the Hall shares with the Grange?"

"Not anymore," he said. "Sir Thomas doesn't row."

"And yet Mr. Lovejoy testified that Sir Thomas had lent Hugh's skiff to Dr. Baines."

"Did he now? Yes, yes, of course—a little more on *that* spot. Excellent. Now, if you rub it just so . . ." He did, and the spot disappeared.

"That's amazing!" I said. "Thank you very much." I picked up the breeches, discouraged by what seemed the end of the conversation, but as I turned, he took them from me to examine them in better light.

"Oxalic acid, well diluted," he said, nodding appreciatively. "There are all manner of newfangled cleansers now, but the inexpensive old ways still work—Yes, Sir Thomas asked me to copy the key to the boathouse for Dr. Baines a month ago." He chuckled. "I'm surprised I'd forgotten. The boat house padlock had rusted shut, and it took all Baines's surgical skill to free it up."

"That's odd," I said. "It doesn't sound like Hugh to tolerate a rusted padlock. Wasn't that sort of thing in Mr. Vanter's care?"

"Care, indeed!" Mr. Parks snorted. "Mr. Vanter 'cared' for the lock by changing it under some pretext, presumably so he would have his own key. When Hugh was last home, there was some unpleasantness about that, during which Mr. Vanter's key ended up in the river. I subsequently received instructions not to give Mr. Vanter the remaining key under any circumstances."

My eyes opened wide. "You mean, Mr. Vanter had been using Hugh's skiff?"

"I think not. He insisted that he had used only his own skiff—one that he had kept in the boathouse until Hugh ordered him to remove it. That may very well be true. When I tested the lock a few weeks after the unpleasantness, there was no skiff in the boathouse except Hugh's, and Vanter had been seen on the river, doing errands, or so he said."

"Errands! What errands could he do in a skiff that he couldn't do in his motor?"

"So people asked themselves after hearing of the disagreement. There are those who speculated, on what grounds I cannot say, that he paid a weekly visit to a lady," said Mr. Parks with a disapproving smile. "I believe her existence, let alone her identity, was never confirmed, but I wouldn't know. I rarely listen to village gossip— Here, take your breeches."

"Thank you," I said. "I greatly appreciate your help."

Chapter 12

It was a point of pride with my father that a gentleman could pass a white cambric handkerchief over any of our horses without dirtying it—a standard, like many others in our stable, set by the kindly but exacting author of *The Guide to Service.* Father had every reason to feel pride when we led the horses to the Hall's front entrance Tuesday morning, for they were perfectly turned out, and Atlas, whose coat had improved immeasurably under our care, positively glinted in the sunlight. Sir Thomas said little, but it was lost on neither my father nor myself that he paused halfway down the steps and looked at the horses with pleasure.

Any concerns we might have had about Atlas's reaction to being ridden by somebody other than ourselves evaporated immediately as my father held Sir Thomas's stirrup. Sir Thomas mounted a little stiffly, but Atlas stood like a rock, not even venturing to move when, after I'd vaulted on, Sebilla began to fret.

Once all was adjusted, Sir Thomas glanced at me. "Should we go through the park or take the bridle path?"

"The bridle path would be more direct, sir," I said quickly, thinking of the hard surface of the Oxford Road.

"Then we shall take it," he said, and moved off in that direction. I was prepared to follow at the distance of the twenty paces my father insisted was proper for a groom, but once the bridle path widened, Sir Thomas turned in the saddle and beckoned to me.

"Tell me the history of this horse again," he said as I trotted to his side.

I repeated the story of Atlas's rescue, adding to it Lady Sylvia's suggestion that there might be blue blood somewhere in his lineage.

"I would say so," he said. "Does he jump?"

"A little, sir. I've worked him over *cavalettis*, then up to two feet six."

He smiled in something like his old way. "And no higher?"

"No, sir. He's powerful, but his strength is in his shoulders, not his hind quarters."

"You've not even been tempted to raise the bar?"

"No, sir. As I'm sure you would not if you had jumped him."

"You flatter me—or at least you flatter the lad I was long ago. At your age, I took horses over every fence in the estate, so long as they would go."

I wasn't sure how to answer without seeming to criticize. Perhaps aware of that, he said, "Tell me about the horse you are riding. He's as handsome as Errant, is he not?"

"Nearly, sir. But he's not as elegant a mover, especially at the canter."

"Ah, yes. The conformation flaw; I remember Hugh's disappointment. But he is certainly a horse on which any gentleman would be proud to be seen. Am I right in thinking your father prefers him to Errant?"

"Yes, sir."

"And why is that?"

"My father values obedience in a horse, sir. And Sebilla, though certainly not passive, is willing to obey."

Sir Thomas's eyebrows shot up. "Surely you're not telling me that the horse that performed so beautifully for you yesterday is disobedient!"

"Not exactly, sir. But his performance has to come from himself, not from his rider. To achieve it, you have to abandon all thoughts of making him submit, and instead be endlessly willing to negotiate."

I looked at him, aware that I had not expressed myself as well as I'd wished, but he seemed to understand me. "Such a horse," he said thoughtfully, "could easily turn rogue in the wrong hands."

I nodded wordlessly, thinking of the way Errant had struck out at the navvy the day before, and of the many times I'd wondered what would happen to him if Mr. Vanter caught me alone again, exposed my true identity, and forced me to leave the stable.

We had reached the bottom of the hill, and he drew Atlas up, peering into the Dell. "Is this where you found Vanter?"

"Yes, sir."

He looked about carefully. "I can't see a place from which a man could throw a stone with great force and not be seen."

"Nor can I, sir."

"A sling, perhaps? I've heard that some poachers are such masters of its art that they'd put David to shame."

He was clearly referring to Goodwin, whose skill with a sling was legendary. I quickly shook my head. "A sling requires more room and more movement than a throw, sir. He would have had to step beyond the trees to use it."

He examined the trees for a few more moments, shaking his head. "Well," he said finally, "we should get on to Farmer Farrington. Shall we try a trot?"

We trotted and, after a few hundred paces, broke into a canter. That was not Atlas's natural gait, and it made Sir Thomas cough so hard that we came back to a walk. Even so, he seemed pleased. "You've done fine work with this horse, lad," he said. "He's as willing as he is steady."

"I'm glad you like him, sir."

He looked at me as he stroked Atlas's neck. "Do *you* like him?"

"Oh yes, sir," I said, smiling. "I enjoy riding him just for his company."

"Well put." He led the way onto the North Road and across the bridge. In a few hundred paces, two lanes forked off the bridle path that paralleled the road, the left crossing it and leading to the Farrington Farm, and the right leading to Chandace Grange. We took the left and, as we neared Farmer Farrington's house, I could almost see a mantle of formality settle on Sir Thomas's shoulders,

When he turned to me, his face had lost all its earlier friendliness. "Let me precede you by twenty paces," he said. "When we get to the farmyard, I may be asked to go inside. If so, you will hold both horses. If not, I will have to ask you to stay out of hearing distance."

"Yes, of course, sir."

We were early for the meeting, but Farmer Farrington was waiting at the farmyard gate, his bent body showing every sign of impatience. His greeting, though visually respectful, was apparently less than cordial, and I saw in a moment that Sir Thomas would not dismount.

According to my instructions, I halted Sebilla outside the gate and pointedly looked across the farm's well-kept walls and hedgerows to the tower of St. Barnabas, hating my circumspection. Here I was, only twenty paces from a man who had some secret knowledge about the murder, and I was shut out.

I knew perfectly well it was my lot to be shut from the affairs of my betters, and that the best servants accepted that lot with grace. I'd been brought up with the example of Mr. Parks and my father and schooled carefully by my ever-tactful mother. I'd even learned to take pride in my deference. But now, as I glanced towards Sir Thomas and Farmer Farrington, I understood the resentment cloaked in the farmer's servile gestures. In fact, they vaguely reminded me of ... of ...

Mr. Vanter. Not the side of him that lorded it over us, savoring every "yes, sir," as if it were a fine wine. The side which made him, alone of all the people on the estate, address Hugh as "Mr. Chandace-Willingford" and who bowed in old-fashioned respect before Sir Thomas. Hugh's response suddenly echoed in my ears: *Watch him, Harry, and you'll see how deference can be used as an insult. He's one of the few who hates the whole wretched system more than I do. Ironically, that very system makes it possible for* me *to believe in an equality denied to* him.

I mulled his statement over, wondering that I hadn't understood its complex truth until now. Mr. Lovejoy had been indignant about

Mr. Vanter's taking so much from a man who had treated him so well; he'd been incensed by the threat to smear Hugh's reputation.

But now it seemed to me it hadn't been Hugh or Sir Thomas that Mr. Vanter had been obsessed with subverting. It was the *system*—the whole parade of "yes sir, no sir," the perpetual march of doing things for "the master" that any sane man could do for himself, the need for obedience without negotiation.

Such a horse could easily go rogue in the wrong hands, Sir Thomas had said of Errant. I sat up with such a jolt that Sebilla moved uneasily under me. I steadied him apologetically, but as we settled back to our waiting posture, I thought of Mr. Vanter's intelligence, and I wondered whether he, like Errant, had had a temperament that demanded respect and compromise, but had received nothing but senseless, demeaning orders until he came, embittered and far too late, to Willingford Hall.

Not that I cared.

Wait! I *did* care. If obedience could have a deeper effect than occasional irritation at a series of orders, what was going to happen to me? *Think of yourself, fifty years on,* Rushdale had suggested; but looking forward all I could see, now that Hugh was gone, was a life of deference and exclusion. Unless, of course, Rushdale was right about there being new times for those of us at the bottom of the heap. But what then?

Without "the system," I might avoid the wrong hands, but would the absence of hands be any better? What guarantee was there that a leaderless world of motors, busses, and houses wouldn't simply enrich ruthless men like Mr. Vanter, while forcing the rest of us to starve or turn rogue?

I tried to shake my questions away, but they continued to plague me, for after concluding his conversation with Farmer Farrington, Sir Thomas was so distracted that he rode to the Rectory without restoring me to his side. Thus, perforce, I remained twenty paces away while he talked cheerfully not only with Reverend Williams and

Richard, but with the Baineses, Lady Sylvia, and some gentleman.

No, not "some gentleman." As he stepped next to Atlas and spoke to Sir Thomas, I recognized the man who had watched me work Errant the day before and admired the stable in my absence. I'd meant to ask my father who he was, but he probably didn't know. A *Guide to Service* groom stood discreetly by as his master brought visitors to the stable, awaiting orders but expecting no introduction. I'd seen it done all my life. I'd done it myself.

But who could he be? A new steward? Impossible. The whole wretched system decreed that no gentleman of quality—his was as visible as breeding in a horse—became a steward. A member of the Council? One who had come to investigate the murder?

If he was, I'd better work even harder on the case, for he would be far more competition than the police, given the way Tim was limited by Officer Morgan. This gentleman would have resources I could only dream of. I had inside knowledge, though. Enough, I reflected, to require the murderer keep an eye on me.

I looked around uneasily, but all I saw was the group twenty paces away. Richard and Lady Sylvia saw me and waved. I tipped my hat, conscious that the gesture, like the distance that separated us, made my position in their world only too clear.

Their conversation lasted quite some time; it was only after the St. Barnabas clock had struck noon that Sir Thomas turned away and rode past me. When we came to the bridle path, he signaled me forward.

"We were talking, among other things, about your further education, Harry. Reverend Williams and his unfortunate son—who wants to talk to you, by the way—think that Hugh wished you to go beyond the village school, as Tim Jenkins and one of the Goodwin boys did."

"That's very kind, sir, but—"

"—I'll discuss the matter with your father soon," he said. "Meanwhile, tell him that Lady Sylvia will be riding with me day after tomorrow."

Well, well! That was interesting. "Yes, sir."

He shook his head. "I confess to being a little disturbed by the prospect. I told her none of my horses were trained for a side saddle—and she said she had never ridden in one! Imagine! The Earl of Atherton's daughter riding astride! Had she been anyone else, I would have said it was indecent, but I had no wish to argue with a lady who sympathizes with the Suffragettes." He glanced at me. "I have offered her Sebilla, not Errant."

"Very good, sir."

"You know, I had been going to suggest that she and I ride tomorrow, but I suddenly remembered that before the inquest, I had told you to come oil my book bindings Tuesday—today—and then had forgotten. In the interest of the book bindings, I quickly decided to have you come to the library tomorrow. Wednesday, that is, at ten. And I will trust you and your father to have the horses ready for Lady Sylvia and me on Thursday at one. Is that satisfactory?"

"Of course, sir."

"Excellent," he said. "And I do like this horse. Let's have a trot."

The action freed my mind from its clouds—until my father's carefully deferential greeting to Sir Thomas raised the specter of my future once more.

Chapter 13

On Wednesday, Mr. Parks showed me to the library promptly at ten, but he hesitated outside the door. "Sir Thomas is engaged. Let me announce you and see if he wants you to wait." He stepped inside and, after a brief conversation, he re-emerged, pointed me to a chair, and stood next to me, his face expressionless.

It was a long fifteen minutes before we heard concluding voices nearing the door and Mr. Parks sprang to attention. As he opened it, Mr. Norton walked out—and stopped with a smile when he saw me.

"I was about to come to the stable to find you, lad. Sir Thomas has kindly said he will allow you to give Master Cyril a few beginning lessons on that black horse you were riding. We have agreed that I will send the boy over at three on Thursday."

I glanced at Sir Thomas. He nodded, so I said, "It will be a pleasure, sir."

"Excellent," said Mr. Norton, beaming. "I will impress upon him the necessity of obeying your directions—not his strong suit, I'm afraid."

"I'm sure he'll be no trouble, sir. He has spirit, but he also respects a horse."

"Until tomorrow, then." Mr. Norton bowed slightly to Sir Thomas, smiled at me, and looking immensely pleased, followed Mr. Parks back through the house.

Sir Thomas gave me a wry glance as I walked through the door with the cloths and special oils Mr. Parks had found for me. "You have your mother's tact, lad," he said. "Spirit indeed! I've heard the boy has been a trouble-maker since he was in the cradle."

"I think his dreams will make him listen, sir," I said, thinking of Cyril's eager face. "He wishes to be a knight."

"So does his father," said Sir Thomas sourly. "Let us hope the boy's aspirations are more chivalric—Well, to business. At the top of those stairs in the corner, you will find yourself facing the oldest books in the library. A few of them are among the first books ever printed in England. Your main concern is the bindings, but if you find any volumes that are losing pages or are otherwise in poor condition, please set them aside and I will have them repaired." Following my awed glance towards the catwalk, he added, "Do you understand?"

"Yes, sir," I said apologetically. "It's just that I hadn't realized the books were so old, and I'd never thought of the binding of a book being separated from . . . from . . ."

"Its pages? You're in the company of many others. But in the fifteenth century, and even the sixteenth, gentlemen bought books in quires held together only by stitching and had them bound in a way that suited them."

"I see, sir. Does that mean that a gentleman who collected books could bind them uniformly so they would look handsome on the shelves, without regard to their subjects?"

He smiled. "Theoretically, but you'll find that my ancestors were a little more careful than that. Books of different sorts—law, history, medicine, poetry, fiction and so on—were bound in different color bindings, and all were stamped with the book's title. The differences will be more visible when you have treated their leather. But have a care. A little damp on the pages will spoil them."

I climbed the spiral staircase with some trepidation, but I found that once I had carefully dislodged a book from its place and dusted it, there was no reason to open it at all, if one were only bent on preserving its binding. Soon, accustomed to hours of cleaning harnesses, saddles, and bridles, I was comfortably involved in my work and rewarded by the beauty of its results.

After an hour or so, the huge library door opened, and Mr. Parks announced Mr. Lovejoy. I expected to be told to leave, but apparently Sir Thomas had forgotten my existence, so I continued to work silently while the two men conversed below me.

"I swear Morgan is going to put me in the local gaol," said Mr. Lovejoy, striding towards Sir Thomas's desk. "They've found nobody who can remember seeing me running. That's no surprise, since there wasn't a soul on the towpath, and the lock keeper was snug in his house when I turned around. But I suspect they're under pressure to make an arrest."

"Who is creating the pressure?" said Sir Thomas, putting down his pen.

"Wouldn't it be the Council?" asked Mr. Lovejoy.

"The Council isn't slated to convene until Friday," said Sir Thomas. "And none of the members have said a word to me. Have you seen Jenkins this morning?"

"Yes, yes. He says I am in 'no immediate danger,' there still being no evidence that's not circumstantial." He sighed. "My friends at The Chandace Arms say the same thing, adding that their odds are on Farrington, because that's apparently the way Norton is betting. On what grounds, I know not."

"Nor do I. I *do* know, however, that Norton visited me this morning, ostensibly to arrange riding lessons for his son, but in fact to inquire into my plans for Chandace Grange. I referred him to you."

"To me!? With the suspicion of blood on my hands?"

Sir Thomas chuckled. "Blood doesn't bother Norton; he's a man of business. I wouldn't be surprised if he talked to you before the week is out. If he does, I'm interested in finding out if he has knowledge that he could have only gotten from Vanter, who shouldn't have had it."

"Knowledge of what kind?"

"Inside knowledge, you might call it. As I told you, it was at Vanter's suggestion that I sold the Hawkins Farm to Norton. At the time, I told him that the Hawkins Farm had been purchased by my great-grandfather for his second son. When the son died in that damn-fool charge in Crimea, his farm became part of the estate, but it was exempt from the entail, and so was the only one I could sell." He smiled. "I thus made sure Vanter believed the remainder of the estate was entailed."

"I believed it myself," said Mr. Lovejoy. "In fact, I remember Hugh's mentioning it."

"Probably with disapproval," said Sir Thomas. "Entail interfered with his egalitarian ideas."

"Well, yes," said Mr. Lovejoy, smiling.

Working quietly above them, I smiled, too. How many times had I overheard Hugh insist that the tradition of fathers' leaving whole family estates to their eldest sons, thus leaving generations of daughters and younger sons without income, was the product of a mind-set that favored property over people?

"Partly because of Hugh's ridiculous ideas," Sir Thomas went on, "but even more because of his shock at discovering the estate's perilous situation on his last leave, he insisted that we break the entail. The procedure was simple; it required little more than a tolerance for legal language and the signatures of father and son. We signed, and we agreed that nobody, especially Vanter, was to be told what we had done. So now, you *should* be the only person besides our London solicitor who knows that I can bequest or partition and sell Willingford Hall to anybody I wish."

Up on the catwalk, I felt a cold sliver of fear slide down my spine.

"But you fear I'm *not* alone?" asked Mr. Lovejoy.

"I'm afraid I do." Sir Thomas coughed several times, then went on. "Consider: when Vanter made his offer on the Farrington Farm, he was visibly skeptical when I said I must refuse it because of the entail. I was surprised, until yesterday evening. That's when I recalled that when I was most seriously ill, my London solicitor wrote that he couldn't settle Hugh's estate until I had looked at a letter and an account marked for my eyes alone." He pulled a folder from his desk and removed a single sheet of paper from it. "This was the result."

He handed the paper to Mr. Lovejoy, who read it quickly and looked up, shocked. "Good God! This gives access not just to Hugh's letter, but to all the other documents in your solicitor's files, including the breakage of the entail! You could have—"

Sir Thomas coughed as he looked unseeingly across the room. "It hardly seemed to matter. Hugh was dead. Nobody expected me to live, including myself. And yet, I have some vague memory of the Almighty's leaning down and telling me on my sickbed to grant Vanter power of attorney only for an hour, as you'll note I did."

"Then we may thank the Almighty," said Mr. Lovejoy. "Still, an hour gave Vanter enough time to look at a great deal. Do you think he told Norton what he'd learned?"

"That's what I'd like you to find out."

"Damn the police!" said Mr. Lovejoy, jumping up and walking to the window. "If I weren't imprisoned here, I'd go to London immediately and talk to your solicitor."

"Sending you there would only arouse suspicions. It would be far preferable for you to talk to Norton directly, trying to determine the nature of his friendship with Vanter."

"I'll be glad to," said Mr. Lovejoy, returning to his seat. "But I assume he's not easy to draw out."

"No, he isn't," said Sir Thomas. "But the Council has found that one can gain considerable insight into his opinions by offering him the public respect one would normally reserve for a duke, while privately observing him with the care one would normally reserve for a brilliant opponent in a game of cards."

Mr. Lovejoy laughed. "I'll be right at home then. My early salary was so meager that I was forced to augment it with my skill at cards, and men of my origins learn deference with our first steps."

"Your origins are nothing to apologize for, Lovejoy. Norton's, on the other hand—"

"Truly?"

"Oh yes. He takes pride in boasting about them in high-bred company. East London, drunken father, beaten mother. He left home at seven, shed his accent at ten, and has been working his way upwards ever since."

As I replaced one book in the shelf and withdrew another, I heard not Mr. Lovejoy's reply, but Mr. Norton's words to me: *Sidelining— making a little money on the side of your regular work. Many a lad has made his way upwards by engaging in it.* It certainly offered a very different "way upward" from the competent, deferential way my father had learned from *The Guide to Service.* The independence that accompanied sidelining's cast of mind was appealing, but . . .

"Before you go, Lovejoy," said Sir Thomas in a tone that broke in on my musing.

Mr. Lovejoy, who had been about to rise, sat back again. "Yes?"

"I haven't thanked you properly for the discovery you made in Vanter's file Monday. Six months hidden! Who would have thought even Vanter would sink so low?" He coughed into his handkerchief. "In any case, the matter has been straightened out with amazing speed, so we—and 'we' includes you—will have an important discussion tomorrow."

Mr. Lovejoy's face brightened. "Wonderful! What time?"

"Let's say eleven. And I need hardly tell you that it will be absolutely confidential."

"Absolutely. The matter is far too important to be anything else."

"Excellent." Sir Thomas rang for Mr. Parks.

"Thank you," said Mr. Lovejoy, standing up. "—Oh, and look! I meant to give you this when I came in!" He handed a note to Sir Thomas and left as Mr. Parks opened the door.

Sir Thomas read the note, jumped to his feet and hurried from the room, his cough echoing through the rooms outside.

Alone with the beautiful shelves of books, I worked my way to the end of the row. Then, sure that even Mr. Parks had forgotten my presence, I tiptoed through the great rooms and managed to pass unseen through the servants' quarters and out the courtyard door, my mind slipping from what I'd heard to the difficulty of scheduling Cyril's lesson.

As I'd expected, my father was displeased. "Thursday at three!" he said. "Didn't you remember that Sir Thomas and Lady Sylvia had planned to ride at one?"

"I couldn't correct arrangements Sir Thomas had made without embarrassing him in front of Mr. Norton, sir."

"True. Well, I can discuss the matter with him, because he's riding today."

"Today!"

He nodded sourly. "You may well be surprised. I learned of the plan only a few minutes ago. Lady Sylvia is to come at half-past one, so we must change into livery immediately. Fortunately, I cleaned harness instead of exercising Sebilla, so he's fresh. All we have to do is groom and saddle."

I glanced at the clock. "What about dinner?"

He smiled. "Remembering that lads are always hungry, I asked Mrs. Middleton to send Agatha to the harness room with sandwiches."

I sighed as I walked to our quarters. Sometimes it seemed that even my father had forgotten I wasn't a lad. But as I changed into my livery and readied the horses, my irritation changed to anxiety. Seeing me so soon after I'd worked on the books in the library might remind Sir Thomas that I'd been present during his conversation with Mr. Lovejoy. And what then?

Fortunately, Lady Sylvia's arrival so distracted Sir Thomas that he once again forgot I existed. She drove herself into the courtyard in Dr. Baines's motor, an independence and skill that plainly shocked him. And when she leapt out, the split skirt of her impeccably tailored riding habit momentarily left him coughing speechlessly. He recovered, however, welcoming her with a courtliness I recognized as a manner that gentlemen automatically assumed for ladies. He offered her his arm, and led her to the stable door, where my father and I were standing at attention.

At Sir Thomas's order, my father led Atlas to the mounting block for him, while I waited a few paces away with Sebilla. But Lady Sylvia walked straight to us, adjusted the stirrups to her liking, and mounted with a businesslike grace even Hugh would have envied. Sebilla, who liked to move off as soon as he was mounted, pranced a little, but she patted him soothingly and collected her reins with such authority that he stood with comparative patience until Sir Thomas led the way out of the courtyard.

"I confess I am relieved," said my father as their hoofbeats faded away. "I expected her to be competent. But as you know, few women ride really well, and I had doubts about Sebilla's behavior with clumsy hands."

"Her hands are excellent," I said. "Did Sir Thomas say how long they'll be out?"

"He said they'd take the bridle path through Chandace Grange, then across the bridge in town and back to the Hall. But he may wish to show her a few of those lovely secondary paths at the Grange, so I doubt they will be back before three. I suggest you work Errant, as he is fretting in his stall."

He was indeed fretting, and so was I, for Lady Sylvia, though she'd smiled and been pleasant, had treated me like . . . well, like a groom. I was torn between resentment and shame at having expected anything else. Since Errant and I were both out of sorts, I decided to take him for a canter instead of schooling him in the manège, and as we returned through the park, we overtook Dr. and Mrs. Baines, who were strolling towards the Hall.

"Hello, you two," said Dr. Baines, smiling as I pulled up and steadied Errant. "We're to meet Lady Sylvia at three. I need the motor at half-past three and she *promised* to be back in time, but just in case . . ." He looked over his shoulder as a motor stopped at the gate house. "Who have we here?"

"I think it's the police," I said, frowning. "Though I can't imagine what for."

"No good news, you may be sure," said Mrs. Baines. "Go on ahead, Harry. We'll waylay them and tell them Sir Thomas will be home within the half hour."

"Thank you," I said, and hurried off to put Errant up, hoping it was Tim.

Unfortunately, it was Officer Morgan alone. I caught no more than a glimpse of him, for he and the Baineses arrived in the courtyard at almost the same moment Sir Thomas and Lady Sylvia returned. By the time Father and I had taken care of unsaddling and grooming, the atmosphere in the courtyard had been transformed from the cheerful one we had left. Father, seeing worried faces, discreetly disappeared, but I brought the five water buckets to the central fountain and made myself busy with scrubbing.

"— impossible!" Sir Thomas was saying.

"Then you can swear that your skiff was returned to your boathouse Wednesday afternoon?" asked Officer Morgan.

"At the inquest, Lovejoy testified—under oath—that he'd returned it."

"But when Lovejoy came to the Hall Wednesday night, he didn't mention the skiff."

Sir Thomas reflected. "That's true," he said reluctantly.

"The omission is of great importance. We have received a telephone call saying that a skiff floated downriver and became tangled in reeds slightly upstream from your boathouse estuary. Yesterday, a walker who had passed it a few times looked at it more carefully and saw that it had "HCW" carved into the inside of its bow. Since those are your son's initials, he called us."

"Who was the caller, that he called the police instead of Sir Thomas?" asked Lady Sylvia.

"It's well known that the Hall doesn't have a telephone," said

Officer Morgan. "And Mr. Vanter's murder has caused quite a stir in the area. Several people have called us with what they consider to be helpful evidence."

"Anonymously?" said Mrs. Baines.

"If they so wish," said Officer Morgan. "Or in confidence if they reveal their names."

"Are they paid for providing 'helpful evidence?'" asked Lady Sylvia.

"The police neither pay for information nor accept payment for investigating accused parties," said Officer Morgan loftily.

"Certainly not," said Sir Thomas. "Yet as a Justice of the Peace, I know that a tip from some quarters carries more weight than one from others."

"Times are changing, Sir Thomas," said Officer Morgan. "The police now feel compelled to weigh all information on the same scale, regardless of its origin."

Looking at the three silent, shocked faces before him, he realized belatedly that what he might have meant as a factual statement had been taken as an insult. He flushed with embarrassment but persisted. "I must request permission to search your boathouse, Sir Thomas. I'm sure I'll find everything in order, but as you must understand, I have to follow every lead I'm given."

Dr. Baines stepped forward. "If you'll excuse me, Officer—."

But Sir Thomas held up a hand. "Of course I understand," he said tersely. "Let me call Parks for the keys."

As he led Officer Morgan to the servants' entrance, the others awaited him in such silence that I found it necessary to take two buckets back to the stable. When I returned for the others, Officer Morgan had started towards the boat house, and Sir Thomas had returned to the courtyard.

"Equal scale, indeed!" Lady Sylvia was saying. "Anonymous calls! Helpful evidence! The police may not be paying for it, but I'll wager somebody else is."

"If so," said Dr. Baines, "it's money wasted. As I was trying to tell

Morgan, the skiff Sir Thomas lent me had no initials carved in its bow."

"Really?" said Sir Thomas with relief. "I'm ashamed to admit I couldn't say so myself. I'm not an oarsman, and though I attended a few races when Hugh was at Oxford, I paid no attention to the equipment I financed for him."

"No matter," said Dr. Baines. "Morgan will find your skiff snug in the boathouse. But that won't prove Lovejoy innocent. Thanks to the wretched errand I asked him to do for me, he was on the river at precisely the wrong time. If the murderer is as clever as he seems to have been, he could easily have seen the opportunity a loose skiff gave him and use a telephone tip to steer the police away from himself."

"You'd think Jenkins would know a frame when he saw it," said Lady Sylvia.

"I'm sure he would," said Sir Thomas. "But he's not here, which worries me. The Council appointed him under-officer precisely because it has occasionally wondered where Morgan's loyalties lie. Morgan was miffed, and he may be retaliating by not sharing his 'tips' with Jenkins, in hopes of proving he has no need of a subordinate."

Lady Sylvia whistled in a most unladylike manner.

"Another difficulty," said Sir Thomas, "is that everybody who attended the inquest knows that Vanter set off Lovejoy's temper last Wednesday. Such knowledge, combined with the unfortunate timing, automatically makes the police doubt Lovejoy's innocence."

"Lovejoy was certainly angry on Wednesday, but it was a matter of righteous wrath, not desire for revenge," said Dr. Baines. Glancing at the clock, he turned to his wife. "We really must go."

As Sir Thomas paid them his respects, I gathered up the remaining buckets, but Lady Sylvia tapped my shoulder on her way to the motor. "Harry," she whispered, "if you should find something out, you'll let us know, won't you?"

I kept my face impassive, but I fear a blush rose into it. "Yes, my lady."

"Good lad." Her wink made me forgive her casual treatment of me two hours earlier.

Chapter 14

Shortly after everybody had left the courtyard, my father remembered with distress that he had not consulted Sir Thomas about the conflict between Cyril Norton's lesson and Lady Sylvia's appointment to ride. As was his way, he remedied the omission immediately, with the result that Sir Thomas ordered me to cycle to the Baineses, deliver a note rescheduling the ride for Friday afternoon, and wait for the reply.

I changed out of my livery, thrust a few coins into my pockets in case I should have time to buy sweets at Mr. Howard's shop, and cycled off, disregarding my father's horror that the message was not to be delivered formally and on horseback. If ever Sir Thomas installed a telephone at the Hall, I thought as I pedaled along the bridle path, *all* errands of this nature would stop, and we grooms would have even less to do. It was a good thing that Officer Morgan was no competitor in the search for Mr. Vanter's murderer; I needed to construct a new future for myself as soon as possible.

I was so busy considering my evidence that I hardly noticed as the Dell and the hedges flashed by, and I was surprised when, upon arriving in Chandace, I heard the St. Barnabas clock chime the three quarters. Given the necessity of grooming and saddling, I could never have delivered the message in a half hour on horseback, I thought as I leaned the cycle against Dr. Baines's wall and walked up the garden path.

I knocked, and after a short pause, Mrs. Baines answered the door, an event that reminded me they kept no servant. "Harry!" she said, worried. "What brings you here?"

"Nothing to cause you concern, ma'am," I said reassuringly. "I have a note from Sir Thomas to Lady Sylvia. I am told to wait for the reply."

"Lady Sylvia is ... er ... dressing," she said. "I'll take her Sir Thomas's note, but it will be a half hour before your reply comes."

Her face told me that she was trying to decide whether to invite me in and, if so, whether to put me in the kitchen or the hall. Fortunately, I could spare her the dilemma.

"That will give me the time I need for my other errands," I said, smiling. "Shall I return at quarter past five?"

"Excellent!"

I touched my forehead and hurried down the walk, reflecting on the difference between the comradeship implied in Lady Sylvia's wink and the *whole wretched system* visible in Mrs. Baines's indecision. At the moment, however, Lady's Sylvia's delay gave me time to do what I had dearly wished to do only fifteen minutes ago: visit The Chandace Arms.

I wheeled my cycle into the courtyard, leaned it against the newly painted wall, and slipped past a large motor into the side entrance. Several workers I didn't recognize were sitting at the tables, but since I wasn't wearing livery, they took no notice of me. That meant that I could chat quietly with Mr. Johnson about skiffs.

As Mr. Johnson and I smiled a greeting at each other, a voice called, "Aren't you Harry?"

Turning in surprise, I saw a stocky older lad in livery wave from an alcove. One glance at his cheeky face allowed me to connect him with the large motor I had just passed. I nodded civilly, but no more. My father had forbidden me to accept friendly overtures from other servants without first consulting him, and my experience with the navvy at Chandace Grange had left me in no mood to make exceptions for Mr. Norton's driver.

"Crikey!" scoffed the lad. "Are Sir Thomas's servants too proud to talk to the likes of me?"

If we had been alone, I would have simply withdrawn, but the workers greeted his remark with laughter I didn't like, so I felt compelled to respond. "No, indeed," I said, walking to his table. "Am I right in remembering your name is Hutchins?"

"Right you are."

"Well, Mr. Hutchins," I said, putting my little store of coins next to his pair of empty mugs and shot glasses, "I'm sure you'll have no objections to fetching yourself a pint of your master's excellent ale."

The laughter changed its tenor, and as Hutchins hurried to the bar with my money, one of the workers said, "Well done, lad."

The others had been gathering themselves to go, but curiosity kept them seated as Hutchins returned to the alcove with his ale. He, however, paid them no mind as he drank off half the mug at one pull. "Must hurry," he said, putting it down with a sigh. "Have to meet His Nibs."

He leaned forward. "Business afoot," he said. "Great plans. That's Norton. Soon he'll own everything in sight, here—" he waved his arm towards the windows. "Farrington Farm, Chandace Grange—"

I glanced at the interested faces behind him and decided to take a risk. "—Surely Mr. Norton knows Sir Thomas can't sell entailed land."

Hutchins drained his pint. "Who knows what he knows? Or what he needs to know, with money like his? 'Many an attorney has been bought,' he says to his solicitor the other day as I'm picking him up in Oxford. His solicitor laughs and says, 'And many an offi—'" He jumped up, his face flushing. "There goes the bloody clock! You should hear His Nibs when I'm late! Last week, *he* was late—over a half hour—and I just waited. But let *me* be behind, and my sermon lasts all the way home. So I'm off. Thanks for the pint, mate."

"You're welcome," I said. "I'll see you tomorrow."

He looked blank. "Tomorrow?"

"At the Hall. I'll be giving Master Cyril a riding lesson."

"Is that a fact? The little blighter'll keep you busy, for certain."

He rushed off, and the workers, seeing that the show was over, left with nods to Mr. Johnson and to me.

Mr. Johnson smiled broadly as he beckoned me over to the bar. "You've got your mum's skill, lad. Friendly, courteous, stopped rumor by making him look the blabbering fool he is—So, what brings you here?"

"I wanted to ask you about Sir Thomas's skiff. There's been—"

"—There's been a right royal row about it, that's what," he said in disgust. "Morgan's such a suspicious bloke. Asked me if I wur sure if Lovejoy took the right skiff when Baines wur called away. As if I'd have Hugh's skiff moored at my dock without keeping an eye on it! The mon's a dunderhead."

I smiled. "I hope you didn't tell him that!"

"Not I," he said. "But it wur a near thing after he'd lorded it over me for half an hour—*wur I sure? Did I watch the boats that came here that carefully?* May the Lord take me! But just as I'm worried aboot losing m'temper entirely, he says he'll to talk to Sir Thomas, and leaves. Whew!" He shook his head.

"Terrible," I said. "Especially for you. Hugh used to say you were the last innkeeper on the river who was careful about boats."

"Did Hugh say that, now?" said Mr. Johnson, his broad face expanding with pleasure. "Well, he wur a real gentleman, for all his crazy politics. And if *he'd* come around today, I'd have slipped him a hint he maybe could have used." He looked around to make sure we were alone, then leaned over the bar.

"See, Wednesday, late aaternoon, a skiff tied up on m'dock. I waited for someone to come in, but nobody did. Well, something aboot that skiff put me in mind of the old days, with the Goodwin lads and Hugh and their little adventures, so I decided to leave it be until morning. And sure enough, in the morning it wur gone. Now, I wur ready to tell Morgan that when he came, but after he'd questioned me like that . . . never."

I was about to respond, but he went on.

"Hugh," he said sadly. "Time passes, and you forget how things wur before the War. What a loss, you know? If Hugh wur still with us, you wouldn't have Norton turning good lond into bungalows fer furriners—Not," he added hurriedly, "that Norton doesn't make a fine ale."

"Does he give you a good price on it?" I asked.

"Good enough," admitted Mr. Johnson. "Can't hold nothing against him if he'd just settle for making ale. It's when he wants more'n that I start waking up nights. Some pubs been selling out to the big brewers—better profit, they say. But *I* say you're never your own master aater you've said 'yes' to any mon's money."

"I'm sure nobody in Chandace wants you to say yes to Mr. Norton."

"There's not many in Chandace, saving maybe Lovejoy and Baines and the Williams lad as knows what it takes fer a mon t'say no to Norton. All he's got to do is stop selling me ale at a good price, or— heaven forefend! Stop selling it altogether, and it's the end of me." He shook his head.

I wanted to ask if he thought Mr. Norton was about to squeeze him, but the St. Barnabas clock stuck the quarter, and I hurried off to collect my note from Lady Sylvia.

She came to the door herself, very beautiful in a frock of what I guessed was the latest fashion. "So, you're giving a riding lesson, are you?" she said, smiling at me over the note in her hand.

"Yes, my lady. If scheduling can be arranged."

"This—" she handed me a note—"arranges it, and just as well. My muscles are reminding me that I haven't ridden for a year. So you and Atlas will be free to teach Cyril Norton tomorrow afternoon. As for tomorrow morning—may I trouble you with a second message to Sir Thomas?"

"Of course, my lady."

She handed me a missive on handsome stationery, folded in thirds and sealed in red. "Such old-world formality in the age of the telephone," she said, half smiling. "It is to be taken directly to Sir Thomas, not given to Mr. Parks."

"Yes, my lady." Keeping my face discreetly impassive, I placed both notes inside my jacket, thanked Lady Sylvia, and pedaled back to the Hall.

Sir Thomas was taking his tea at his desk when Mr. Parks showed me into the library, but he called me over and nodded as he read Lady Sylvia's note. "Very gracious," he murmured. "And this one . . ." He broke the seal, read the contents, and looked up, smiling.

"Just as I'd hoped. Please tell your father that Lord Sandford will be riding Errant tomorrow morning before our meeting. Have him ready at ten o'clock."

I had difficulty containing my surprise, for Hugh had trusted nobody to ride Errant but my father and myself. But there was no possibility of questioning the order.

"I'll be prompt, sir," I said.

Chapter 15

The next morning, Sir Thomas and Lord Sandford arrived at the stable as the clock struck ten. We had Errant groomed and ready, and as my father led him out, he pricked up his ears at the sight of visitors.

Both men paused in admiration, and his lordship whistled. "What a stunner!" he said.

"Thank you, my lord," said my father. "Shall I take him to the manège?"

"I'll do it, thanks," said his lordship. "It'll give us a chance get acquainted."

He took the reins from my father and stroked Errant's neck while the horse sniffed his jacket. "Okay?" he asked—the horse, not my father. And I suddenly realized the accent that had puzzled me must be at least partly American.

He led Errant across the courtyard and down the path. Sir Thomas started to follow them but turned back towards us, smiling. "Wouldn't you like to watch?"

We thanked him and hurried forward, arriving at the manège as his lordship lengthened the stirrups, checked the girth, and vaulted on. My eyes met my father's as he and Errant became perfectly balanced within four or five strides. As they moved into a sitting trot, then into serpentines, I realized that Lord Sanford, like Hugh, knew a hundred times more than I did.

Watching Errant's collection and graceful transitions as his lordship spent the next half hour guiding him through our usual routine, I saw with sorrow that he was capable of performing the most difficult movements of haute école, but that without Hugh, there was nobody to . . . I returned to the present as his lordship halted him in front of the three of us.

"Would it delay our meeting unconscionably, Sir Thomas, if I followed Harry's example and took Errant for a short trot and canter to reward him?"

"Not at all," said Sir Thomas, smiling. "Follow the path at the end of the manège, then turn right at the footpath that parallels the North Road, then right again at the bridle path that meets the bridge. That will bring you back here in a quarter hour."

"Perfect!" said his lordship, and they were off.

Sir Thomas turned to us. "So, what do you think?"

"He's a very fine rider indeed, sir," said my father, in a tone of voice he seldom used.

"Absolutely!" I added enthusiastically. "He's a master horseman!"

"So Lady Sylvia told me," said Sir Thomas. "When I see her tomorrow, I will have the pleasure of agreeing." He turned back towards the courtyard, where Mr. Lovejoy was waiting next to the side door. As my father and I returned to the stable, I wondered absently what they and Lord Sandford were about to discuss at their 'confidential' meeting.

I had just time to fill two buckets at the fountain before the sound of hoofbeats announced Errant's arrival. His lordship dismounted quickly and gave Errant a friendly pat on the neck as he handed the reins to my father, who began to walk him. I picked up the two buckets, but to my surprise, instead of hurrying to join Sir Thomas and Mr. Lovejoy, Lord Sandford stopped me.

"Harry," he said quietly, "I don't want to get you in trouble, but are you in the habit of stopping off to chat with your mates when you're exercising the horses?"

"Oh no, my lord!" I said, shocked.

"I thought not," he said, "but when Errant and I came close to the spot where the bridle path turns at the bridge, a young man was leaning on the parapet. He called out, 'Harry! Stop a minute, will you!' When I drew up, he realized he had the wrong person, and he said, 'Oh, sorry, mate!' and hurried off. It was nothing, really, except I didn't like the look of him, and I hoped you hadn't been being tempted into bad company."

"Never, my lord!" I said.

He looked at me keenly, and to assure him that I had told the truth, I returned his gaze. As our eye met, a fleeting surprise crossed his face, and he half smiled. Something sad about that smile puzzled me, but it was soon gone. "Forgive me for doubting you," he said. "I just know that the really talented youngsters—whether horse or human—are the easiest to spoil. Have a care, Harry." He glanced over his shoulder as Mr. Parks appeared in the side door, clearly waiting to escort him through the house. "Don't worry," he said, starting off. "I'll say nothing."

I did worry, and I wished I had asked his lordship if the man he'd encountered had been wearing a green jacket. But as I put Errant up, I reflected that no man, in any jacket, could possibly have known to lie in wait for me at the bridge. Until Lord Sandford left the manège, none of us had known he was going to ride out. No doubt it was all, as his lordship had said, nothing.

*   *   *

Cyril Norton was driven into the courtyard shortly before the clock struck three, his face so filled with awe and excitement that I would have had no concerns about the lesson if he hadn't been accompanied by his father. Remembering Hugh's diatribes about the impossibility of teaching boys whose fathers coached them incessantly from the sidelines, I was momentarily discouraged, but since there was no possibility of asking Mr. Norton to absent himself, I forced myself to step forward with a smile.

"Thank you for coming so promptly, Master Cyril," I said to the boy, and turning to Mr. Norton, I added, "Generally I begin a first lesson by asking the student to tack up his horse and lead it from the stable by himself. I trust you will permit that?"

"By myself?" breathed Cyril. "Oh, Papa!"

Mr. Norton's stance stiffened, a resistance made more obvious by a snicker from Hutchins, who had not yet backed the motor from the courtyard. But the concern drained from his eyes as they met mine. "Yes, yes," he muttered. "Go ahead."

Cyril trotted by my side in handsome boots that must have been made for him, telling me proudly that he was six years old, that he'd been breeched early because he could read real books, that his special cat had had kittens . . . but as we stepped into the stable, he became silent and reached for my hand. I gave it to him, remembering the comfort of Hugh's hand when, much younger than Cyril, I'd felt the same mixture of fear and elation.

He greeted Atlas with grave enthusiasm, and the horse, whose checkered history had obviously included being handled by children, walked patiently with him to the cross ties and halted at the shaky command, "Whoa." After we'd saddled and bridled Atlas, talking about each step, we emerged into the courtyard, Cyril holding the reins with whitened knuckles, Atlas with his head kindly lowered.

"Up you go," I said, boosting Cyril into the saddle. "Now take your reins, one in each hand—thumbs pointing up, three fingers over, little fingers under."

"I know," he said. "I looked at pictures in *The Gentleman's Magazine,* and I practiced on my hobby horse with a piece of string."

"So I see," I said, smiling. "That's exactly right."

He straightened his back and tucked his chin in. "Am I sitting like a gentleman?"

"You're sitting like a horseman, which is much more important, because it means the horse that is carrying you is comfortable."

"Was Sir Lancelot's horse always comfortable?"

"You may be sure he was," I said, walking with the two of them towards the manège. "If he hadn't been, Lancelot couldn't have defeated all those other knights."

We had reached the point where Mr. Norton was standing, but Cyril was so intent on guiding Atlas that he didn't even glance at him. Out of the corner of my eye, I saw that his father was not so much hurt as astounded.

As the lesson progressed, I was occasionally astounded myself. Cyril was one of those rare people who instinctively moved with a horse and, as he gained confidence, he performed all the exercises I set him without losing his balance for a moment. By the end of the hour, he had learned to post Atlas's trot with only an odd bounce here and there.

"Very fine," I said as I walked him to the gate where his father, miraculously silent, had hung on every detail of the lesson. "Have you really not ridden before, Master Cyril?"

"Never, except in Chandace the day Mama fainted," he said. "Can I ride tomorrow?"

"Not tomorrow," said Mr. Norton. "We're going to Oxford, remember?"

Cyril stuck out his lower lip, and foreseeing an unhorsemanlike tantrum, I said quickly, "You can come ride some other day. Your father will arrange it with Sir Thomas. But now, you must dismount and lead Atlas to the stable. That's what good horsemen do."

All the sulkiness disappeared as he slid the long way to the ground, and he talked to Atlas all the way to the stable. I lifted him so he could undo the girth and take off the saddle, and he insisted on carrying them to the harness room himself.

Mr. Norton had been standing in the stable door, but as I emerged from the harness room, he stepped towards me quickly. "I hope you'll be willing to give Cyril regular lessons," he said.

"I'll be glad to, if Sir Thomas agrees," I said. "He's very talented."

"It's amazing," he said. "I've never seen him so happy. My wife will be delighted."

Cyril joined us as we walked into the courtyard and, to my surprise, he took my hand as Hutchins drove Mr. Norton's motor through the archway. "I wish you were *my* servant instead of Sir Thomas's," he said. "We'd have such larks."

Hutchins, who had descended from the motor and opened its door, laughed in a way that made me wonder how he managed to remain employed. But when I glanced at Mr. Norton, I saw interest, not disapproval.

"Learning to ride isn't all larks," I said—for somebody clearly had to speak. "There are a great many things a good horseman needs to know. He must work hard, practicing the way Sir Lancelot did. Remember how we talked about that?"

"Yes," he said earnestly. "I'll practice just as hard as he did."

"Good," I said and, to prevent argument, I lifted him into the motor.

Before stepping in after him, Mr. Norton touched my shoulder and pressed something into my hand. I glanced at it as they drove off, then blinked and looked again.

A five-pound note.

For a single lesson, he'd tipped me my wages for a month.

I shoved it in my pocket, but its presence distracted me for the rest of the day. I intended to consult my father about it that evening, but he fell asleep on the settle again, so I put it off until morning.

But when morning came, Goodwin and Jimmy were so quiet when they arrived at the stable that I forgot the tip altogether.

"What's amiss?" I whispered to Jimmy as we went to fetch the harnesses.

"Trouble at home," he whispered back. "See, Dad was offered a pig yesterday."

"A pig! Wonderful! You'll have food all next winter! Whose sow farrowed?"

"It makes no matter. Dad wouldn't take it." Jimmy sighed as he hefted one of the horse collars. "He was talking aboot it to Mum last night—that and his wager with Farmer Farrington—but they caught me listening and sent me on an errand."

"His wager—you mean the pint Farmer Farrington didn't collect on?"

"That's the one, but being sent off, I couldn't learn any more than we'd heard Dad tell Officer Jenkins and your father on Monday, when we were supposed to be fetching the harnesses. I know Dad must've paid Farmer Farrington his pint Tuesday e'en, because we're a mite short. But he's been twice to Farmer Farrington's house since then and not found him. He sent me on by myself yester e'en, so he could look in the barns. When he came home, he wouldn't say aught except Farrington was likely at the Arms, but something's ailing him. Mum's fair wild to know what it is, because last time he shut into himself, it was aboot Mr. Vanter and the corn. And—well, look at him."

I looked as we carried in the harnesses, and I saw what he meant. Goodwin's face was always tired, but his eyes were usually full of the humor that often came from his tongue. Now, they were filled only with worry and what, if he'd been anybody else, I would have called fear. Exchanging a glance with my father, I realized he saw it too, but a shake of his head told me to say nothing.

We finished harnessing the horses in awkward silence, and after Goodwin trudged off to his long day at the farm, I slipped Jimmy a chunk of bread and cheese. A pig, I thought, as I watched him start to the garden, munching voraciously. A family "short" until pay day because of a single pint. And me with a fiver. Hmm.

After breakfast, I asked Mrs. Middleton casually what a shoat cost, and amidst a long complaint about high prices, she gave me a figure well within my present means. Excellent. As I hurried after my father, I decided to put off telling him about the fiver until I'd used it in a way that made me less ashamed of having accepted it.

Chapter 16

My assignment that morning was to ride Errant to Chandace along the bridle path that went through the Dell, then, after a quick visit with Richard Williams at the Rectory, to come back through Chandace Grange. It would have been a pleasant prospect if I hadn't been concerned about Errant's possible fear of the Dell, but I tried not to think about it, lest my own worry be communicated to him. As it happened, he was only a little nervous, and after I'd made him walk by the Dell in both directions, he trotted cheerfully on to Chandace, enjoying his usual shenanigans with lambs.

Richard had apparently been watching for us, for he came to the gate the moment we arrived. He greeted me, of course, but it was Errant who received his real attention.

"What a treasure!" he said after he'd finished his scrutiny. "He has everything Hugh hoped for: beauty, conformation, spirit—it's wonderful. I thought Sir Thomas was exaggerating when he described him Tuesday, for even at a distance, I could see that the Austrian you were riding was merely a good looker. But this is the horse of a lifetime." He smiled. "Am I right?"

The horse of a lifetime. The phrase crystallized all my thoughts about Errant, and I said, "Yes," with enthusiasm. But even as I spoke, I thought of Hugh's lifetime, already spent, and Richard's, cloistered by his injuries, and as for my own . . .

"Does anybody ride him but you, Harry?"

"Not usually, but Lord Sandford rode him yesterday," I said. "You should have been there! He's as good as Hugh!"

"A real master, I've heard, and supremely dedicated to what's coming to be called Equine Sport. He was one of the men who got Dressage and Eventing into the 1912 Olympics.

"Oh, ripping!"

"That's what Lady Sylvia's brothers and I all said, when Hugh told us about Sandford in the spring of '14. We were all going to meet here in August, but Sandford got sent to the States on some business of his mother's, and the rest of us got sent to the Front. We all wrote to each other, though, until . . . well, until." Richard's face darkened.

"But I've kept up the correspondence, and Sandford's still keen. He thinks competitive riding is going to save horsemanship from simply fading away as motors take over transportation. It wouldn't have to depend on the Olympics, either, he says; we could start competitions in England, on private estates. We were talking about it just the other evening, in fact. He has the right contacts to make a go of it. The right money, too, between his father's wireless business and his mother's fortune. All he needs, he says, is the prestige that comes from being known for a top-notch stable.

"And he's looking—" He broke off. "In any case, he's a splendid horseman, and it would be wonderful if he could help you with Errant now and again. Father and I want you to continue your education, but nobody wants to leave this magnificent horse standing in a stall."

He pursed his lips. "Confound it! I'd take him on in a second if I were a whole man!"

"Don't say that!" I said. "You're—"

"—a coward. A cripple! Have the courtesy to tell the truth!"

"I *am* telling the truth!" I said, so vehemently that Errant began to fidget. "You *know* what Hugh thought! A coward is a coward through and through. You're terrorized by only one thing, and when it's not there, you're no cripple. You're just a man walking around with a bullet in him that can't be dug out."

"And you think I should walk further, do you?"

"How far you walk is up to you," I said. "But if you were to walk to Willingford Stable, I'd saddle Errant for you and listen to Hugh cheer from heaven as you rode him."

He looked at me, the resentment in his face gradually fading into sadness. "Such faith," he murmured. "Ah, Harry."

The sound of a slowing motor made him turn towards the North Road. "A visitor, it seems. If it isn't for Baines, it'll be the parish records bloke. I'm custodian now. Easy work for the most part, but recently some chap has come back time after time, checking, re-checking. He's civil enough, but something about him worries me." He gave me something like his old wry smile. "He's probably just trying to find out who his father is."

"I wish him luck!" I vaulted on Errant, who had begun to paw the cobblestones. "Take care, Richard."

"You too, lad. And come back soon."

I wanted to assure him that I would, but the parish records bloke drew up at the Rectory gate with hardly a glance at Errant, leaving us very little room. As we squeezed past his muddy, ill-kept motor, I thought of Joey Rushdale's remarks about flivvers. "Good thing he owns a motor, not a horse," I muttered to Errant.

We'd crossed the Chandace bridge and neared the bridle path to the Grange when Errant pricked up his ears. A minute later, the police motor turned into the lane that led to Farrington Farm and stopped. I looked away and hurried Errant towards the bridle path.

"Harry! Wait!"

Tim?! My heart jumped as I turned back. "I'm sorry," I said. "I thought you were—"

"—on business?"

I decided not to say I'd thought he'd been Officer Morgan.

"I *am* on business," said Tim, easing himself stiffly out of the motor and leaning against it. "I'm looking for Farrington. It seems that Morgan missed meeting him yesterday when I was out of town. But I have a little time for a cheering investigative report if you have one." He shifted his weight off his game leg. "I need all the cheer I can get."

"Well," I said, wishing he'd told me where he'd been and why he looked so drained, "to begin with, Mr. Parks gave me the details of the 'blazing row' about the boathouse I mentioned on Monday." Steadying Errant as he began to prance, I told the story of the changed lock and the key that ended up in the river. "And so," I said, enjoying Tim's broadening grin, "It's pretty clear that Mr. Vanter has been mooring his skiff in the Dell for over a year."

"It certainly seems so,'" he said. "And I'll tell Morgan as soon as I can. He was disturbed when he had to admit the skiff the telephone tipper found in the reeds wasn't Hugh's. Maybe Mr. Parks's tale will persuade him to reconsider his adamant belief that there could have been no dock in the Dell."

"Reconsider! You mean he just ignored—?"

"—Harry," he said wearily, "any soldier can tell you that some officers have difficulty considering evidence they missed finding themselves. But to be fair, until Wednesday, it was easy for Morgan to brush your evidence aside. When Farrington checked in with us on Tuesday, I asked him point blank where Vanter had moored his skiff. He looked up, down, and around—the way he does— and finally, he muttered that last time the two of them had talked, Vanter had said he kept his skiff in the Hall's boathouse. That kind of equivocation is hard to get around without evidence that directly confronts it. So in addition to reminding me that Hugh in a temper was a wonder to behold, your sleuthing has given me a fair chance of drawing Farrington out. Good work, lad."

"There's more," I said, pleased. "The Wednesday of the telephone tipper, Sir Thomas sent me on an errand in Chandace. On my way, I remembered Hugh's saying that Mr. Johnson knew every boat between Lechlade and Willingford Hall, so I stopped off at The Arms to talk to him."

Tim patted Errant to stop him from fidgeting. "Morgan tried

that, but he said Johnson couldn't tell him anything."

"Sometimes it's hard getting Mr. Johnson to talk," I said with feigned seriousness that made Tim chuckle. "But he told *me* that a skiff tied up at The Arms' dock late afternoon on the Wednesday of the murder, and nobody came in. Remembering Hugh's shenanigans, he decided not to meddle with it— and it was gone in the morning."

"Hm," said Tim thoughtfully. "I wonder what happened to it." Suddenly he smiled. "I can *see* you thinking that somebody loosed it from The Arms and let it drift downstream to an inlet where it got caught in the reeds. Can you prove it?"

"Not really," I admitted. "But think. If the murderer used Mr. Vanter's skiff to escape, he had a skiff to get rid of. He also probably had to get back to wherever he'd come from. So he quietly tied it up at The Arms, where a lot of boats come and go, and bunked. Later that night, he let it loose, and slowly, the skiff bumped its way down the river to the reeds where the telephone tipper found it." I met his eyes. "To prove that, I'd need to know that Mr. Vanter's skiff had HCW carved in its bow. But I can offer my theory for consideration."

"It's very much worth considering," said Tim, with respect that made me proud. "And I'm going to discuss it with Morgan, along with Parks's story. I think he'll consider them seriously."

"I hope he does," I said. "Lady Sylvia said that the telephone tip was a frame. Sir Thomas and Dr. Baines as good as said that Officer Morgan's compliance had been bought."

Tim's face suddenly took on an impassive expression that reminded me I'd criticized his superior. "Harry, in an unsolved case, such opinions always crop up."

"Yes, but I heard another opinion when I was at The Arms!" I said, and I told him how Hutchins had repeated what Norton's solicitor had said about the ease of buying police officers.

Tim's face clouded. "Good god! Did anybody hear him besides you and Johnson?"

"Just some workers I didn't recognize. But I promise you, they were interested."

He shook his head. "Norton should get himself a new driver," he said. "But the best way to stop negative opinions about police incompetence is to solve the case, which I hope I am going to start doing this morning. I'm sure Farrington has a fair idea about what happened."

"I'm sure he does," I said. "And I suspect somebody besides the two of us knows that. Remember the man Errant caught on Monday at Chandace Grange?"

"I certainly do! I looked for him right after you left, but none the chaps loading the lorries wore a jacket that color."

"I think he didn't go back to the lorries," I said. "On our way home, Errant saw somebody skulking in the woods by the bridge. Whoever it was disappeared, but I had an uncomfortable feeling that he might have stopped me if Errant hadn't been snorting so. "

"My God, Harry!" he said, horrified. "Why didn't you *tell* me?"

"I *am* telling you! I've had no way to find you since we met Monday. The only time I leave the stable is when I'm exercising the horses or taking a message."

"And Sir Thomas is hopelessly prejudiced against telephones," he grumbled. "Look, Harry, you may be in real danger. Who knows where you exercise the horses?"

"My father and I usually decide that at the last minute."

"What about messages?"

"Sir Thomas sends me out now and again, but yesterday, for instance, he sent me to Chandace at four o'clock on fifteen minutes' notice."

"Well, that's a mercy," he said. "Still, be careful, and don't ride by the navvies. I have no proof, but lately I've been perplexed by the speed at which news from Chandace reaches town."

"No fear!" I said and told him about the navvy Errant had struck down. "But that had nothing to do with a man in green," I said, looking at his troubled face. "Unless . . . do you suppose . . . I mean, *could* a navvy from the Hawkins Farm have got to the Grange before I did? Even if he knew the shortcuts, how would he escape the minders?"

"If any one of them followed you, it'd *be* a minder," he said grimly. "That's not good. The minders are more brutal than the navvies, and they have lorries if they need to travel quickly. I'll look into it, right after I see Farrington." He sighed. "I wish there were some way I could thank you properly for your danger."

"I'll be fine," I said, with a confidence I wished I felt. Then suddenly an idea flashed through my mind. "Actually, there might be."

He brightened. "A way I could protect you?"

"No, just advice for a way out of an awkward situation."

"Say on," he said, and added, "quickly," as Errant began to paw the ground.

I told him about Cyril's lesson and the fiver. "I handled it poorly," I added. "I'm not used to being tipped, and I didn't look fast enough."

He shook his head. "You have nothing to be ashamed of, Harry. He tipped you because he was pleased. To him, there's hardly a difference between a quid and a fiver, and he wouldn't have slid it into your hand as he left if he hadn't been afraid that you might refuse it. The next time he comes, thank him for his generosity, and tell him how much to pay you in the future. Your father will know a just price." He looked at me, his brown eyes sympathetic but firm. "The important thing is to make it clear that he can't buy your loyalty."

"But do you think he considers my loyalty bought already?" I asked anxiously.

"If you talk to him frankly and respectfully, he'll understand it isn't for sale."

"Thank you," I said, much relieved.

He watched as I made Errant stand still. "There's something else," he said, smiling. "I can feel it."

"Well, yes," I said. "Jimmy's family has been offered a shoat, which is providential, because with Mrs. Goodwin too ill to work for so long, they've been living on bread, dripping, and rabbits. But Goodwin has refused, saying the price is too high. If I gave you my fiver, could you take it to a bank and get two quid so I could buy them a shoat?"

"How do you plan to buy a shoat, Harry? You never get to market."

That was true. I steadied Errant once more, trying to think.

"Listen," said Tim. "I'll be at the Hall this afternoon to talk to Lovejoy before he leaves to pay the workers at The Arms. If you bring me your fiver, I'll give you three quid and keep two. Then on market day, I'll buy a shoat, deliver it to the Goodwins with your compliments, and bring you the change."

I stared at him. "You'd do all that? For me?"

"I would indeed, " he said. "I came back from France convinced that Hugh's kind of generosity had been drowned in the mud of the trenches. But you're walking proof that some of it has survived. God bless you—and go on, lad, before your horse digs up the lane." He held the reins, which by now was necessary; I vaulted on, waved, and started up the bridle path to Chandace Grange.

After a good trot that took the kinks out of Errant, I slowed to a walk at the top of the rise where the bridle path ran briefly parallel to Chandace Grange's narrow lane, looking out across the river valley. It was a quiet, understated vista, the river running randomly through walled squares of varying greens, the red tint of the woods that promised leaves, the groups of sheep and cattle. Gradually, my thoughts drifted from its beauty to Hugh's love for it, and from there to the warmth in Tim's pain-filled face when he'd talked about Hugh's generosity and praised mine.

Errant swung his head to look behind us, and looking back myself, I saw a lorry round the corner of the lane. Odd. Tim had said the workers had finished emptying the Grange on Monday. Errant stirred uneasily, and my mind stirred with him as I remembered what else Tim had said: *They have lorries if they need to travel quickly.*

There was nothing but a wall between us and the lane, but two hundred paces on, the lane turned north towards the house, and the bridle path swerved east through the wood and the bridge to the

Hall. I urged Errant forward at a canter, pulling him up only as we were well into the trees. "Halt," I whispered, driving my seat forward in the signal for a salute. Miraculously, he stood still, his ears pricking forward as the lorry reached the top of the rise and started down to the house. I expected to hear its engine change tone, but instead it slowed, then stopped entirely. Errant startled as its door slammed.

I wheeled him around, and we made the trip back to Chandace at a speed I knew even the lorry couldn't match, because it couldn't reverse direction until it drove the half mile to the house. As we rounded the corner by the North Road bridge, I thought suddenly of Lord Sandford's encounter with the man whose looks he didn't like. "Nothing really," he'd said. But it wasn't nothing. Nor was it an accident. The man who'd hailed him had been waiting for Errant to come by.

He'd hurried off when he'd realized Errant was being ridden by a stranger. Which meant . . . I trotted home along the familiar bridle path by the Dell, wondering anxiously how whoever was following me knew where I was going.

Chapter 17

Arriving home, I said nothing to my father about my fears, as that would have involved considerable explanation and caused him alarm. Fortunately, he was so busy preparing for the afternoon ride that he didn't notice my preoccupation. Sir Thomas had come to the stable a quarter hour early, and amidst the bustle of saddling, he and Father were chatting about feed, straw, Goodwin's team . . . in short, everything and nothing . . . just as they had in the days before Hugh's death.

By the time Lady Sylvia arrived and we'd brought out the horses, I'd realized with pleasure that Sir Thomas had regained a little of his old self. Ten days earlier, I had hardly recognized him. Now, though his cough remained worrisome, and he was still thin, pale and stooped, his face had lost the deep sadness that had struck me at the inquest. Maybe it had something to do with his starting to ride again.

Or . . . or could it have something to do with the "confidential" meeting he'd had yesterday morning with Mr. Lovejoy and Lord Sandford?

"Harry?"

My father's voice made me jump. "Yes, sir?"

"What did you ask Mr. Norton to give you for Master Cyril's lesson?"

"Nothing, sir," I said, thankful for the way he'd phrased his question.

"So I thought. When you were fetching the saddles this afternoon, Sir Thomas told me that Mr. Norton wishes the boy to have more lessons, and it won't do to let you go unpaid again. Best you settle the matter yourself, but I'll speak to Mr. Norton if you'd like."

I could hardly believe the ease with which the situation was becoming manageable. "I'd prefer to settle it, sir. What do you think I should ask?"

"I watched enough to see how carefully Mr. Norton was studying you and how he admired your skill in handling the boy. So I'd ask for a bob." He looked out into the courtyard. "Here's Lovejoy to meet with Jenkins."

He hurried out, greatly to my relief. My failure to tell him about Mr. Norton's fiver was adding to the burden of the other secrets weighing upon my conscience. Expecting

Tim at every moment, I ran to our quarters and slipped the fiver into my pocket before going on with my duties.

Tim was usually punctual, but a quarter hour passed with no sign of him. My father went back to the stable, telling me to re-sweep its floor in preparation for Sir Thomas's return. When I completed the task, Tim still hadn't come. Mr. Lovejoy sat by the fountain and drew a book from his haversack. He looked restless and worried, so when I took the water buckets out to fill, I asked him what he was reading.

"A book Richard Williams lent me, by a chap called Kenneth Grahame," he said, with a smile I'd come to like. "It's called *The Wind in the Willows*, but if I told you what it's about, you'd think I was off my chump."

"No, I wouldn't, sir. It's about Rat, Mole, Toad and 'messing about in boats.' Hugh read it to me when I was a kid."

"You mean Hugh . . . ?" He took a breath. "Hugh *read* to you?"

"Oh yes," I said. "Whenever he was home. And when he wasn't, he gave me a list of books to read when he was gone and asked me questions about them when he returned." The way Mr. Lovejoy was looking at me made me finish quickly. "In any case, *The Wind in the Willows* was one of his favorites."

"So I've heard. Richard said it came out when they were at Oxford, and all the Blues started joking about Toad's rowing, and making a fetish of hot buttered toast—"

"—With butter running through its holes like honey," I said, laughing. "Hugh said he used to dream about it."

"So did Richard, especially in the trenches. Landlubber that I am, I had no idea that Richard rowed in the First Boat with Hugh the year they won the Oxford-Cambridge match. But I suppose you did."

"I'm sure I was told, but I was still in toddlers' dresses when they were at Oxford. All I knew was that Hugh said Richard was as good in a shell as he was on a horse."

"Well, they were champion oarsmen. Richard showed me their photo the other day. Beautiful shell—fast and sleek. And eight men, all rowing in unison. Richard said winning the race was all very well, but what was really wonderful was the harmony." His face clouded. "Then he let drop he's the only one of that First Boat still alive."

The bucket rattled on the cobblestones as I put it down. "*All* the others died, sir?"

"Every single one. And Richard . . . well, you've seen him. What a bloody *waste!*" He glanced at the courtyard clock. "Why I didn't think of that waste until I came home from the Front, I don't know. The comradeship Richard was talking of, the harmony, was there, you see, especially among us Signals men, laying wire right up to the front lines so the troops could talk to the higher-ups. The stuff of adventure! Was *The Thirty-Nine Steps* on the reading list Hugh gave you?"

"Oh yes, sir. Ripping good yarn!"

"That's the world I lived in over there. The officers at the top told us we were fighting 'the war to end all wars,' and I believed it, the way I believed what Hugh said about there being equality at the end of it all." He looked bitterly into the fountain. "But you know, nothing has changed. Except Hugh's gone, and Richard's shut in his room, and Jenkins will never see Oxford . . . You ever talk to Jenkins?"

"Now and then, sir."

"He's brilliant! Cooped up the way I am, I've talked to him a good deal. The bloke knows his history inside out, puts out philosophical arguments that leave me spinning. He belongs at Oxford, where Hugh and Sir Thomas were all ready to send him. But where is he now? Limping around the Cotswolds in the shadow of Officer Bought and Sold Morgan—"

"—You mustn't say that, sir!"

"You're right," he said. "But it makes me furious to see him wasting Jenkins's competence." He slapped the book down on the fountain wall. "The case can't be that complicated, Harry! You and I could find the murderer ourselves if it weren't for our hopeless tactical disadvantage."

"Tactical disadvantage, sir?"

"No bloody telephone at what should be headquarters," he said. "Due to Sir Thomas's belief that it's simply 'a trifling convenience' he can do without. So, all important pooling of evidence has to wait until somebody happens to see somebody else."

"Have you urged Sir Thomas to install a telephone, sir?"

"Indirectly. That is, I've urged Lady Sylvia to tell him that he can't guide the investigation because he can't collect the information that would allow him to. He's *beginning* to consider it, but it's hard for a man of his generation to see what a difference the telephone has made. Meanwhile, here's Jenkins over an hour past his time, and me needing to be in Chandace in a half hour—and no way of communicating! If the army had worked on Sir Thomas's principles, the Huns would've wiped us out in a few weeks!"

He slipped *The Wind in the Willows* into his rucksack and pulled a pen and paper out of its exterior pouch. "I'm afraid you're going to have to deliver this to Jenkins when he comes," he said apologetically as he scrawled a few lines. "Morgan will want written proof that I was here at the appointed hour and left word of my whereabouts."

"Of course, sir," I said, taking the folded paper he handed me.

"Godspeed," he said, sighing. "Go back to your horses and memories of being read to by the finest man in England." He looked hard into my face, adding, "And if you can see your way clear, lad, do Hugh's ghost a favor and drop the 'sir' when you speak to me."

I thanked him, promised I would, and stepped into the quiet stable, where Errant was dozing in his stall, and my father was dozing over the unused bridles he'd been cleaning. Having nothing to do before Sir Thomas and Lady Sylvia returned, I remembered that I'd promised to sweep the alcove in which bedding for the straight-stall horses had once been kept. Good, I thought, quietly picking up a broom and shovel: a mindless job that would enable me to think.

Careful not to disturb either of the sleepers, I turned away from the box stall wing and walked softly along the straight-stall corridor, trying not to be distracted by the ghosts of its one-time inhabitants. The bedding alcove was a few paces past the ladder to the dormitory that had been home to the stable lads. I passed it moodily, wondering what had happened to them all.

I stopped at the edge of the alcove, peering through the murky light that came in under the eaves, past the wooden tack trunks stored on the far side, to the large double doors designed to admit carts of straw. The right-hand door contained a smaller door that permitted easy access to the far side of the stable, and so was securely fastened on the inside with a heavy bolt and socket. Or it should have been. It seemed to me that too much light was shining around the door's edges, and it rattled as a breeze blew past. Frowning, I crossed the area, placed one hand on the door's latch, and raised the other automatically to release the bolt.

There was no need. The bolt had been pushed forward, as it always was when it was fastened. But the socket into which it should have slid was nowhere to be seen.

Slowly, my heart pounding, I pulled the little door open and looked out at the faded wagon track that led around the outside of the stable. Rooks cawed, and a few doves flew up as I stepped outside. There seemed to be nobody about. I stepped out as quietly as I could and crossed the track, searching for the path that led—as the elder lads had well known—to a great oak that grew conveniently near the park wall.

The path's entrance had always been carefully disguised and, by rights, it should have grown over entirely in the five years since the lads had left. But no, there was the familiar opening behind the clump of nascent cow parsley. Careful not to leave tracks, I walked slowly down the path—and saw not only boot marks but soil that had obviously been disturbed.

I was about to investigate when I heard Errant's welcoming neigh, and within seconds, the sound of hoofbeats. Sir Thomas and Lady Sylvia! I hurried back into the stable, closed the un-bolted door behind me, and reached the courtyard just as they rode in.

They dismounted in fine spirits, and because Sir Thomas turned immediately to my father with some words about Chandace Grange, I had to put up both horses. I expected the courtyard to be empty long before I was again free, but when I emerged, they were still there, speculating on the reason Dr. Baines had not yet arrived to drive Lady Sylvia to Chandace.

Just as Sir Thomas offered to send me to fetch Rushdale and the Lanchester, the police motor drove in. I moved forward, full of news for Tim, but I stopped in confusion and concern. For Officer Morgan was driving, his face grim. And the seat next to him was empty.

Chapter 18

Scarcely heeding the general greeting, Officer Morgan stepped out of the motor, cleared his throat, and said in a voice the suggested he had been rehearsing the line, "I regret to inform you, Sir Thomas, that your tenant, Farmer Robert Farrington, is dead." Sir Thomas grasped my father's arm for support "What ... ? How ... ?"

Officer Morgan continued as if there had been no reaction to his news. "His body was found in his root cellar this morning. This afternoon, examination by Dr. Baines and Coroner Davis has determined that he did not die of natural causes." He paused, surveying our four shocked faces. "It appears that he drank a corrosive liquid."

"Good heavens!" said Lady Sylvia. "A suicide!"

Officer Morgan gave her the kind of look men give women who interrupt them. "I'm afraid not, my lady," he said. "His mouth and throat were severely burned in a way which the two medical authorities take to be evidence that he ingested a drink that had been mixed with Oxalic Acid Dihydrate, a common cleaning agent. However, no cleaning agent of that kind was found on the premises."

"No," said my father, unexpectedly. "Farrington detested old-fashioned cleansers. He repeatedly warned me that the Oxalic Acid we used for cleaning boot tops was poisonous."

"Thank you, Green," said Officer Morgan, shortly. "But I was about to add that while Oxalic Acid caused him injury, the immediate cause of death was a severe blow to the back of the head."

"God save us!" breathed Sir Thomas. "Who would do such a thing?"

Officer Morgan's face remained grave, his voice almost a monotone. "There is a suspect," he said. "He is known to have been seeking Farrington—and in fact was seen entering his kitchen door late Thursday afternoon." He gave me a distracted glance as I stifled a gasp, but went on. "He's a laborer of yours: Barth Goodwin. I plan to question him when he returns here with his team."

"Impossible!" said Sir Thomas and my father together.

"Officer Jenkins claimed he's much trusted on this estate," said Morgan. "But there are reliable witnesses." He looked over his shoulder as the sound of an engine drifted up the sweep. "If this is Doctor Baines, he'll be able to give you the medical details."

It was Dr. Baines, and to my relief, Tim was with him, whole and unhurt. Sir Thomas, Lady Sylvia and my father hurried towards the doctor as the motor stopped, but Tim climbed out and limped towards me, his face set and ashen.

"You've heard the news," he said quietly as Dr. Baines talked to the others.

I nodded. "Were you the one found him?"

"Yes." He looked past me. "I thought the Front had hardened me, but the horror will haunt me for the rest of my days. Farrington died in agony. Baines thinks the internal burning had gone on for half an hour before the murderer finally finished him off."

I shuddered. "Officer Morgan thinks *Goodwin* would do that? To a friend?"

He sighed. "Goodwin was seen at Farrington's door, and Morgan needs a suspect."

"But *you* don't think—"

"What I think is no longer relevant," he said tersely. "But I'm worried. Half an hour before I found his body, you and I agreed that Farrington knew a good deal about Vanter's murder."

My eyes widened. "You're saying Farmer Farrington was murdered because he knew too much?"

"I can't think of any other reason." He touched my shoulder. "So, for god's sake, be careful. Whoever has been following you may never do it again, but—"

"—but he has!" I said. "And I think I know how!" I told him quickly about the unbolted stable door. "Do you see? With the back door unbolted, anybody could enter the stable, creep up to the old dormitory, and listen as my father and I discuss where I should ride."

I broke off as the sound of heavy hoofbeats rang on the cobblestones. Officer Morgan suddenly looked very formidable, and Sir Thomas, seeing him touch the handcuffs at his belt, stepped forward, presumably to interfere. He drew back, however, as the horses plodded into the courtyard, for the driver wasn't Goodwin, but Jimmy.

Officer Morgan signaled him to halt, looking like a cat whose mouse had disappeared into a hole. "Where is your father?" he asked.

"At The Arms, sir," said Jimmy. "Collecting his wages from Mr. Lovejoy with the others. He sent me on with the horses because they were too hot to stand."

Something in Jimmy's voice told me he knew more than he was saying, but Officer Morgan seemed unaware of it. "I suppose," he said with a forced smile, "that having received his money, your father will stay at The Arms for some time?"

"No, sir," said Jimmy. "He always takes his wages straight to Mum."

"I see. Is he cognizant of the unfortunate recent demise?"

"Sir?"

Officer Morgan raised his voice. "Does he know Farmer Farrington is dead?"

"Oh, yes, sir. Everybody knows, sir."

"May I assume your father will be at home if I drive there to question him?"

"I should think so, sir."

"Thank you, lad. Your name again?"

"Jimmy, sir."

"Excellent. Well, put the horses up, Jimmy, and hurry home to your Mum."

Jimmy clucked to the team, looking neither right nor left. I reluctantly started to follow him, but to my surprise, my father shook his head and started to the stable himself, laying a hand on Jimmy's thin shoulder.

"Well," said Officer Morgan, "It appears that I must go to Goodwin's cottage."

I. Not *we?* I looked at Tim, but his face was expressionless.

"Surely," said Sir Thomas, "there's no evidence that would require the use of those." He pointed at the handcuffs. "As I'm sure Officer Jenkins has told you, Goodwin was Farrington's tenant. There would be many reasons for him to visit his landlord."

Officer Morgan looked around the circle of unsympathetic faces. "I'm sure you realize how serious the matter is, Sir Thomas. I cannot risk letting a suspect escape. I must talk to Lovejoy, too. I notice he has not kept his appointment here."

"Excuse me, sir," I said, stepping forward. "Mr. Lovejoy was here at the appointed time. He waited for Officer Jenkins over an hour. Finally, he left me this note to give to you."

I gave it to him; he glanced at it and gave it back. "I can't accept this as genuine without seeing another specimen of Lovejoy's handwriting," he said. Then, suddenly aware of my indignant face and the others' collective growl, he added, "I'm sure Sir Thomas, as a member of the Council, will agree that it would be wise to question Lovejoy as well as Goodwin."

Dr. Baines exchanged an angry look with Lady Sylvia. "You'll find Lovejoy at my house, if he has left The Arms, officer. We had engaged his company for supper."

"Thank you," said Officer Morgan. "I hope your evening plans continue without change." He bowed to Lady Sylvia and Sir Thomas, started the police motor, and drove off.

Lady Sylvia turned to Dr. Baines. "There seems to be something Officer Morgan is unwilling to tell us."

"Several things, I should think," said Dr. Baines. "What *has* he told you?"

"That yesterday, Farmer Farrington was poisoned ineffectively, then bludgeoned very effectively, and that he suspects Barth Goodwin of the murder," said Lady Sylvia.

Dr. Baines frowned. "Did he say the murder was committed yesterday?"

All of us looked at each other. Finally, as nobody else spoke, I volunteered: "Actually, sir, he didn't say, in so many words. Merely that Farmer Farrington's body was found this morning."

"Well remembered, Harry," said Sir Thomas. "I was so shocked at the news I paid no attention to its date."

Dr. Baines's tired face grew a little more fatigued. "I fear you weren't supposed to. In emphasizing the discovery of the body, Morgan allowed you to assume Farrington was killed Thursday, which he insists is the case—even though Coroner Davis and I agree that Farrington had been dead for two days by the time we saw his body this afternoon."

"That's odd," said Sir Thomas. "Why would Morgan ignore medical evidence?"

"He says he received a telephone call on Wednesday evening, telling him that Farrington, contrary to the orders at Vanter's inquest, had plans to look over sheep at the market in town Thursday morning. Morgan spent most of Thursday searching for him."

"Were you with him, Jenkins?" asked Lady Sylvia, looking at Tim.

"No, my lady," he said quietly. "I was in London."

"In London!"

"Yes, at my behest," said Dr. Baines. "His leg has been painful, and I arranged for him to meet with a specialist." He smiled. "As I'd hoped, a great deal can be done, and will be, within a few weeks."

"Oh, ripping!" I said, before I could stop myself.

Sir Thomas smiled; Lady Sylvia laughed. "You've spoken for us all, Harry," she said. "But if Jenkins was in London, who joined Morgan in the search for Farrington?"

Tim looked uncomfortable. "I'm afraid I don't know, my lady."

She glanced at Dr. Baines. "Was the search successful?"

"It was not," he said. "But Morgan has insisted that he received word that Farrington was seen near Chandace on the North Road, Thursday afternoon. And he repeated the assertion many times over, as he argued with Davis and me about the time of death."

"Did he say *who* saw Farmer Farrington near Chandace?" said Lady Sylvia. "And *when*?"

"When we pressed him, he'd only tell us that the information was telephoned in by a 'completely reliable' party."

"Jenkins," said Sir Thomas, "can *you* assure us that the witness was reliable?"

Tim's face became a mask. "I . . ."

"Come, Jenkins," said Dr. Baines. "Out with it! Better Sir Thomas should hear it from you than from Davis and me."

As Tim looked from him to Sir Thomas, I somehow thought of a man facing a firing squad, but he drew himself up and spoke calmly enough. "I feel badly telling you this, Sir Thomas, because I know I was made an officer on the basis of your recommendation and the Council's support. But today, Officer Morgan dismissed me."

"The devil he did!" Sir Thomas's voice rose angrily. "For what reason?"

"The cause he stated was that my leg made me unfit for service in the police. The issue had arisen before: for example, when he insisted that I was physically incapable of examining the riverbank after Vanter's murder, and he told me to stay with Dr. Baines."

"By Jove!" said Dr. Baines. "So *that's* what was going on! I thought something was."

"A fair amount of it went on," said Tim. "Enough to warn me that my position was tenuous. But as my parents depend upon my income, I was careful not to give him any reason for dissatisfaction until Wednesday evening, when Dr. Baines asked that I travel to London on Thursday for medical reasons. Morgan's dissatisfaction was exacerbated when I returned to the police office this morning with news of Farrington's murder. He assumed I was accusing him of negligence."

"Knowing the story," said Sir Thomas dryly, "It would be difficult *not* to accuse—"

"—Excuse me, Sir Thomas, but I did *not* know the story," said Tim. "When I went off to find Farrington, I assumed he and Morgan had simply encountered the kind of scheduling difficulty that made me miss Lovejoy today."

"And yet, when you brought news, Morgan angrily dismissed you?"

Tim shook his head. "We hurried off together after we'd telephoned Dr. Baines and Coroner Davis, and I thought he would forget his fear of criticism as we dealt with the murder. Unfortunately, I was unable to carry Farrington's body up the ladder from the root cellar unassisted—"

"—and so, as Davis and I arrived at the scene, we became involuntary witnesses to the most unjust and intemperate dismissal I've ever encountered," said Dr. Baines. "Davis tried to reason with Morgan, but he was as irrational as a surgeon whose error has resulted in the death of a patient. He actually tried to blame Farrington's murder on Jenkins's absence!

As for the 'incompetence' that prevented Jenkins from carrying Farrington up that ladder, *nobody* could have done it alone. The body had been chucked head-first into the cellar; it was wedged in a corner and so stiff that extricating it was difficult even for Davis and me together."

"What a horror!" murmured Sir Thomas, shuddering. He turned to Tim. "At what time did Morgan say your dismissal was effective?"

"Immediately, sir. I believe he sent official word back to town with Mr. Davis."

"Yes," growled Dr. Baines. "And he refused to talk with Jenkins further on any subject. He even refused him transportation back to his home! In the middle of this very difficult case! I tell you, guilt, or fear, or whatever ails him, has left Morgan without his wits."

"This is a matter for the Council to take up," said Sir Thomas, frowning. "In the meantime . . ." He glanced at Tim. "A word with you, Jenkins." He started to the fountain, beckoning Tim to follow him.

Dr. Baines smiled ironically. "As I'd hoped," he muttered. "In some cases, one's political principles fly out the window."

"Excuse me, sir," I said quietly.

He turned to me. "Yes, Harry?"

"When did you and Officer Jenkins make his appointment in London?"

"Oh, quite at the last minute," he said, surprised. "The specialist I'd told about Jenkins suddenly had a cancelation and telephoned me Wednesday afternoon. I telephoned the police station, and we arranged it in five minutes. I knew Morgan wouldn't be pleased, but if I'd had any idea that Jenkins's position depended on his presence, I would have put it off." Suddenly he caught my meaning. "Are you suggesting that somebody could have learned of Jenkins's coming absence and realized that it would be comparatively easy to send Morgan on a fool's errand Thursday?"

I nodded.

"Clever lad. But why would a man who had murdered Farrington on Wednesday be concerned to mislead the police on Thursday?"

"Because Farrington's workers had seen him—the murderer, that is—visiting the Farm on Wednesday, and he wished to distract Officer Morgan so he wouldn't discover it until today."

"That sounds a little complicated, Harry," he said.

"Not really, sir," I said, but as I began to explain, Sir Thomas and Tim returned.

"So," said Sir Thomas, clearly pleased. "Jenkins has kindly agreed to take a position at the Hall, temporarily helping Lovejoy with the many administrative duties connected with Lord Sandford's— er, presence, and performing some private investigating for me. Accommodations for him and his parents will eventually be arranged, but he has expressed a willingness to spend this night at least in the old dormitory above the harness room. Harry, it is in habitable shape?"

"Yes, sir," I said, forcing myself not to dance with joy. "I clean it once a week."

"Well done. You can show him his quarters as soon as he has talked with Jimmy Goodwin. Meanwhile, nip over to Rushdale's cottage and ask him to move the Lanchester to the old carriage house and be sure it has petrol. Jenkins will be wanting it a fair bit in coming days."

He turned to Dr. Baines. "Perhaps you will be good enough to use your telephone to call the White Stag, which Jenkins assures me will tell his parents where he is tonight."

"You may have that pleasure yourself, if you'd do us the honor of dining with us," said Dr. Baines. "Sandy, er, that is, Lord Sandford, will be there."

"I'd be delighted," said Sir Thomas. "But I'm afraid my dinner jacket isn't—"

"—We never dress for dinner," said Lady Sylvia and Dr. Baines nearly together.

"Excellent," said Sir Thomas. Then, frowning at me, "Harry! You're still here!"

"Yes, sir," I said. "Rushdale will want to know what time you'll need the Lanchester this evening, and whether he's driving."

"I'll need it immediately. And I'll drive myself. Off, now!"

Chapter 19

I returned from Rushdale's cottage to find my father and Tim in the harness room, gently easing a meat pie and a rhubarb tart into a rucksack, Jimmy nearby. Tim threw me a look that made me stop sniffing the tempting smells.

"Sir Thomas has been kind enough to send Agatha out with his tea here, since he's going to dine with the Baineses," he said. "But your father and I decided it was best sent to the Goodwins."

I nodded, but the atmosphere in the harness room kept me from speaking. In a moment, Jimmy, his face lined with dirt and worry, shouldered the rucksack, looked at the three of us and jogged off, saying no more than, "Thank'ee."

As he rounded the corner, I asked, "Does he know where his father is?"

"We didn't ask," answered my father, "lest we have to lie should Morgan come back here with awkward questions. The food won't go to waste. The poor lad could probably eat the whole himself. And as for his mum, Jimmy says she'll be fair desperate if she can't get Goodwin's wages, they being short already. He also says that with everybody knowing that Goodwin was looking for Farrington Wednesday and Thursday evenings, his father would be a fool to go home. Morgan would arrest him, not question him."

Tim shook his head. "I'm afraid his disappearance will be taken as admission of guilt."

"How can it?" I said hotly. "He was seen *asking* where Farrington was! You don't ask a man's workers where he is if you're planning to murder him!"

"That's true," said Tim, "But unfortunately, I think Morgan feels compelled to perform an arrest before the inquest. Just who is compelling him, I can't say, but his irrationality today—not just with me, but with Baines and Davis, and even with Sir Thomas—makes me suspect that he is afraid of whoever it is."

"Serves him right, the way he treated you," observed my father, standing up. "Harry, it's time for you to show Tim his quarters. I'll go tell Mrs. Middleton that we three will be at supper. And I'll make her swear not to tell Mrs. Baggum that Sir Thomas's tea went to the Goodwins." He smiled wryly as he stepped into the courtyard. "Wish me luck."

"I'm missing something," said Tim as we left the harness room for the straight stall wing. "Why should Mrs. Baggum not want the Goodwins to have Sir Thomas's tea?"

"Because years ago, Nellie Goodwin got in trouble when she was a parlor maid."

"Oh, that's right. Goodness. All that time past, and still ... ?"

"And still," I said. We walked to the foot of the ladder to the dormitory, and I looked about, suddenly uneasy. "You'll be sleeping up there," I said, very quietly.

"Let's nip up and look," he whispered, and was up the ladder far faster than I'd have thought his leg would let him.

There was nothing there except the familiar musty warmth that came from the sun on the roof, the four beds the lads had once used, each with a blanket I shook out and folded every week, a washstand, and a dangling electric lightbulb. Tim limped from one end to the other, saying what comfortable quarters he was going to have in a voice belied by the care with which his eyes were taking in every detail. At the far end, he stopped, moved a bed slightly to one side, and beckoned. Hurrying to his side, I saw a knot hole—and through it, the harness room.

"I thought I saw something in this corner when we were down there," he said quietly.

I felt myself turning red. "And to think I've swept this room every week!"

"No," he said. "Look." He opened his palm and showed me a piece of cork, whittled so it was wider at one end than the other. He fitted the narrow end into the hole. "You see? It's been cut so it's level with the floor. And of course, it's right by the foot of the bed. What I saw downstairs was just a mark in the ceiling—not a place one looks at in a well-cleaned dormitory."

"Who taught you to see things that little?"

"Sniper training," he said brusquely, moving the bed back to its place. "Now, you were talking about a back door? Let's go look."

I led the way, my pride in my detection skills chastened. Tim made me feel much better by noting how hard it was to see that the door's bolt had shot into nothing; and if, when we stood outside, he noted that I'd left boot marks as I'd run back to greet Sir Thomas and Lady Sylvia, he didn't say so.

"Now," I said, "this is the secret footpath to the wall. And look." I pointed to the disturbed earth. "Isn't that odd?"

He stared at it a minute, then said, "Let's follow it—careful where you step—let's see where it leads."

He started into the wood, stepping so softly I became angry all over again at the thought of Morgan finding Tim "unfit for service." After fifty paces, he stopped. "There it goes, by Jove."

He was looking at what seemed an ordinary tree, one supporting, as many trees in the wood did, a vine of some sort . . . except a vine would never shine like that in the filtered late-afternoon sun.

"What is it?" I whispered.

"What does it look like?" he said, amused.

"A wire."

He nodded. "A copper core cable. Chaps like Lovejoy risked their lives running cables like that from the advance lines to headquarters."

I followed the line of the wire as it wound behind the vine up the tree, and saw an occasional glint among the branches, heading towards the park wall. "Telegraph?" I said.

"Field telephone," he answered. "Two-way communication. Usually buried, but of course there's little danger of discovery here. Let's go back to the storage room. There may be a very useful piece of equipment there, unless . . ." He stopped, listening.

I listened, too, suddenly thinking of the eerie silence in the Dell.

A rustle. Another.

Tim stepped silently off the path and flattened himself against a tree. I chose a thick oak and knelt behind it, my heart thumping.

For several seconds, all was silent.

Then . . . it was hardly even a sound. Just the merest whisper of last year's leaves. Again. Silence. Again.

Whoever was coming towards us was an expert in the woods.

Chapter 20

As the silence in the wood drew on, my heart stopped thudding and my brain began to assert its rights. Whoever it was must have heard us. We'd been talking, after all. The intelligent thing for him to do, then, was to make sure we didn't see him, either by waiting us out or by leaving. Which meant that if I wanted to know who he was, cowering behind an oak tree put me at what Mr. Lovejoy would call a tactical disadvantage.

Up. I reached for the massive branch above me and pulled myself slowly onto it in a way that stretched every muscle. Slid behind the trunk. Inched noiselessly up two opposite branches. Stretched up for the sun-touched limb above me.

"No, no lad," said a voice. "Never climb into the sunlight before the leaves come. A warden'd catch you in a second."

Through the bare branches below me, I made out a familiar figure almost indistinguishable from the beech in whose shadow he was standing. "Goodwin!"

"Good fortune it's nobody else," he said, pointing to the copper core cable that ran through the branches above him. "There's more set here than snares."

I clambered down the tree, shaking with relief. "I know. We thought you were one of the men who'd set them."

"We?" he said anxiously as Tim stepped forward. "You wouldn't be handing me to the police, now would you, Harry?"

"I'm no longer 'the police,'" said Tim wryly. "I'm in Sir Thomas's service. I was let go without warning, so until I can gather civilian clothes, I'm still in uniform."

"So, it's true," said Goodwin, moving towards us. "Not that I'd thought aught else after Mr. Lovejoy told us aboot Farrington." He shook his head. "Said he'd heard aboot Morgan handing you the slip from the coroner himself. Then he took me aside, told me to let m'lad take the horses back here, and not to go home, or Morgan would slap me in gaol in a trice. 'Find Sir Thomas,' Lovejoy said. 'Him being a magistrate, he can keep you in custody.'"

"An excellent idea," said Tim. "Sir Thomas knows there is a problem with Morgan, and as he's dining with Lovejoy and the others at the Baineses this evening, he's probably been put in touch with Coroner Davis and a few council members. As for tonight, it might be well for you to share the dormitory above the stable with me." He looked meaningfully around the wood, then down at his game leg. "If some fellows came to keep us company, one of us, at least, might need to chase them."

Goodwin smiled. "Not so fast as I wur—but if the bloke who set this up had known his way in the woods, it wouldn't show like it does. D'you know what this is?"

"Telephone line," said Tim.

"Here?! What for?"

"To spy on the stable," I said. "Somebody listens from the dormitory, creeps down the ladder and calls to tell somebody else where I'm going. And when."

"*You*, lad? What have you done, that a mon would go to all this trouble to find you? You ride out every day."

I looked at Tim. "May I tell him?"

"Tell away," said Tim. "Farrington's murder has made it very important."

"Well," I said, "the Sunday after the inquest, I went to the Dell, looking for Bailiff Vanter's cycle—"

"—Ha," said Goodwin. "Thought of doing that myself, but didn't dare, for fear of being thought a murderer."

"I thought of that, too, so when I heard somebody rowing towards the shore, I climbed a tree, most likely into the light, but I was lying along a branch by the time he came ashore, and he didn't look up. It was Farmer Farrington."

"Farrington!" Goodwin's face went so gray that I hurried on with my little tale, and finished, with a glance at Tim for support, "Then as he was untying his skiff, he saw Mr. Vanter's cycle in the water and said the police were bloody fools."

Goodwin frowned at me. "So, you thought Farrington wur the—"

"No," said Tim. "When Harry told me what he'd seen, we agreed that Farrington was probably comparing what he knew with what was—and wasn't—said at the inquest."

"It just meant he knew something," I added, seeing Goodwin was still upset.

"I knew something, too, more's the shame," he said. "Lord forgive me, if I'd told all when Mr. Davis asked if I owned a skiff, maybe Farrington would still be walking aboot."

Tim frowned. "What could you have told us at the inquest?"

"A long story. See, the skiff m'lads sold to get to the Front had been a present from Hugh back in '08, when Sir Thomas gave him the new one. 'For moonlit nights,' said Hugh, laughing because the lads spent so many of those together. Hid it in the Dell, m'lads did. Made a dock in the reeds so clever you'd have to know where it was to see it. To thank Hugh, my Charlie—he wur always one with words, wur Charlie—carved their initials in the bow. 'Henry, Charlie, Willie' he said. 'Same as Hugh Chandace Willingford,' see, to show whose it was and whose it had been."

"Crikey!" I said, "Those initials that made Officer Morgan think Mr. Lovejoy—"

"—so Johnson told me Dr. Baines had told him," said Goodwin. "And so I told Mr. Lovejoy this aaternoon, being grateful for his tip. Point is, though, the one who bought my boys' skiff from m'lads wur Vanter."

"Vanter!" said Tim and I, both astonished.

Goodwin nodded unhappily. "He wur the only one with money enough. That's what I should have said at the Inquest, d'you see?"

"But you weren't asked about it!" I said.

"My good luck I wasn't, I thought at the time," he said. "Wish I could set the clock back. Anyways, Vanter took the skiff and kept it in the Hall's boathouse. Not sure how long, it being the time of all those losses. But one evening last Eastertide, when I wur traveling homeward with a rabbit, I thought to pass m'lads' dock for old time's sake, and there wur the old skiff Vanter had bought, tied up.

"Odd, I thought. So I talked to the mates as had used m'lads' skiff now and then, Farrington being one. And they took it by turns to keep watch for the next few weeks, hoping to find Vanter wur doing something so untoward he didn't want anyone to see his motor. But it seemed that he took the skiff out only on Wednesdays at three or thereabouts, coming home late." He grinned. "Farrington, he wur beside himself. 'No shenanigans. Just a wench,' he told me." Goodwin turned to Tim. "Likely you heard the talk."

Tim nodded. "But what you're saying is that only a few people knew Vanter's skiff was kept in the Dell. And Farrington was one of them."

"Yes. But what Harry saw tells me that Farrington might have told somebody else about the dock. And that after the inquest, knowing nothing wur decided, he wur curious to know if that same somebody might have done Vanter in. Question is, who'd he told?" He looked expressively at the copper core wire.

"All respect to you, Harry," he said, looking back at me, "I'd say this wur a line set to catch a bigger hare than you. And unless the trees are lying, it wur set long afore Vanter and Farrington passed on. See how the wire's worked its way into that joint, there?"

We looked. Tim pursed his lips, probably thinking, as I was, what duffers we'd been not to have noticed. "Let's go back to the stable," he said. "The line goes underground there."

I followed the two of them, fidgeting because the courtyard clock was striking five. I was about to excuse myself when we came out of the wood and Goodwin bent down.

"See here," he said. "This is new. Not a few days, but likely wintertime, when digging was hard. But see the earth over there? It wur dug up in summertime. And it goes . . ." He followed the almost indistinguishable line for some fifty paces along the stable's foundations, then stopped and looked up at the two windows above him. "There. A clever mon made him a hole in the frame there on the right, to slip his line into the stable. Seems he moved it later for some reason."

"That's too far to be in the stable," I said, "And there are no windows in the carriage barn. It's the steward's office."

They both stared at me, and not to tell me I shouldn't correct my betters, either. But before they could say anything, my father's voice boomed my name across the courtyard.

"I'm late for feeding time," I muttered, starting towards the back door.

"We'll come in with you and explain," said Tim, limping beside me. "How much have you told your father about all this?"

"Nothing," I confessed. "Wish I had, now. He'll be hurt that I didn't trust him."

"It's not trust," said Goodwin, smiling. "Long as there's been children, there's been secrets kept to save mums and dads from worrit. Always so thoughtful, you rogues." He gave my shoulder a friendly thump as we hurried across the empty storage room. "No fear, lad. We'll make it well."

I never learned what exactly they said, only that it must have been plenty, because my father's face told me he would have said plenty himself if he hadn't seen Tim and Goodwin behind me. As I distributed grain, hay, and water, I heard their voices in the harness room and the dormitory. By the time I'd finished, they were standing in the doorway, waiting for me, and I hadn't seen my father so troubled since we thought Sir Thomas was dying.

"Harry . . ." he began, then swallowed and stopped.

I looked down. "I'm sorry, sir," I said. "I found out about the bolt only this afternoon, just as Sir Thomas was returning. I was going to tell you—honor bright!"

"I should have checked the bolt myself," he said heavily. "It's your danger I'm thinking of."

"I'm all right, sir," I said, and added, with sudden inspiration, "Now that you're helping, it's just a question of time before there's no more danger to me or the rest of us."

My father's face relaxed, and Tim's smile told me I'd said the right thing. "We're about to look amongst the trunks in the bedding alcove," he said. "Come, lead the way."

I did, of course, but as we walked by the deserted straight stalls, I glanced up at the ornate plastered ceiling, half expecting to see it obscured by the fog of sadness I felt drifting through the stable. The handsome trunks we were about to examine had once graced the harness room, and we had packed them dozens of times for Hugh's visits to other stables. After Hugh died, my father had taken to opening them time after time under pretense of airing and cleaning their contents. The review had invariably filled him with such sorrow that he could hardly do his duties.

Finally, at Mum's quiet suggestion, I'd moved the trunks to the back wall of the bedding alcove, where they were practically invisible in the poor light. Father had never mentioned their absence. He had merely assigned the upkeep of the straight stall wing entirely to me.

I stopped in front of the trunks. "Shall I move these? What are we looking for?"

"First tell me if they're in the order you remember," said Tim.

I peered at them, marveling, as I had several times since Tim had spotted that hole, at how little I saw of what I looked at. "I . . . I think so—no, wait! They used to be a little short of the whole wall.

Now they fit exactly."

"Then we must be extremely careful not to change their order," said Tim. He glanced at my father. "Are there lights in here, Green?"

"There were," said my father, "but Vanter insisted we remove the fuse as an economical measure."

Tim nodded and limped slowly along the row of trunks; a short way before he came to the far end, he stopped. "By Jove!" he said triumphantly. "Here it is." He lifted up a box smaller than the trunks, but evidently heavier than it looked. "Let's have some daylight."

Hurrying across the room, I realized my father had already walked to the small door to examine its bolt. He opened it just as I arrived, his eyebrows raised. "It was well done," he muttered. "From a distance, it looked just as it should. Even expecting it, I didn't see it until my hand was on the latch."

I could hardly believe it: he was excusing my incompetence. I was about to thank him, but he had already stepped to Goodwin's side to look at the box. Tim put it down in the pool of late-afternoon sunlight and stiffly lowered himself next to it.

Looking at it myself, I could see how easy it had been to hide it amongst the trunks. Like them, it was made of well-finished pine, its corners reinforced by black metal. Its top was hinged on the short side and closed with a catch that Tim was unfastening.

"No lock," he said, shaking his head. "Whoever uses it seems not to fear sabotage." With a practiced hand, he tilted the lid back, revealing a paper covered with diagrams on its underside. Reaching into the box itself, he drew out a black handle—no, not a handle. I recognized it from the contrivance I'd seen at The Arms, with two bell-shaped ends that allowed one to listen and to speak.

"See?" he said, showing it to us. "A telephone." He moved his hand along the cord attached to one end. "The battery that powers it fits neatly into the box, and this"—he held up another cord—"attaches with these pinchers to the lines outside."

"And where do the lines lead?" asked Goodwin.

"Presumably, through the wood and over the wall, where they're probably grafted to the Chandace telephone lines that run along the high road to the exchange in town. The fellow to ask is Lovejoy. He was in Signals, so he understands the details better than I do."

My father looked at the box with loathing. "And this is the contraption that lets some spy know where Harry is riding?"

"I'm sure it is," said Tim.

"You're saying there's two blokes in on it, then," said Goodwin. "One to pass on the word after spying from the dormitory, and one to get it. Where's the one who gets it?"

"Well, judging from what Harry said about a lorry following him this morning, I'd say somewhere near where the navvies are working," said Tim. "I've been wondering about them for some time."

"The navvies!" My father's eyes widened in horror.

"Could be more'n them," said Goodwin. "Let me think on it a little. Are we going to talk to Sir Thomas about this?"

"We have to!" said my father. "These people are intruding on his property!"

"Absolutely," said Tim. "We'll talk to him first thing in the morning. Given a gentleman's hours, however, I don't think we can see him much before half past nine."

"Then I can't join you," I said. "I have to give Cyril Norton a lesson at ten."

"Ah," said Goodwin, in a tone I didn't quite understand. "Hutchins'll be driving him in that Rolls of Norton's?"

"That what?"

Tim laughed. "Rolls Royce. You'll have to learn more about motors, Harry. They say as much about the way a man wishes to be seen as horses once did. Vanter's motor was the equivalent of your Atlas— solid, well put together, not flashy. The Lanchester, though—that's a Thoroughbred. As for the Rolls . . . well, think of a carriage with liveried panels and six dapple grays."

Six dapple grays! Even on formal occasions, Sir Thomas and

Hugh had never driven more than their matched pair of chestnuts. But I hadn't answered Goodwin's question. "Cyril did come to his first lesson with Mr. Norton in the Rolls," I said hurriedly. "And yes, Hutchins drove them."

"All right," said Tim, as Goodwin looked thoughtful. "Tomorrow, I'll ask Parks to catch Sir Thomas at breakfast and arrange for us to confer with him at half past eleven. And I'll ask him to include Lovejoy, who understands field telephones. Does that suit?"

We agreed that it did, and I hurried up to the dormitory to make beds for Goodwin and Tim, half-wishing I could sleep up there myself, awaiting adventure.

Chapter 21

Next morning, Cyril arrived at the courtyard exactly on time, as before—and also as before in the company of his father. This time, however, Mr. Norton immediately began talking to my father, pausing only to tell Hutchins, who was eying the laundry girls, to stay with the Rolls. It struck me as odd that he felt compelled to give that order, for the rules about men and women servants on duty were unbreakable, at least in public. But Cyril's excited chatter soon occupied all my thoughts as we walked patient Atlas to the manège.

The lesson went well. Cyril listened intently to my pointers on using his legs and seat to keep Atlas moving smoothly, and he seemed to feel instinctively how and when to apply them. The result was such mastery of the trot that if Atlas's uncollected canter hadn't been so ponderous, I would have been tempted to let him try it. Instead, I had the two of them work on halts, salutes, circles, serpentines, and figure eights, allowing the boy to develop sensitivity with his hands—which, again, he did with surprising speed.

He was so enthusiastic, and Atlas so willing to please him, I didn't notice that the lesson had drawn spectators to the manège until the final halt, when Cyril said, "Is that Sir Thomas next to Papa?"

His voice carried across the arena and, to my surprise, instead of looking annoyed, Sir Thomas smiled, bowed, and said, "It is indeed, at your service."

Cyril's expression suggested he was disappointed to see that Sir Thomas wore tweeds, not armor, so I whispered, "Salute him, the way you practiced."

Instantly the boy sat straight, bowed, and touched his forehead in a salute that would have warmed Hugh's heart. Without instruction, he added, "I am honored, sir."

I held my breath, willing Sir Thomas not to crush the boy by laughing. And greatly to his credit, he did not. "You ride very well, Cyril," he said.

"Yes, indeed," said Mr. Norton, with a smile that softened his usually hard face. "Sir Thomas, Green and I have been talking about finding you something closer to your size than Atlas, here."

Cyril's face lit up. "A pony?"

"Either that or a small horse," said Mr. Norton. "Sir Thomas and Green have extensive contacts in the right circles, and they've promised to help."

"Will it come tomorrow?" the boy asked eagerly.

"I'm afraid not even your father can work miracles like that," said Sir Thomas drily. "But I'm sure we can find something in the next month or so."

"Meanwhile," I said, to ward off his disappointment, "you have a horse to cool." Cyril slid off obediently, but he chattered on about "his pony" the whole time we were putting Atlas up, while I listened with a sympathy increasingly mixed with irritation at his unspoken assumption that anything he wanted would be instantly forthcoming. By the time I sent him back into the courtyard, I was hard pressed to remember that the boy was not to blame for his upbringing.

My reflections quickly moved to the coming interview with Sir Thomas. I was trying to put all our information together in my mind when I heard the sound of breaking glass, and a shout from Hutchins: "'Ere, you little villain! Look wot yer rock's done!"

I set down the water buckets I'd been gathering and hurried to the stable door. Sir Thomas, my father, Mr. Norton, and Hutchins were all grouped around Mr. Norton's Rolls, and even from where I stood, I could see that its windscreen was broken.

I ran back to the box stall wing to fetch a broom and shovel, and as I returned, I heard the harness room door shut. I walked towards it, feeling the hairs on the back of my neck prickle, but then it occurred to me to survey the courtyard. No Cyril.

Ah. I opened the harness room door quietly and looked in.

Cyril was in the far corner, half hidden under the pile of neatly folded winter horse blankets. His face, when he saw me, was so filled with terror that for a moment I almost sympathized with his plight.

"Don't tell them I'm here!" he whispered tearfully.

"Come, Master Cyril," I said. "You've broken a windscreen. You can't hide forever."

"I didn't do it on purpose! I meant to hit a rook and it—" He broke off.

"And what?"

He shook his head wordlessly.

"Never mind," I said. "The windscreen will speak for itself. Let's go into the courtyard and tell your father you're sorry. I imagine he'll be angry, but apologizing always makes things better."

He glanced at the horse blankets, then at me, his face filled with a fear that made me wonder about the extent of the punishment he faced. I knew from remarks of Hugh's friends that far gentler fathers than Mr. Norton thought nothing of beating their sons into manhood. Unfortunately, I had as little hope of preserving him from a beating as I did of teaching him the world wasn't his to command. "Come, Master Cyril. It will only make matters worse if they find you here."

He got slowly to his feet. "Will you hold my hand, Harry?"

"Are you sure you want me to? It will look as if I'm bringing you to them, instead of your walking out on your own like a true knight."

"True knights don't do wrong things," he said desolately. "So, I can't be one."

I stooped down and looked directly into his tear-stained face.

"Yes, you can," I said. "Knights don't always *begin* by being true. They *become* true knights by admitting they've done something wrong and promising not to do it again."

"And true knights *always* keep their promises," he added anxiously.

"Exactly. Even when it's hard."

"All right." He gave me one despairing look; then, squaring his shoulders, he walked out the stable door and across the courtyard without a backward glance. I watched him from the door, reflecting that there might indeed be a true knight there . . . if only Hugh were present to help him find his way.

*   *   *

The task of sweeping the windscreen glass out from between the cobblestones naturally fell to me. Under my father's meticulous eye, the job required a dustpan and brush as well as a broom, and it took so long that Mr. Parks came outside and stood over me with dignified impatience for nearly a quarter hour after Goodwin, Tim, and Mr. Lovejoy had followed Sir Thomas into the library.

At the last moment, my father decided to stand guard over the stable, so Mr. Parks conducted me through the house in offended silence that I had to endure alone. None of the men in the library were irritated by my tardiness, though; they were listening with such attention to Goodwin's story about the skiff that they didn't even notice when I was announced.

Goodwin finished the story in fine style; then he added, "Last night, I couldn't sleep—no fault of your dormitory, Sir Thomas— and one of the things tossing aboot in my head was, when I bought Farrington a pint Tuesday last, he mentioned that when he'd gone to The Arms Wednesday—the Wednesday of the murder, that is—he might've seen Vanter's skiff tied up there."

"There was no skiff tied up there at three, when I talked with Baines!" said Mr. Lovejoy. "Just a small barge and a couple of . . .

dinghies, I guess you'd call them. What time did Farrington say he saw it?"

"He didn't say, but it must've been e'enmost dark, he being finished with his work."

"Good lord, man!" said Sir Thomas. "And he said nothing about it at the inquest?"

Goodwin shrugged. "He wurn't asked. And even if he had been, he wurn't certain. And being no fool, he didn't see a point to offering information that could be twisted to make him look guilty. I can't fault him, having done the same m'self."

Sir Thomas looked so disapproving that I wondered if he'd forgotten the way he'd privately schooled me in circumventing the truth under oath. "And now, of course," he said, "there's no confirming his tale—"

"—Oh, but there is, sir!" I said.

I instantly had to beg pardon, for they startled like a herd of horses. But after Sir Thomas called me forward from the door where I'd been standing, I told them about Mr. Johnson's having seen a skiff tied up at The Arms the evening of the murder, and of its disappearance by morning.

The irritation gradually fell from Sir Thomas's face, and when I finished, he turned to Mr. Lovejoy. "With evidence like this, not even Morgan can accuse you of escaping Vanter's murder in Hugh's skiff. When Davis hears it, I'm sure he'll set you free to go to London."

"Excellent," said Mr. Lovejoy. "As soon as he does, we can conclude the matter we discussed last Thursday."

Sir Thomas turned back to me, smiled, and to my great surprise, thanked me for sweeping the courtyard. "As you know, a shard of glass could cause a horse's frog serious harm," he said. "I made sure the little scapegrace learned that."

"He'll be doubly sorry then, sir," I said. "Where horses are concerned, he's no scapegrace."

"I suspect that horses aren't the only influences on his behavior," said Sir Thomas, turning to the others. "No boy that age would have thought for himself of walking up to the men who were surveying the damage he'd done to offer a dignified, sincere apology to his father— and, I might add to me—for the disturbance he'd caused."

Mr. Lovejoy looked at me. "Did you put him up to that, Harry?"

"More or less," I said. "But I told him only that he should apologize, not how to do it. His dignity was his own."

"Dignity like that gives a father hope," said Sir Thomas, smiling at Goodwin. "As you may recall. High jinks, pranks . . . apologies stayed my hand a score of times, and I was never sorry later. Wish I could think Norton will stay his. He seemed more perturbed than the situation warranted, though of course it is a nuisance."

He pointed me towards the last empty chair facing his desk; as I sat down, I saw Tim had been taking notes in his little book.

"Now, Goodwin," Sir Thomas continued, "To avoid any surprises at Monday's inquest, we need to know why you were looking for Farrington on Wednesday and Thursday evenings."

"Why, for sure, sir," said Goodwin. "To warn him."

Sir Thomas stiffened. "Warn him about *murder*?"

"I wurn't thinking murder, sir. There's other kinds of trouble, and I feared it would come to him."

"What exactly made you fear for him?"

"Well, as I told you, sir, there wur rumors about Vanter's rowing to town for a wench—"

"—Hold up," said Tim, suddenly. "When did you say Vanter began those trips?"

"Easter last, when we wur most feared of losing Sir Thomas."

"Why do you ask, Jenkins?" asked Sir Thomas.

"Because I just put something together. Thursday morning, when I was waiting for the train, the station master took me aside and told me that starting last spring, Easter or thereabouts, Vanter met a 'London toff' in a bowler hat at the 4:20 up train every Wednesday. Never for long, he said: the toff and his hat left by the 5:10 down train. The stationmaster said he didn't give it much thought, since he assumed Vanter was on business for you. But after Vanter's murder, he got to wondering, so when he saw me, he slipped me a word."

"You mean Vanter *wur* doing something untoward?" said Goodwin.

"He was certainly meeting a London man on business that wasn't mine," said Sir Thomas.

"Always ran true to form, Vanter," said Goodwin. "But no wench— what a laugh *that* news would get at The Arms! Truth to tell, a lot of us just shrugged the story off, but Farrington treated it like the Gospel. Then, aater he felt he'd been cheated out of his farm, he got to thinking aboot making Vanter pay for his sins. Supposing, he asked me, a story got about saying Vanter wur bedding not just a wench, but some banker's wife or daughter—*then* who would loan Vanter money t'buy farms?"

"Good lord!" said Mr. Lovejoy. "Would he really sink to ruining a woman's reputation just to avenge himself?"

Goodwin shrugged. "No question he *would*. Just whether he'd *dare*, knowing he might someday need a loan himself. I wagered him a pint he'd never risk noising such a story aboot."

Sir Thomas leaned forward. "When was this?"

"The Sunday aaternoon afore Vanter was kilt," said Goodwin. "Then the very next day, Farrington told Rushdale and some mates he'd fixed Vanter so he couldn't get loans. But see, he didn't call me on the pint. Not then, and not afore the inquest when we wur talking. A whole week passed afore I heard Rushdale's story from Jenkins, here. Odd, I thought. So last Tuesday e'en after darts, I asked Farrington, did I owe him a pint? He said, no, he'd done something different from what we'd wagered on. I asked what that 'something' had been, but he wouldn't tell me. With the murder and all, I left it be, but I could see he wur worrit, so I bought him a pint of Norton's best, just for good cheer."

He shifted in his chair. "It happened Rushdale and I left the Arms together, so I asked him if *he* knew what Farrington'd done to keep Vanter from getting loans. He couldn't say for sure, but he did say that on the Monday morning afore the murder, he'd seen Farrington talking private with that son of Norton's."

"Farmer Farrington was talking to *Cyril?*" I asked, incredulous.

"No. T'other son, drives the Rolls. Seems he's come to be a regular at the Arms."

"Wait!" said Sir Thomas as we all stared at each other. "You're saying Hutchins is Norton's son?"

"Well, Farrington *said* he wur—wrong side of the blanket, given the surname. But Norton being who he is, and Farrington not being above twisting the truth, nobody'd credit it if it wurn't for the way Norton protects the lad."

"Hm," said Sir Thomas. "I confess I'd wondered a bit. Cheeky driver, isn't he?"

"More'n often," said Goodwin, "But that's nothing serious. Talking in his cups, though, that's something else."

"Oh!" I said, suddenly remembering the two pairs of empty mugs and shot glasses I'd seen on Hutchins's table at The Arms. Then, urged on by Tim's nod, I told them what Hutchins had said about Mr. Norton's money, Chandace Grange, and the police.

"Well, I see what you mean about protection!" said Mr. Lovejoy. "During the War, fear of talk like that made Prime Minister Asquith cut pub hours back to zilch in munitions areas and big cities. Doesn't Norton know about Hutchins's loose lips?"

"You'd think word would get back to him," said Goodwin. "Coz it happens more than now and again. Nobody's seen the lad drunk, but Johnson says it's nip, nip, nip any time he's free. You hate to watch that happen. But more than that, what with how much time a driver has free, and what with the cost of drink, and what with a driver's pay being low, you know a lad in that fix'll do just aboot aught for a few shillings."

Sir Thomas tapped his fingers together. "Are you suggesting that includes murder?"

"Hutchins is no more a man to murder than Farrington," said

Goodwin. "It's his tongue that causes trouble. So Tuesday e'en, when Rushdale tells me Farrington and Hutchins had been talking private, I'm worrit. Then Wednesday aaternoon, when I'm plowing the rye field, I reach the end of a furrow and see the Rolls and Hutchins talking to a navvy minder in a lorry atween the old Haskins Farm and the Home Farm. Well, it could be business. On the other hand, it could be something else, so I think, I'll stop by Farrington's to warn him not to trust Hutchins with any secrets."

Tim stiffened. "What time was this?"

"Which? When I saw Hutchins or when I went to find Farrington?"

"Both, if you can tell us," said Tim, his pencil poised.

"Seeing him . . . hard to . . . no, wait. It wur a half a furrow aater the St. Barnabas clock struck four."

I shivered. My father had given me the message to take to Lady Sylvia at four. Apparently, my orders had gone out by telephone, too.

"Later," Goodwin continued, "I heard the half hour as I put up the horses . . . likely it wur half past six, so sommat after seven when I got to Farrington's. Late enough I thought he'd left for The Arms."

He shook his head. "Then, early Thursday aaternoon, I'm plowing the field nearest to Chandace, and when I look up, there's the Rolls, and who should get out but Hutchins. Comes right up to the hedge, waits. So I pull up, and he asks, did I see someone on the road an hour or so past? Something's odd, I think, so I say I'd seen some bloke, but I'd not been paying mind. And he says, the navvies say it wur probably Farrington.

"*More* than odd, I think, for there'd been no bloke at all. I shrug and turn the horses. Then he says I should think hard, because if I can remember seeing Farrington, there'll be a shoat in my pen right after market. I say, over my shoulder, I'll have to see if I can recollect who it wur."

Goodwin looked at Sir Thomas. "When I get back the hedge, next furrow, he's gone, but I'm so worrit for th'rest of the day, I put the horses up early, go to see Farrington—even open his door, call—ask his dairy lasses, his hedger . . . nobody's seen him." He lifted his right hand. "That's God's truth, and I'll say it at the inquest Monday."

"I'm sure it's true, and I trust it fits with the facts you've gathered, Jenkins," said Sir Thomas. "Does it?"

"Yes, sir," said Tim. "Including this one: at about the time Harry was giving Cyril Norton a riding lesson Thursday, Officer Morgan received a telephone call from 'a reliable witness' saying Farrington had been seen on the North Road, heading towards his fields."

"Hutchins couldn't possibly have made that call," objected Sir Thomas. "He would have had to drive to the Arms, and . . . well, I don't know where he went, but the Rolls was in the courtyard all through Cyril's lesson."

"Begging your pardon, sir," said Tim, "Hutchins could easily have made the call. But to show you how, we'll have to ask you to step to your stable and see what has been laid out there."

Sir Thomas rose slowly to his feet. "Nothing could possibly have been laid out in the stable! Green and Harry are there all day!"

"I'm sure you don't expect them to be there at night, sir," said Tim.

"Harry!" said Sir Thomas in an exasperated voice I'd never heard him use before. "Don't you and your father lock the stable at night?"

"Of course, sir. But . . ." I looked down. "Yesterday, I found that the bolt in the old bedding alcove had been tampered with."

"It was well done," said Tim, before Sir Thomas could speak. "From the doorway, it looked as if all was well. As for the rest—yesterday evening, we found a set-up that had existed for quite some time, probably before the bolt was altered."

"If you please, sir," added Mr. Lovejoy, "Jenkins has told me about this set-up. I think we all need to see it before making any further judgments."

Sir Thomas looked from one to the other, then to Goodwin. To my astonishment, all three of them met his eyes.

"Very well," he said stiffly. "Let's go to the stable."

He led us out through the formal rooms and the hall. At the top of the portico stairs, he paused to look out over the sweep and the park. I looked too, awed by its elegance and . . . and . . . permanence. It was a landscape in which war, murder, field telephones, navvies, embezzlement, all seemed impossibly out of place, even to me. To a man who had looked out from these stairs every morning of his life, and who had always had servants to protect him from change—

A shout from my father echoed from the courtyard below. Forgetting all protocol, I sprinted down the stairs past Sir Thomas and towards the stable, with Mr. Lovejoy only a few strides behind me. I dashed around the corner just in time to see Hutchins break away from my father, who, though a much smaller man, had been holding him by the collar.

Hutchins could easily have escaped into the stable if he'd seen us coming, but instead of looking, he knocked my father down with a vicious punch. Realizing I could never hold Hutchins myself, I dove for his legs in a rugby move Hugh had taught me.

He went down hard, and in a matter of seconds, Mr. Lovejoy had hauled him up and held him in a double nelson. "Harry!" he said breathlessly. "Get me some rope!"

"No need," snarled Hutchins. "I'll stand. It's not like I've done anything wrong."

"Nothing wrong, eh?" Sir Thomas, coughing hard, turned to him after Goodwin and Tim had helped my father to his feet. "Just snuck into a private stable without permission and assaulted a groom."

"*He* was the one who assaulted," said Hutchins. "I was just stopping by to look for a toy the kid left here after his lesson."

"Right in the harness room, he was," panted my father indignantly, pressing his side. "Moving things about—"

"—as you would've been, if you had to find something," retorted Hutchins.

"Now wait," said Tim soothingly. "Let's get the record straight. Hutchins, did Mr. Norton tell you to come fetch Master Cyril's toy?"

It was a clever question. If Hutchins weren't a duffer, he'd say yes, and that would be an end to it, except for his hitting my father. But he muttered, "The kid's a right howler when he's lost something. I was doing him a *favor*."

"I see," said Tim. "And how did you get here?"

"Walked from Chandace ..." Hutchins hesitated. "Wot I mean is, I asked Mr. Norton to drop me off at The Arms and take Master Cyril on home himself. Told him I could get a lift home with the navvies."

Sir Thomas glanced at Tim. "That's an extremely odd statement for a chauffeur to make, Hutchins," he said. "So while we won't tie you, we'll lock you in one of the stalls—a clean one, mind—and ask your master to confirm your story."

"You're wasting your time and his," growled Hutchins.

"Not much time," said Tim. "It can be done very quickly on the telephone we found in the bedding alcove."

Hutchins shrank about three sizes. "I'd nothing to do with that, y'hear? It was Vanter as had it put in. I didn't even know that until lately, when—" He stopped.

Sir Thomas stepped forward. "Are you saying my steward installed a telephone for his own private use?"

Hutchins would have backed up if Goodwin hadn't been standing squarely behind him, "Not a regular one. Just the kind they used at the Front. And only since ... I dunno. A year ago spring."

"And you didn't know that 'until lately,'" said Sir Thomas, his voice dangerously quiet. "How did you find out, 'lately?'"

Hutchins tried a knowing smile. "Well, a driver isn't supposed to listen, but he can't help hearing."

Mr. Lovejoy took one of Hutchins's elbows, and Goodwin took the other. They exchanged a nod behind his back, and Mr. Lovejoy said, "Once Hutchins is situated, we'll go look at that telephone. I'll be able to tell if he's used it."

"You never!" exclaimed Hutchins, his face distorted in fear.

Mr. Lovejoy smiled. "You'd be surprised."

He and Goodwin put Hutchins in the broodmare stall, which,

besides being impeccably clean, had barred windows and double bolts on its sliding door. Sir Thomas quieted Hutchins's indignant complaints by pointing out that we'd set him free within the hour instead of arresting him for trespass, so he slumped on the stool I'd brought from the harness room. But when my father told me to groom Errant and Sebilla in their stalls so I could keep an eye on 'the intruder,' Hutchins gave me such a sly look that Goodwin, catching it, said he'd stay and do the job. Sir Thomas said that would be wise, as Goodwin had already refused to sell his word for a shoat.

Seeing the renewed fear in Hutchins's face almost made up for the implication that I might be easy to bribe; and as I was keen to see how the field telephone worked, I held my peace.

Once we had Hutchins settled, everything went forward quickly. As my father showed Sir Thomas how difficult it was to see the altered bolt from across the room, Tim and Mr. Lovejoy extricated the telephone box out of its place among the tack trunks, and in a few minutes we'd all gone outside and looked at the wires. Sir Thomas was clearly indignant at having been betrayed in his own house, but he was also interested, which I thought a good sign. And when Mr. Lovejoy pulled out the telephone and connected it to the woods wire with the pincher-like things at the end of its own wires, he was as amazed as Goodwin, my father, and myself.

Mr. Lovejoy held the receiver up to his ear, nodded, and beckoned to Sir Thomas. "Hear that sound?" he said. "That means we're connected. Now, what I do is ask the central operator . . . Good afternoon. Norton's brewery, please . . . Hello, may I speak to Mr. Norton, please? No, not a sale. I'm calling for Sir Thomas Chandace-Willingford."

He looked at Sir Thomas. "Do you want to handle this, Sir Thomas, or should I?"

"I suppose I should brave the instrument," said Sir Thomas, taking the receiver.

"You may get the secretary back, if Norton's busy."

Sir Thomas shook his head hastily. "Hello, Norton? Sir Thomas here. Excuse me? No, no, not a horse, unfortunately, but I do have a lead on a fine pony . . . We shall see. But in the meantime, there's a problem. Green has caught your chauffeur rooting around in our harness room. Excuse me? Yes, Hutchins. I'm afraid he was quite obstreperous, threw a punch . . . You didn't? Ah. So I suspected. It may be perfectly innocent, of course; he said he was looking for a toy Cyril had left behind after his lesson."

He frowned as Mr. Norton said something in an indignantly apologetic voice all of us could hear. "No, no—no personal offence, of course, but I will have to ask you to promise that Hutchins will testify at the inquest Monday. He seems to have some information. "Excuse me? Oh, that would be excellent. Ten minutes, you say? Wonderful. Your man should give your name at the gate, and he'll be admitted right away. Thank you very much. I'll look forward to seeing you Monday."

He gave the telephone back to Mr. Lovejoy. "Whew!" he said, reaching for his handkerchief. "This contrivance works very well, so far as it goes, but it flattens out the voice. Hard to tell exactly what a man's thinking, too, when you can't see his face."

"I'd be the first person to agree," said Mr. Lovejoy, and Tim nodded.

"Norton was shocked, though. Had no idea Hutchins was here. Very apologetic, but more to the point, he is sending his secretary to fetch him. Dunster, his name is. He seems to be somewhere in the area and will arrive in a few minutes—Green, let's go be sure all is well in the stable."

My father, clearly impressed by the powers of the telephone, fell into step with him. They probably expected me to follow them, but I turned to Mr. Lovejoy and Tim instead.

"If Mr. Norton's secretary is so much 'in the area' that he can be here in a few minutes, he must have a telephone," I said. "If he didn't, Mr. Norton couldn't reach him from Lechlade."

Mr. Lovejoy exchanged a glance with Tim. "Sharp lad."

"What I'm wondering," I said, "is whether it's the same telephone as the one that's been sending lorries after me."

"Lorries?" said Mr. Lovejoy. "What's this?"

As Tim explained my encounters briefly, my father called through the back door. "Harry! Does Goodwin have to exercise the horses as well as groom them?"

I looked at the two men apologetically. "I'm sorry. I have to go."

"But Harry—" began Mr. Lovejoy.

"I know, I know," I said. "But I must. Father's very upset that I'm involved in all this, and he's trying to protect me"

"As well he might, if you're being followed!" said Mr. Lovejoy.

I nodded and started off, but so did they, for a motor was roaring up the sweep. The three of us rushed through the straight stall wing and breathlessly joined my father, Goodwin, and Sir Thomas at the main stable door.

I think we all expected a motor to drive through the archway, but instead we heard footsteps, and a man strode out of the shadows. For a moment, I was dazzled by his handsome boots, impeccably tailored tweeds, and fashionably parted hair. Then I realized that he was the man who had silenced the navvy that Errant had knocked down on Monday.

Tim and Mr. Lovejoy immediately turned back into the stable, fetching Hutchins, I assumed. Goodwin remained at the door, but my father and I followed Sir Thomas part of the way across the courtyard, stopping discreetly a few paces from the fountain.

"I take it you're Dunster," said Sir Thomas as they met. "I'm sorry to trouble you."

"It's no trouble at all," said Mr. Dunster, with a courteous movement that fell perfectly into the gray area between a respectful nod and a bow. "I'm sorry that Hutchins's hunt for Master Cyril's toy has caused such a disturbance. He'll be firmly corrected; I can assure you."

He cast his eyes around the courtyard, taking in the clock tower, the stonework, and the fountain. "I confess that while I regret the occasion, I welcome the opportunity to see the handsome place whose gates I've passed so often, and the stable of which I've heard so much."

"Ah," said Sir Thomas. "Then you ride?"

"Not so well as I would wish," said Mr. Dunster. "My father was Head Groom at Chatsworth Hall, but he died when I was seven, and my mother moved us all to London. Still, in my early years, I heard your son's name often, and I was extremely sorry to hear of your loss."

"Thank you," said Sir Thomas stiffly. "Now, as to Hutchins. I'm afraid we had to put him in a stall after he hit my groom—"

"—Hit your groom!"

"I'm afraid so. If he hadn't, I would simply have sent him off, but as it was, I felt it necessary to call Mr. Norton. Do you know, by the way, what toy it was that Cyril left behind? I'm sure Green and his lad will keep an eye out for it."

"I'm afraid I can tell you nothing," said Mr. Dunster regretfully.

"Very well," said Sir Thomas. Then, as Tim and Mr. Lovejoy emerged from the stable with Hutchins sulking between them— "Ah, here he is."

Mr. Dunster cast Hutchins a look that should have frozen him in his tracks. "Very well, Hutchins. I trust you've excused yourself to Sir Thomas and his staff?"

Hutchins nodded, though he'd done nothing of the kind.

"Excellent. Then we'll be off. Mr. Norton has instructed me to take you to his office. He wishes to ask you some questions about the information Sir Thomas said you gave him." Ignoring the panic that spread across Hutchins's face, Dunster bowed to Sir Thomas, nodded to the rest of us and, laying one hand on Hutchins's shoulder, ushered him out of the courtyard. We watched them disappear into the arch's shadows.

"Harry," said my father gently.

"Coming, sir," I said. But then I finished the arithmetic I'd been doing in my head. "Excuse me, sir," I said to Sir Thomas. "What he said about Hugh . . . I can't quite make it out. He's Hugh's age, as I figure it, wouldn't you say?"

"Approximately," said Sir Thomas. "Why do you ask?"

"Because he said he'd heard Hugh's name often 'in his early days.' But if his early days were the same as Hugh's . . . Hugh didn't yet have a name among riders."

"That's true," said Sir Thomas. "But Harry, there is such a thing as being ingratiating, and it sometimes involves a subtle distortion of the truth. He probably heard Hugh's name later and was just being complimentary to cover the embarrassment of the situation."

It was a rebuke. A subtle one, but enough to make me apologize and start towards the barn.

When I led Errant out a few minutes later, Sir Thomas was gone, and Tim was engaged in starting the Lanchester, which Rushdale had moved to the carriage house. Mr. Lovejoy, however, was sitting on the fountain bench, and as I pulled down my stirrups, he walked towards me.

"You're a sharp lad," he said, stroking Errant's neck. "What you said about the arithmetic was absolutely right. And say, did you see the way Dunster looked at you?"

"Yes," I said. "But that's no surprise." I told him about Monday's episode with the navvy, and the way Dunster had intervened. "He was dressed differently then, though," I added, thinking of his muddy boots and crumpled jacket.

"I suspect he does a variety of work for Norton," he said. "It took me a little while to see past the tweeds and the center part, but the way a man stands and moves doesn't change. As he walked out, I remembered that in early fall before armistice, a new bloke was assigned to the lads working telephones. He was supposed to be a genius with the things, though some of the lads said his real genius was pleasing officers who'd promote him.'"

I stared at him. "That was Mr. Dunster?"

"I'm almost certain it was, though he was no 'mister' in those days, and I wouldn't swear to the Dunster. But . . . well, he was very careful not to meet my eyes. That's unusual if you recognize a man you've worked with at the Front. He *was* talented. No question. Fully capable of setting up the system here." He frowned. "Harry, don't ride out today. Work the horses in the manège."

"You're as nervous as my father," I said, trying to smile.

"I'm *more* nervous than your father. Listen, when we were laying out wire up to the front lines, Dunster, or whatever his name was then, worked like the rest of us. But unlike the rest of us, he took a rifle, a bayonet, a pistol. He said it was to protect us, but that wasn't it. He *enjoyed* picking off scouts and messengers."

Mr. Lovejoy looked across the courtyard. "Last night, Baines said the really shocking thing about Farrington's murder was that whoever did it apparently let the poison burn away his throat and gullet for quite some time before he dispatched him. Just. Stood. And. Watched." His eyes locked onto mine. "So, promise me to stay in the manège. Just for a day or two, while Jenkins and I work this out."

While Jenkins and I work this out put me on the sidelines, instead of the place I'd be if Tim and *I* worked this out. But truth be told, what Mr. Lovejoy had said about Mr. Dunster made me fully as nervous as he and my father were, so I made the promise easily. And as Errant and I trotted to the manège, I reminded myself that since tomorrow was Sunday, I'd have plenty of time to 'work this out' for myself.

Chapter 22

I'd been looking forward to Sunday's service, because the choirmaster had finally persuaded Jimmy to sing a solo anthem. Jimmy had told me, but he'd also said that he'd promised Richard not to say what he was singing. Knowing how easy it was to worm information out of Jimmy, I had spared him questions.

Goodwin walked to St. Barnabas with my father and me. He'd worried that he might have to miss Jimmy's solo, but Sir Thomas had pointed out that he could be considered still in custody, and that so long as he went back to the Hall after the service, he would be in no danger of being arrested.

In the churchyard, we were joyously greeted by a flock of Jimmy's sisters. All five of them worked within a few miles of the Hall, and between the fame of the murders and the kindness of their employers, they had managed to get Sunday off. But the real treat was that Mrs. Goodwin was finally well enough to make the trip to church on foot. When Goodwin saw that she was there, he threw his arms around her in front of everybody. Quite a few of us cheered.

Seeing the Goodwins all together made me think of Mum, and how she'd died almost exactly a year ago. I knew from my father's face that he remembered too, but always concerned to be punctual, he didn't offer to join me when I said I wanted to visit her grave before the service. He just said to be quick.

I hurried along the gravel path that led from the church to the Chandace-Willingford family vault, threaded my way between the graves on the left . . . and there was my mother's modest stone.

Edith Haddon Green

2 August 1875—28 March 1918

Behind it, wooden markers commemorating my infant brothers and sisters rose through the spring flowers Mum had planted and which had, over the past twenty-one years, spread into a carpet of silent remembrance.

She'd visited them weekly, but since my father had rarely joined her, I'd followed his example out of fear of showing un-masculine grief. As I looked at the markers now, however, I was surprised by a woman's thoughts—of the miracle of carrying life, feeling it move, looking forward to its arrival and fearing, after losing the first seven-month child, that the others might also come too early to live.

The fading inscriptions made it only too clear they had, for none of the five had lived longer than three days. I looked from one marker to another, suddenly aware of the sorrows Mum's cheerful warmth had masked: the deaths, the tiny coffins, the doctrinal urgings of resignation. *The Lord giveth, the Lord taketh away.*

Was it the Lord? Rushdale's words echoed in my mind: *Your mum, she lost five babies coz she couldn't pay for the care grand folks' children would've got.* And yet, Mum, whom I'd never heard speak a bitter word, had accepted the loss of her children with the same patience she'd accepted orders from Mrs. Baggum. Faced with her goodness, I regretted my indignant questioning of the Lord, wishing instead that I'd been more of a comfort to Mum. Every time I'd caught her looking at me sadly, I'd tried to cheer her by being a better son. Never once had I offered her a daughter's sympathy.

Inside the church, the organ music swelled. I gave my mother's chilly stone a penitential kiss, then ran back and slipped into the servants' pew next to my father just as the choir and Reverend Williams began the procession. Amidst the readings and hymns, my thoughts kept reverting to the churchyard, but I reined them in and tried to reach the God whose infinite wisdom had guided and comforted my parents.

After the sermon, Reverend Williams turned slightly to the choir, and Jimmy stood up, his face deadly pale as the organ played the opening of an unfamiliar hymn. Then drawing a visibly deep breath, he began to sing:

> *Turn back, O man, forswear thy foolish ways,*
>
> *Old now is earth and none may count her days.*

As Jimmy's voice gained confidence, I sat in wonder—how was it possible that for years I'd heard him sing at his work without knowing how sweet and pure his voice was? Then, as he sang on, I realized it wasn't just his voice that had made Richard and Reverend Williams choose him to sing the new hymn. It was his three brothers.

> *Earth might be fair and all men glad and wise.*
>
> *Age after age their tragic empires rise,*
>
> *Built while they dream, and in that dreaming weep:*
>
> *Would man but wake from out his haunted sleep,*
>
> *Earth might be fair and all men glad and wise.*

Glancing at my father, whose eyes were filled with tears, and Sir Thomas, who sat alone in the grand Chandace-Willingford pew, I knew they were thinking of the loss of Hugh and the village boys who had once been seated in these pews. Maybe the two men were comforted as Jimmy's beautiful soprano finished, "Earth shall be fair and all her people one." That had been Hugh's hope—the equality, the one-ness, that he'd fought to create. Mr. Lovejoy, too. Tim. Richard. Surely all of us thought of that now, as Jimmy finished, and the congregation sat for several seconds in silent remembrance. Then Reverend Williams finished the service and dismissed us with a blessing that had always been my favorite, but this time made me sad: *May the Lord lift up his countenance upon you and give you peace.*

The Hall's servants sat in the front pews, so it took us a long time to move out the church doors, and by the time we emerged into the chilly churchyard, Jimmy was surrounded by his family and practically everybody else. He looked so embarrassed by all the praise that I hesitated to add to it, and as I stood indecisively, a hand fell on my shoulder.

"What a stunner that hymn is, eh?" said Richard. "Bax at his very best—He sent it to me a few weeks ago, after I got up the courage to write him."

"Bax?" I asked, frowning.

"Clifford Bax. Playwright, editor, journalist, man of letters. After I wrote him, he asked to see some of the gloomy stuff I've written lately. Polite, I thought, but I sent him a few things—and he wrote back, very encouraging. New way of writing, he said. Coming thing. The War's changed everybody's outlook, so we need more than Victorian leftovers. Good cheer, right?"

"Oh yes!"

"Well, we'll see. It may come to nothing, but at present, it's better than sitting at my window and dwelling on tragic waste." He pointed to the dormer that looked out over the churchyard from the second floor of the rectory.

Behind him, a motor started up in the lane; he looked back uneasily but didn't move. "Anyway, Jimmy did a bang-up job. The Reverend's trying to find him a place at one of the Oxford choir schools. Late, of course. Most boys start much earlier. But if he sings Bax's hymn for them, they'll take him as soon as they dry their tears."

"That would be A-1, except Jimmy has his heart set on being a groom."

"A groom!" he shook his head. "Harry, there'll *be* no grooms by the time he's on his own! But if he can get into musical circles, he'll be looking at a whole new world."

I must have looked sad, for he gave me the smile I remembered from my childhood. "All in good time. Meantime, there are horses, music, writing—enough to make even a man with a bullet in him want to walk further, eh? I owe your sharp tongue a debt, lad." He turned quickly and strode to the fringes of the gathering to talk to Tim.

Rather than ponder the mixture of my happiness at Richard's renewed cheerfulness and my sadness at confronting a world with no grooms, I moved towards Jimmy. But Goodwin, who had been talking to some of his Chandace Arms mates, broke away and led me to the bench where his wife was sitting. She held out both hands, and I took them, surprised by the tears that were standing in her eyes.

"Bless you, Harry," she said. "I wur still thinking of you as a lad like Jimmy, not having seen you for so long. But when you turned and walked with Barth, it put me in mind of our boys and Hugh at aboot your age. Can you ride by our new cottage soon to hear some things about old times before I'm back to working?"

"Absolutely!" I said, pleased. "It can't be tomorrow because of the inquest, but maybe Tuesday. I'll ask my father."

She smiled. "He has already said he'll be sure you have time to come." She was about to say more, but Goodwin broke in. "Say, Harry, who's the chap talking with Sir Thomas?"

"Oh," I said, pressing Mrs. Goodwin's hands before I let them go. "That's Lord Sandford. He's been visiting for a week or a little more."

"A lord, is he?" said Goodwin. "Well, that accounts for the posh clothes, but Friday, when we wur waiting for our wages, he wur standing aboot at the Arms like the rest of us, and there was no 'my lord' aboot him. He got us all talking of the things Vanter had done, and after we'd had our say, he asked wouldn't it be better for us to have Willingford Hall belong to all of us? Small farms. No rents. No stewards. I wur all for listening, but Lovejoy came, and then Davis burst in with the news of Farrington's murder, and I had to leave without finding who he was."

Mrs. Goodwin shook her head. "A dreamer, like Hugh."

Goodwin shrugged. "He *said* dividing up estates like that wur all in an Act of Parliament over ten years back, but the blokes who'd have had to enforce it were the same blokes who'd lose their rents, so nothing happened. Still, as Rushdale said, it could be a coming thing."

"Dad!" said Jenny Goodwin, leading the thinning crowd towards us. "Give poor Mum a rest from Arms politics!"

"Give me a rest, too!" said Jimmy, with a grin I hadn't seen for a long time.

I thumped Jimmy on the back and told him he had the best voice I'd ever heard, and soon everybody was talking at once, the way we had when we'd all lived in the cottages behind the stable. Afterwards, as Goodwin, my father and I trudged back to the Hall, I reflected that it was strange that we could all talk and laugh like that, with Henry, Charlie, Willie and Hugh all killed, Mum dead, Mr. Vanter and Farmer Farrington murdered, and Goodwin sheltering from arrest.

Surely it wasn't a sign that we'd forgotten our troubles—we'd shared our sadness and worry for over a year. But I couldn't even remember the last time I'd heard all of us laugh together. Maybe it was good that we'd remembered how.

*   *   *

Dinner at the servants' hall was as miserable as the morning had been wonderful. Any pleasure we might have taken in eating an excellent mutton stew was ruined by Mrs. Baggum's silent disapproval of Goodwin's presence at the table and Mrs. Middleton's far from silent disapproval of Sir Thomas's absence from the Hall. After church, I learned, Sir Thomas had suddenly agreed to eat Sunday dinner at the Baineses', along with Tim and Mr. Lovejoy. I suspected the change of plans less to do with Sunday dinner than with investigations that required a telephone, but Mrs. Middleton, knowing only that she had been given no prior warning, was near tears, and Mr. Parks, who at Sir Thomas's request that morning had specially decanted a fine old wine, was indignant. Altogether, I was glad when the meal was over, and I could escape to the stable and my thoughts.

Among the first of those thoughts was the dropping temperature, which after a half hour made me return to our quarters for the winter jacket whose ragged sleeves and torn lining had made me stop wearing it as early in the spring as I could. As I was hunting for my gloves, my father looked up from the cribbage game he and Goodwin were playing.

"Is it that cold?"

"Yes, sir. And the wind's coming up strong."

"And a good thing, too," said Goodwin. "It'll keep frost off the new wheat."

"Should I bring the horses in, sir?" I asked.

The two men looked at each other, and as if in answer to their unspoken question, the courtyard clock struck three.

"Give them a half hour more," said my father. "But when you bring them in, put the winter blankets on Errant and Sebilla. Atlas has enough coat still to do with his regular blanket—and yours, Goodwin?"

"They'll be fine. Good English stock knows not to shed full out until Whitsun," he said, grinning at me. "Not like your high class furriners."

I smiled back, but I returned to the stable with a sinking heart. It had taken me a long time to wash the winter blankets—the laundresses would have nothing to do with them, being squeamish when horsehair clung to their arms. Well, if we used them only tonight, and the horses didn't lie down, maybe Father wouldn't make me repeat the task.

I checked briefly on the horses; they were bunched together in the lea of the wall, except for Errant, who was looking uneasily into the wood. When I whistled, he nickered and trotted towards me. I scratched him behind the ears as he leaned over the fence; then I walked to the harness room to gather the blankets.

They were exactly where I'd left them three weeks before, but as I lifted Sebilla's off the top, I saw a peculiar lump in the folds of Errant's. Irritated at myself for folding sloppily, I shook it as I picked it up, and something clattered to the floor.

It was a wooden Y, cut from a branch but carefully sanded and finished. Attached to each prong of the Y was a strip of rubber expertly cut from the tube of a cycle tire. The two pieces of rubber were sewn in the middle to a flexible but substantial piece of leather. I'd never seen anything like it, but clearly it was Cecil's toy.

I set it on a tack trunk, my thoughts whirling. When I'd found Cyril after he'd broken the windscreen, I'd thought he was planning to hide under the horse blankets, but I'd been wrong. He'd been hiding the toy, and he'd said nothing about it. Including where it was. Hutchins hadn't known where to find it when he came back to look for it.

What did Cyril Norton know that I did not?

The clock chimed the quarter hour as I carried the two blankets to the stalls. Fifteen minutes before I had to bring the horses in. Plenty of time to experiment. Back in the harness room, I picked up the Y and gave the rubber a pull, surprised at its resistance. It was easy to see how it worked; how *well* it worked was a matter of testing. I hurried through the deserted straight stall wing and out the door, noting absently that I must re-affix the bolt's socket, which I'd thought my father had done.

Outside, I placed a stone in the Y's leather pocket, pulled it back as far as the straining rubber would allow, and let go. In spite of the stiff headwind, the stone shot so far into the wood that I couldn't see where it fell. I pursed my lips. In the hands of a six-year-old, a stone could easily be shot awry, simply for lack of wrist strength. But in the practiced hands of a grown man—

It could raise a welt on a horse's neck from over fifty paces.

Or deliver a stunning blow to a man's head so he could be dispatched at leisure.

I stared into the wood, trying to believe what I knew to be true. Oddly enough, when I finally convinced myself, I felt neither horror nor triumph, only sadness for my true knight. He'd clearly promised never to talk about the "toy," and he'd kept that promise even though he didn't know the reason for it. But he had unwittingly revealed his father's secret. I drew a deep breath and brought the horses in, blanketed our three, and filled all the water buckets.

The clock chimed three quarters just as I finished. An hour and a quarter until feeding time. If I took my cycle, I could give "Cyril's toy" to Tim and the others in Chandace and be back before my father needed my help. I slid the long side of the Y into the torn lining of my jacket and pedaled off.

Chapter 23

I rode fast, hoping to outpace my thoughts, but they marshaled more and more evidence. Hutchins's annoyance at his master's being a half hour late when he'd met him 'the other day.' The skiff tied up at The Chandace Arms, and later allowed to drift down the river. The telephone calls that led to Officer Morgan's repeated misjudgments, including Tim's dismissal. The promise of a shoat in return for a lie. I'd been suspecting Mr. Dunster since I'd talked with Mr. Lovejoy, but if he was involved, it wasn't to protect himself. It was to protect—Crikey!

I braked at the opening of the North Road just in time to avoid a motor going so fast that it would have hit me if it hadn't skidded to a stop. It wasn't a motor I'd seen before, but as the driver jumped out, I realized in a terrified flash why Errant had been looking into the wood when I checked on the horses, and why the bolt's socket had been missing from the back stable door. My follower this time wasn't Hutchins or even Mr. Dunster. It was Mr. Norton, clad in a heavy motoring coat, with heaven knew what concealed beneath it.

And nobody knew where I was.

"Harry!" he said, smiling as he pulled off his driving gauntlets. "Well met!"

"Indeed, sir," I said, trying to keep my voice from trembling. "I trust your family has had a pleasant Sunday."

"Yes, yes," he said dismissively. "But meeting you here—so unexpectedly—will make it far more than that. Windy, isn't it? Let's get off the high road and stand in the shelter of the wall of that lovely churchyard in the village. I have an offer to make you."

"That's very kind of you, sir, but—"

"—No 'buts,'" he said, leaping back into the still-running motor. "Walk your cycle towards the church. I'll be right behind you."

For a moment, I had hope. To turn the motor around, he would have to drive across the bridge, giving me ample time to—but no! He backed rapidly to the corner of High Street and beckoned impatiently. Given how easily the Y in my jacket lining might be replaced, my chance of surviving a dash along the unsheltered bridle path was exactly nil.

He did indeed follow 'right behind' me. There was at most a foot between his motor's bumper and my cycle as I wheeled it towards the churchyard. I prayed that somebody, preferably the Baineses and Sir Thomas, would see us, but the smell of coal fires made it all too clear that the cold and wind had driven the villagers to their hearths. Just past the Rectory, I paused at the gate to the churchyard, but Mr. Norton pointed ahead and, as I'd feared, followed me to the end of the lane, which stopped at the double gate used in funeral processions. Just short of a steep drop to the river.

Behind me, the motor shut off, and before I could think where to run, Mr. Norton stood beside me, still smiling. "You needn't look so apprehensive, Harry," he said. "It's not every day a lad gets an offer that will settle him for life. Don't you want to hear it?"

"Oh, yes, sir," I said. "It's just . . . unexpected."

"I hope you'll soon come to expect good fortune. Your talents deserve it, and Sir Thomas has assured me that they're every bit as exceptional as I've suspected, watching you teach Cyril." He smiled again. "He also assured me that Cyril could be a fine horseman."

I nodded. "The boy's very promising, sir."

"Promising students require exceptional teachers, Harry. And that's what I want to talk to you about. I have been talking to Sir Thomas's agent—Lovejoy, is it? —about purchasing Chandace Grange, so unfortunately emptied by the death of my friend Mr. Vanter. Lovejoy temporized, saying that Sir Thomas was considering another offer, but I know a bargaining technique when I see one. Once the details are settled, I will own the farm and move there with my family. My wife would benefit greatly from country air and be an ornament to country society and, as for Cyril, he would be in heaven riding daily on the pony your father and Sir Thomas are going to find for him.

"Furthermore, I've heard that Sir Thomas's son was interested in starting a new breed of English horses that could excel in haute école. The gray you ride would be the beginning of such a line, and I will soon make an offer on him. Soon there would be mares of the same quality. None of these plans, of course, can come to fruition unless I have a skilled groom. I am asking you to be that groom."

I stared at him, trying to juxtapose the wonders of the offer with my knowledge of the man who offered it.

"Come, have you nothing to say?"

"I hardly know what to think, sir. It is extremely generous, but—"

"Ah, yes . . . *but*. I realize why you hesitate. You're concerned because you fear I would not make this offer if I knew you were a lass, not a lad." He smiled as a wave of shock went through me. "Harry . . . Harriet, so far as I am concerned, you may pass for a lad—and later a man—if you wish; but if you would prefer not to, I have no objections to having a female groom." His expression became notably less benign. "And as for your other secret, it will always be safe with me."

"I have no other secret, sir."

He frowned. "Don't bother to lie, Harriet."

I shook my head, dumb with fear.

"You expect me to believe that you don't know why you've had to pass as a lad all these years?"

One look at his face made me realize what he could—and surely would—tell Sir Thomas if I revealed the story that Mum had told me again and again. "No, sir."

"By Jove!" he said. "It almost passes understanding, but I believe you really don't know! Well, well." He put a heavy hand on my shoulder and turned me towards the gate. "Well, come with me, and I'll show you who you are."

He marched me between the graves to the Vault, turned at its pillared corner, and halted at the modest family plot brightened by the jonquils my mother had helped Jimmy and me plant in memory of his brothers. "Here lie the Goodwins at the feet of their betters," he said. "Four generations."

"Yes, sir."

"The fourth-generation war heroes: Henry, Charles, and William."

I thought of their skiff, and how he had distorted its evidence. "Yes, sir."

"And who's over here?"

"Their sister Nellie, sir."

"The disgrace. You know what kind of disgrace, I presume?"

"Yes, sir."

"Righteousness is dreadful stuff," he said caustically. "As I know all too well. But it's not a universal disease, and your parents weren't infected. It seems that after Nellie was dismissed from the Hall, she lived at the Head Groom's cottage so she could help your mother, who was also expecting a baby and feared it would come into the world before it could survive. That baby—a boy—was indeed born early, but Nellie nursed him so carefully that everybody rejoiced, confident that he'd live. But a day or two later, Nellie had a very difficult labor and, in spite of your mother's efforts, she died as her baby was born.

"Just as well, said local gossip. But what the gossipers didn't know was that your parents' baby boy died the same night Nellie did. Your mother laid both corpses out, while caring for Nellie's healthy baby girl. The next day, the Goodwins placed Nellie and 'her' child in a single coffin and buried them here."

He looked at me. "Do you see what happened?"

I stared at him. "You mean, Mum . . . *stole* Nellie's baby?"

"That's exactly what I mean. And because all the manor knew that your parents' baby was a boy, they raised you like one, so nobody would discover their crime."

Crime. The jonquils tossed in the wind as I stared at Nellie's grave. My mother ... my kind, loving mother ... had stolen ... ? Unless, of course, the story was another of Mr. Norton's distortions.

"How do you know this, sir?"

"At third hand, I confess, but reliably. One afternoon some months ago, when I got off the up train, I saw Vanter meeting a man clearly from London. They parted after a brief exchange. Vanter didn't see me, so having previously suspected him of dealing behind my back, I accosted his friend and ... encouraged him to tell me what he and Vanter were doing."

He cocked one eyebrow. "Don't look so shocked, Harriet. Very few men come without a price, and the price of a London dealer in East End housing is relatively low."

"Didn't that low price make you doubt his veracity, sir?"

"Very sharp," he said, smiling. "We'll make you a businessman yet. But to answer your question, I gave him ten pounds, told him that my London contacts could ruin him, and he told me what he knew. It seems that when Sir Thomas was ill, he received a letter from his solicitor saying a matter in Hugh's estate urgently needed his personal attention. Sir Thomas foolishly gave Vanter power of attorney and sent him off. Thus, Vanter learned that Willingford Hall was no longer entailed—which, of course, implied that Sir Thomas was planning to sell parts or even all of it. Even more interesting was a sealed letter from Hugh dated 1905, leaving a more than ample bank account to his daughter, of whose existence Sir Thomas was evidently unaware."

He paused, watching me as I slowly grasped the implication of his words.

"Vanter told my London informant that the account had only a few pounds left in it; Sir Thomas's solicitor said Hugh had used it to pay Sir Thomas's most pressing debts. But where, and who, was the daughter? The letter gave no indication. Vanter assumed she was a London brat, and he had hired this London dealer to find her."

"Did he tell Sir Thomas?"

"Of course not! He hoped to use the girl for his financial advantage. It's odd, though. Wouldn't you think he'd have looked for her closer to home?"

"I suppose so, sir," I said automatically. But as my mind flashed to the harness room and Mr. Vanter's leering words about "lads' fair faces," I realized that he *had* looked closer to home. Within days of his return from London, he'd used the old slur to search for proof that I wasn't a lad, in the most obvious way possible. If my father hadn't appeared . . .

"In any case, looking closer to home was *my* first thought," Mr. Norton went on. "I set Dunster searching the parish records, which duly recorded the birth of two babies within days of each other and the death of one mother and her daughter. Subsequently, I had him talk to your Mrs. Baggum on her day off, and he charmed out the story of Nellie's disgrace, including her being sheltered by your parents. However, not even she had made a connection with Hugh, because he'd been studying at some famous Paris riding school. But then, I met you in Chandace the day after Vanter's unfortunate demise. A few days later, I saw the portrait of Hugh that hangs over the mantel in the Willingford Hall drawing room."

He shook his head. "It's a mystery to me that anybody can look at that portrait, then look at you, and *fail* to see that the young lord of the manor had indulged in classic aristocratic exploitation of a pretty housemaid."

I thought of Sir Thomas's shock when I entered his study the night of Mr. Vanter's murder. I thought of Hugh's devotion to Mum, of his frequent visits to our cottage, of his interest in my education and riding. I thought of Tim's comment: *There was something . . . unusual . . . about Hugh's attachment to you.* I stared across Nellie's grave at the Chandace-Willingford vault. Hugh, whose middle name was honor! Hugh, who'd hated inequality! *Classic aristocratic exploitation.*

Through the haze of distress that surrounded me, I heard myself say, "That's all very well, sir, but you've offered nothing to confirm your theory."

He looked at me with something close to respect. "You're made of solid material, Harriet. Most girls learning of their illegitimacy would cry."

"Girls learn there is sympathy to be gained by crying, sir. Boys learn, as I did, that tears are scorned as a sign of weakness."

"You think it's just a matter of training?" he said, with real interest. "I confess that had never occurred to me. In any case, you are correct: I've not been able to confirm my suspicions about your parentage. I've been waiting to discuss it with you."

"Oh, is that why I've been followed, sir?"

"You've been followed? How disturbing. I will have to speak to a few people about it this evening. But leaving that aside, I was waiting to catch you away from the stable, because I assumed you would be able to confirm your parentage yourself, thus avoiding the necessity of ruining the man you call your father."

"My father, sir?"

"Certainly. Surely, he knew what your mother did. And when I tell Sir Thomas of the crime he helped her commit concerning his son's daughter, he will naturally—"

"Oh, please, sir!" I broke in. "*Please* don't tell Sir Thomas! If it's just a matter of pressing me to consider the position you've offered me, I'll accept it! It would be a pleasure to work with Master Cyril, and to serve you!" I stretched out my arms in supplication, and for a moment, I thought my plea might succeed.

Unfortunately, the movement swung my jacket open—and the Y teetered out of the tattered lining and fell to the ground. I stooped to retrieve it, but Mr. Norton snatched it up and sprang to his feet, his face ashen. In the terrible silence between us, Hugh's warning flashed across my mind: *the most dangerous horse isn't one that's vicious or angry, but one that's frightened.*

"Where did you find this, Harriet?" he said finally.

"In the harness room, sir. Master Cyril apparently hid it in the winter horse blankets after he broke the windscreen on your motor. I knew you were looking for it, because Hutchins said he'd come to search for 'Cyril's toy.' When I met you just now, I was riding to Dr. Baines's house so he could telephone you to say it had been found."

"And nobody but you and Cyril knows where it was and what it is?"

"That's right, sir. Except I don't know what it is."

"Surely Cyril told you that it's a catapult—a sling shot, if you're an American."

"No indeed, sir. Master Cyril told me nothing about it, not even that it existed. The boy is true steel!"

"Ah," he said, laying the catapult softly on Willie Goodwin's gravestone. "But when you found this, you realized he must have promised not to tell anybody about it, and you saw why."

Treat him with the respect you would reserve for an extremely skilled player of Ecarté. I'd made a beginner's misplay. But maybe . . .

"Immediately, sir," I said, smiling. "No father would give his son such a toy without making him promise to use it only under supervision."

"Well, that's true," he said. "But you were riding to Baines's house to telephone me about it. Did you not know there was a telephone closer to home?"

"I don't know how to use it, sir."

"Ah, so you know the telephone exists."

Trapped! I nodded.

"Perhaps you suspect that the telephone has had some influence on the murder investigations currently underway."

"If I do, I'm not alone. Everybody—"

"— everybody! How interesting. Whom do you include in that group?"

I fought down rising panic. "You didn't let me finish my sentence, sir," I said. "I was going to say, everybody who discusses the case at The Chandace Arms and such places agrees that Officer Morgan has been influenced by the telephone calls he said he'd received."

"Let's try again, Harriet. Of the many people discussing the murders and the investigation, how many of them know about the telephone in Willingford Hall's stable?"

"I'm not sure, sir."

"I warned you not to lie, Harriet."

"I'm not lying, sir. I don't know how many men are on the Council."

His face twitched. "Then Sir Thomas knows?"

"The telephone is on his property, sir. He had to be told before tomorrow's inquest."

"Who told him?"

Tim. Goodwin. My father. Mr. Lovejoy. If I named them, I'd be risking their lives. "I did, sir. After I found the unlatched door and the wires in the woods."

"And so," he said, almost sadly, "you betrayed me."

"No, sir. I told Sir Thomas only about the telephone and its possible connection to my being followed."

"And no more?" he asked, looking straight into my eyes.

"No, sir."

"But you do know more."

"Not . . . not certainly, sir."

"You're planning to reveal your lack of certitude at tomorrow's inquest, I imagine."

"I've not been asked to testify, sir."

He looked thoughtfully over the gate to the river beyond his motor. In the silence, the church bells began to ring and, glancing towards them, I saw a few people hurrying towards St. Barnabas.

Evensong. Prayer. All men glad and wise.

Mr. Norton whirled around, his hand falling on my shoulder with a grip that made me gasp. "What do you see, Harriet?" His eyes scanned the churchyard, and though the parishioners had fortunately disappeared, his free hand had reached into his driving coat in a way that warned me to be wary.

"I see nothing but the clock that makes me realize it's feeding time," I said, keeping my voice as steady as I could. "May I go, sir?"

"I've been debating that in my mind," he said, loosening his grip. "Perhaps we could strike a bargain. I suspect, but have not revealed, the secret of your birth and your parents' crime, one serious enough to imprison your father at worst, and ruin him at best.

"You suspect, but fortunately have not revealed, that I'm in some way responsible for the deaths of two local men. While your suspicion is completely unfounded, even a whisper of it would ruin me.

"Suppose we were to promise each other that neither of us would reveal what we suspect about the other, and that you would become my groom and the teacher of my son."

I tried desperately to think, but my mind refused to function.

"What do you say, Harriet?" he said quietly. "Could we be partners?"

I looked at his waiting face and saw fear mixed with reluctance. He liked me; I knew he did. He'd murder me unwillingly if I refused his offer. But I would be no less dead for his regrets. "Possibly, sir," I said.

"Ah! So you believe that I'm innocent?"

"I could do so more readily if I knew who was guilty, sir."

His smile chilled me. "They were victims of their own corrupt natures."

"They killed themselves?" I said, trying not to sound incredulous.

"In a manner of speaking. One of them informed an honorable man—not directly, but by a sealed note delivered to him by his chauffeur—that his wife had taken a lover who left Willingford Dell every Wednesday at three o'clock in a skiff and rowed upriver to their secret meeting place. After several local witnesses confirmed the weekly trips, the honorable man sought out the lover and punished him.

"A day or two later, however, the honorable man heard a distinguished lady say, quite by-the-by, that she'd been working with his wife at the local hospital at the time the tryst was alleged to have taken place. You'll agree, I'm sure, that the lying informer was as guilty of murder as the man who'd defended his wife's honor."

A lifetime of saying what my betters expected to hear came to my aid. "Oh yes, sir."

"And you'll agree, therefore, that the only honorable thing for him to do was to discover the informer's identity and punish him before being betrayed again, this time with an accusation of murder?"

"Indeed, sir. He'd been terribly tricked." *And watched his victim suffer terribly*, I thought, *until Goodwin came to warn him of his danger, making it necessary to finish the job quickly.*

"Your understanding is yet another token of your intelligence and maturity, Harriet. It's a pity that two corrupt men brought their fates upon themselves, but the unpleasant incident is concluded. The man of honor can go on, making this lovely part of the world into a paradise for people to visit." He smiled.

"By the time I've enabled you to become a famous groom and rider of twenty-four, my property will overlook one of the major motor routes from Oxford to Cheltenham and the finest racing in England. People will buy the bungalows I've constructed so they can walk in this beautiful countryside and share the excitements of the turf and the beauties of haute école. You, Cyril and I can make the Cotswolds the glory of England and the home of its finest horseflesh."

As he finished, a movement near the Vault caught the corner of my eye, but when I looked, I saw only shadows. There was no hope of escape. I drew a deep breath and inwardly asked God to forgive me.

"It's a wonderful vision," I said, "and one I'll be proud to share." I held out my hand. "We are agreed on our bargain, sir?"

"We are agreed." His hand, warm and soft, closed over my icy fingers.

"Very good, sir. I'll say nothing to my father about the position you offer. You can talk to him about it at Cyril's lesson Tuesday." I forced myself to smile. "May I go back to the Hall and feed the horses now, sir?"

"You may."

I thanked him once more and hurried towards my cycle through the graves.

After a few paces, I realized he hadn't followed me.

Some instinct made me duck as I turned to see where he was. A stone whizzed over my head and shattered the wing of the angel on a monument just beyond me. I dove behind a gravestone and peered, shaking, around it. For a moment, I thought terror had made me see double, for where there had been only Mr. Norton, there were now two . . . no, three . . . no, four men.

One of the men said "Stand, Norton!" in a voice used to being obeyed.

But instead of standing, Mr. Norton dropped the catapult and reached inside his coat. In a second, he'd whirled around and pointed a pistol at the man who'd spoken.

Sir Thomas.

Not far from where I crouched, a fifth man limped from behind a gravestone and raised a rifle so quickly that he'd fired it before I realized what it was. The shot cracked across the churchyard, followed by a terrible scream as Mr. Norton's arm jerked and the pistol flew out of his extended hand.

Another man— Mr. Lovejoy—picked up the pistol, rushed in front of Sir Thomas, and aimed it at Mr. Norton. The screaming became a series of sobs, but, confusingly, Mr. Norton was silent as he looked from Mr. Lovejoy to Sir Thomas, to Dr. Baines, to Tim, who stood just behind me. Then slowly, deliberately, he reached into his coat with his left hand and pulled out a second pistol.

"No!"

"Stop!"

"Don't, Norton!"

Tim raised his rifle, but before he could shoot, Mr. Norton had pointed the pistol at his own head and pulled its trigger. The screams that filled the churchyard couldn't possibly have been his.

Dr. Baines and Mr. Lovejoy rushed forward, but Sir Thomas turned away from the horror, supporting himself on one of the Vault's pillars. Tim limped towards my protecting gravestone, his face deadly pale. "Are you hurt, Harry?"

"I . . . I think not," I whispered.

"Don't look," he said, putting an arm around my shaking shoulders. "I'm terribly, terribly sorry. The others crept through the graves to the Vault, but I can't bend well enough to do that, so I went around by the lane. Unfortunately, I couldn't move fast enough to stop him from shooting at you with that contraption."

"You saved Sir Thomas, though."

He nodded. "Clear shot. Poor Richard."

"Richard's here?"

He nodded. "He saw you and Norton from his window. This morning, I'd told him about the telephone and your being followed, and he realized you'd been caught. He rushed to Baines's house, where we all were, and insisted on coming with us."

"The rifle?"

Tim looked at it appraisingly. "It's Richard's Lee Enfield 303," he said. "Beautifully kept, thank heaven. He said I should take it because he suspected Norton was armed." He pointed towards the huddled, sobbing figure some fifty paces off. "Next to you, Harry, he's the bravest of the brave."

I slipped from behind the grave that had sheltered me and walked unsteadily across the grass. "Richard," I whispered, touching his shoulder gently. "Thank you. Bless you."

He shivered convulsively, his glazed eyes fixing themselves on me. "Hugh!" he murmured. Then a kind of recognition dawned, and his hysterical moans merged with tears of another kind.

I sat on the ground and pulled him into my arms, rocking him like a child. "K'mathee," I said softly. "K'mathee, k'mathee."

*   *   *

A few minutes later, Sir Thomas hurried over to us both, coughing and stammering so badly that I could hardly understand that he thought we had both been shot. I assured him we were all right, but he was so frantic that I wasn't sure he believed me. I was greatly relieved when Dr. Baines joined us and, laying a hand on Sir Thomas's shoulder, suggested that the two of them walk back to his house and telephone Council members and Mr. Davis. That seemed to have a calming effect, and they went off together.

In what seemed no time at all, various motors swarmed at the back entrance, and Tim helped Mr. Lovejoy direct official-looking men who arrived to take care of details. That done, the two of them walked to the spot where Richard and I were still huddled and sat down beside us.

"Harry, lad," said Mr. Lovejoy, "what can we do for you?"

"Can somebody tell my father that I'll be home soon?"

"Does he know where you are?"

"I'm afraid not. When I found the catapult in the harness room, he was playing cribbage with Goodwin, and I didn't want to bother them. I just cycled off to give it to you and the others, thinking I'd be back in an hour."

Mr. Lovejoy scrambled to his feet. "Good God, he'll be frantic! I'll go right away. Sir Thomas is recovering from shock; he badly needs a ride back to the Hall. I'll take him there, then tell your father you're a hero—And listen, Harry, don't even think of riding your cycle home. The devil knows who's out there, waiting. One of us will give you a ride back after things settle a bit."

Tim nodded. "Meanwhile," he said, "you can help me walk Richard back to the Rectory. Between the shots and the motors, I'll wager that a fair number of people will be asking what happened."

He was right. As we started slowly down the path with Richard between us, the village was filling with people hurrying into the streets from nearby houses and fields, offering help and shouting questions in a way that made Richard cringe. I tried to tell him it was just his neighbors, but Tim interrupted.

"Hush, Harry," he said gently, "You're seeing what's here, not what Richard's seeing."

Something in Tim's face made me think he, too, might be seeing more than what was here, too, so I said nothing more as we helped Richard stumble to the Rectory and up to his room.

"There, old chap," said Tim, laying Richard on his bed and covering him with a blanket. "You're safe now." He glanced out the window. "Evensong is over. Harry, will you tell Reverend Williams what has happened?"

I dashed down the stairs and met Reverend Williams as he emerged from St. Barnabas into the street.

"Harry!" he said, looking from me to his congregation, which was being absorbed into the excited crowd. "What is it, lad?"

"It's Richard, sir," I said. "At least, partly. He's going to be all right, I think, but there were shots . . . that is, Mr. Norton shot himself."

"In the churchyard?" he said, shocked.

As I started to explain that Mr. Norton had murdered Mr. Vanter and Farmer Farrington, Tim limped out the rectory door, nodding. But before I had finished, somebody cried "There he is!" And suddenly, a roar of voices called out, "Here's Harry Green! Here's the lad who caught the murderer! Well done! What a winner!"

Reverend Williams looked at me. "You seem to have left a few details out."

"He did," shouted Tim over the crowd. "Harry was the one who found what Norton had done. Somehow Norton got wind of that and caught Harry as he cycled into Chandace to tell Sir Thomas and the rest of us. Richard saw them from his window and warned us—but we could never have crossed the churchyard in time to save Harry, if the lad himself hadn't been brave enough to keep Norton talking until we got there."

I tried to explain that he didn't have it quite right, that I hadn't been brave at all, and that it had been horrible, but Mr. Johnson and a couple of men from The Arms pushed their way through the crowd and boosted me up on their shoulders. Looking around, I saw the Baineses cheering with the rest, along with Lord Sandford and Lady Sylvia, who had apparently just arrived by motor.

Held helplessly above scores of friendly faces, I thought of the days I'd longed to become Somebody, so I could show everybody who I really was. But ironically, it was Mr. Norton who had showed who I really was: a child resulting from Hugh's "classic aristocratic exploitation" of the Goodwins' daughter; a baby Mum had stolen; and a lass who had lived a lie so long that she had promised to shelter a murderer rather than reveal the truth.

As Johnson and his friends set me down and clapped me on the back, I smiled and thanked everybody in the way their kindness deserved. But after I finally got home that night and apologized to "the man I called my father" for not telling him before I'd cycled to Chandace, I lay cold and tearless in my bed, alternatively reliving Mr. Norton's words and reflecting that far from being Somebody, I was less than nobody.

Chapter 24

In place of Monday's inquest, the Council began an immediate investigation of Mr. Norton's actions in the area. Consequently, I spent an uncomfortable hour in Sir Thomas's library, as two elderly Council members asked me about the men who had followed me when I exercised Errant. They also asked me to repeat what they called "Norton's confession." I was afraid they would ask what else Mr. Norton might have told me, but they just said I was a brave lad and dismissed me, shaking, to the stable.

Outside the Council, anybody who wanted information about the murders' offshoots was forced to rely on observation and rumor. Polly and Agatha, the two maids who lived at home, told us at breakfast that Hutchins, Mr. Dunster, and two others had been seen shortly before dawn, driving three familiar lorries towards London. The navvies' horses had been spotted grazing hungrily in the overgrown Haskins Farm fields, which suggested the navvies had gone, too.

Further news arrived in the afternoon with the greengrocer, who'd heard that the navvies were now working on a railway cutting just south of London, and that the minders had last been seen boarding a train to Dover. The source of this information was unclear, but Tim, who had been using the field telephone to connect with police officers between Lechlade and London, nodded when he heard it.

When the Council called Tim to a meeting, I kept a close watch on the bedding alcove as I cleaned stalls and tack, but there was no sign that the new padlock my father had put on the rear stable door had been disturbed. Mr. Lovejoy, busily preparing sheaves of papers for the trip he and Tim were taking to London with Sir Thomas, said that Mr. Johnson had been scanning the river at The Arms for unfamiliar skiffs, but had nothing to report. By Monday night, even my father said it would be safe for me to ride to Farrington Farm the next day for my visit with Mrs. Goodwin.

I spent most of Monday struggling with distress that haunted me every hour. The more I thought about it, the more the idea that my parents had stolen Nellie's baby became as unbearable as the exposure of Hugh's hypocrisy. As I miserably oiled harnesses that would probably never be used again, I remembered how thoughtfully Mrs. Goodwin had nursed Mum when I became too sick to do so, and how she'd later helped me lay Mum out, even though she was becoming ill herself.

Belatedly, I realized it hadn't been just the eviction that had made her influenza linger for months; it was the exhausting days she'd spent nursing Mum and me. As I hung up the harnesses, I wondered despondently how I could bear to tell her what I knew.

*   *   *

The next morning, as I saddled Atlas for my ride to visit Mrs. Goodwin, I heard the harness room door close softly behind me. Turning, I saw that my father was watching me—not in his usual way, but with an expression that rarely appeared in his disciplined face. I had seen that expression last when he'd found me in tears because my monthly bleeding had started, and I'd despaired of hiding the evidence from the laundresses. His face full of embarrassed sympathy, he'd quickly found the rags Mum had stored for me, carried in washing water, and pointed to a place in the rafters where the clouts could be dried.

"Harry . . . ," Father's voice broke in upon the memory. "When you and Mrs. Goodwin talk today, remember . . ." He stood straighter as his voice thickened, but his unfamiliar expression hovered in the silence between us. "Remember," he repeated hoarsely, "that your mum and I always loved you as our own."

I nearly dropped the bridle I'd been holding—he seemed to think that I knew what Mr. Norton had told me about my history! But that was impossible! I hadn't shared any of Mr. Norton's tale with Father; I'd feared that if I began, I would unleash all my anger, hurting both of us. And yet his words, his commiseration—

That expression disappeared in an instant as the clock struck the three-quarters. "You'd better hold a steady trot," he said, "or you'll be late."

"Yes, sir," I said, and as I led Atlas into the courtyard, I added, "Thank you, sir." I pondered the possible implications his words for the entire half hour it took Atlas and me to reach the Goodwins' cottage.

I found Mrs. Goodwin sitting outside, thinner and pale, but enjoying the sun that was drying her graying hair. "Turn your horse out with the cows," she said. "He'll fancy the new grass." I did, and as we both laughed at the way Atlas rolled in the dust by the gate before settling down to graze, I noticed that the shoat Tim had promised to deliver was already rooting in the sty next to the barn.

We strolled back to sit on the rugged bench I remembered from my childhood, and she said, "So now, lass—"

"Lass!" I said, staring at her. "You mean, you know?"

She smiled. "How could I *not* know, having changed your nappies when you were a little one and seen you grow up beside my own?" Her face changed as she looked at me. "I thought your mum had told you all aboot it."

"Mum had promised to tell me on my fourteenth birthday, last December."

"Who would have known she'd be with the good Lord then, and I near joining her?" she said sadly, putting an arm around me. "And Hugh, too. Poor lass. So many losses. Did nobody tell you, then, that your dad and mum aren't kin to you?"

"Mr. Norton did, on Sunday." Stumbling and trying not to cry, I told her everything, including the dishonorable bargain I had made with him. "And," I sobbed as I finished, "I'm so sorry—"

"Sorry!" she said, so angrily that Atlas looked up from his grazing. "That wicked man! To frighten a lass into standing between him and hanging, by saying he'd keep her secret! It wur never your secret. 'Classic aristocratic exploitation,' indeed! Hugh and Nellie wur head over heels in love, but they wur too young to marry without their parents' say-so. Hugh asked Sir Thomas, never thinking it mattered that he wur a baronet's son and she a plowman's daughter. But it mattered to Sir Thomas. He sent Hugh away to a riding school in Paris for a year."

"But the baby! Why didn't Hugh tell Sir Thomas about that?"

She shook her head. "He didn't know. Nor did she. They must have made a baby—you, that is—just before he set off. And when Nellie found out, she couldn't tell Hugh, because Sir Thomas had made them promise not to write to each other for the whole year. He wur sure pretty French lasses would make Hugh forget all aboot Nellie. So sure, he didn't even tell Hugh when she died."

"He didn't?!"

"It wur a terrible thing. Hugh wur half-crazy when he came back, having waited so faithfully—and he never looked at a lass after. Sir Thomas wur sorry, and he tried to make it up with him, but Hugh never forgave him. He wouldn't even speak to him until your mum and I said he had to honor his father. After that he wur polite, but he spent most of his time in the stable and our cottage row when he wur home from Oxford and such places."

"Did he know Mum stole . . . ?"

"Your dear mum never stole you! That's a wicked murderer's lie! I begged her to take you, her little one having stopped breathing, me nursing twins with no milk for a third, and Nellie suddenly still." A tear trickled down her face as she looked at me. "What a dreadful night that wur. Please God you'll never know what it is to watch your child slip away, knowing you have nothing to stop her but love."

I took her hand in mine, wondering bitterly if "the care grand folks would've got" would have saved them both.

"Before we buried Nellie," she went on, "we told Reverend Williams what we wanted to do aboot the two babies. He said it wur sensible, and no sin, things being as sad as they wur. But it would've cost money to draw an adoption up legal, so your mum and dad decided to raise you as the boy everybody had been so glad your mum had had, so long as Hugh agreed when he came back. And Hugh did agree, loving your parents like his own, and never trusting Sir Thomas to know."

She looked at me seriously. "That makes it harder for you now than Hugh wanted. Being born out of wedlock means that even though he wur heir to Willingford Hall, you have no claim on it."

"I'd never take it, even if I had a claim!" I said angrily.

"So you say, never having gone hungry and being young enough to be proud. But it's hard to find work when you've been brought up to be something a lass can't be. What if you wur to tell Sir Thomas, and he would give you sommat?"

"How could I do that, after what he did to Hugh and Nellie?"

"Think a little before you take sides. Sir Thomas wurn't a bad father to Hugh. He wur just acting like a baronet, with lands and marriages to plan. How wur he to know that his pride would take his son from him long before the Kaiser did?"

"How am I to know what would happen if I asked Sir Thomas for 'sommat'? He might let my father go, the way Mr. Norton said. A baronet can do that easily! It's the whole wretched system! And the minute I took help from him, I'd be part of it."

"You're your father's daughter, surely," she said with a wry smile. "Well, if you truly want to leave Willingford Hall, there's plenty who'll help you."

"Even when they learn I'm a lass?"

She smiled. "There's more than a few who know already, though with you riding so well as you do, Rushdale, Johnson and even Barth let it slip their minds oft-times. Reverend Williams can help you most. But Sunday last, he told me you've skittered away every time he has tried to tell you that Hugh gave him money to send you to the Lechlade School, where Sir Thomas sent our Charlie and Tim Jenkins."

"But the Lechlade School is only for boys!"

She shook her head. "If you'd just talked to Reverend Williams, he would have told you it that it wur once, but some bluestocking ladies got fired up about that, and now there's lasses, learning the same things as lads. Our Charlie wur sweet on one of them, a storekeeper's daughter as smart as he wur, and twice as fast, when it came to maths. She's in London, now—been working for some Parliament bloke all during the War. No 'wretched system' for her."

London. Parliament. I'd never even thought of them as places I might see. I bit my lip as I remembered how my fear of being found out to be a girl had made me leave the village school, and how many times I'd avoided Reverend Williams.

Atlas interrupted my regrets by neighing, and turning, I saw Goodwin's team clattering up the lane. Mrs. Goodwin glanced at the sun and stood up, holding the back of the bench to steady herself. "You're before your time," she said to him, her voice trembling. "Is something—?"

"Oh, it's something," he said, pulling up the team. "But not something wrong—Harry, do you remember the lord I wur asking about at church? Well, he's planning to start a big stable at Willingford Hall."

I looked at his grin suspiciously. "You're pulling my leg."

"Always one for a prank," agreed Mrs. Goodwin. "As if we'd believe you, knowing you've been plowing three miles from The Arms."

"It's no prank! I heard it from the man himself," he said, raising his right hand. "He wur riding with Lady Sylvia, a handsome sight on Hugh's two grays. But they'd stopped at the fork in the lanes, which wur where I was working. When I reached the wall, they asked me which lane went here, because they had good news for Harry. Naturally I asked them what the good news wur, and his lordship said—but here he is to tell you himself."

He urged Pip and Squeak to the side as Errant and Sebilla came around the bend. Walking, I was happy to see, so they'd be cool enough to stand.

The riders dismounted in the yard, greeting us all as I stepped forward to take their reins. Both horses shook their heads, but Errant nickered when he saw me. "Damnation!" said his lordship, smiling ruefully as he stroked Errant's neck. "That rather takes the edge off my news."

"Oh, don't be sentimental!" said Lady Sylvia, "It makes no difference to Errant if Sir Thomas owns him or you do! He's Harry's horse."

I gulped. "Are you saying Sir Thomas *sold* Errant?"

"Errant and Sebilla and Atlas—and the whole of Willingford Hall," she said.

The Goodwins and I looked at each other in a combination of doubt and wonder.

"I'm afraid it's a bit sudden, announcing it like this," said Lord Sandford, "but I didn't dare even drop a hint until it was confirmed. That happened this morning, and I wanted to tell the grooms and the tenants before the rest of the county—and I suppose, the country—finds it out from the newspapers that are already ogling the murders.

"To be short—last fall, Richard Williams suggested that I write to Sir Thomas, saying I was interested in buying his estate and establishing a stable that could become a center for English haute école. Sir Thomas was enthusiastic, so I made an official offer within a week. He didn't reply, but I'd heard that he was ill, so I waited more or less patiently. Then two weeks ago, I received a telephone call from Lovejoy, saying he had found my offer, opened and re-sealed, buried in Vanter's files."

"You mean—?"

"I mean Vanter had deliberately hidden the offer because, so Lovejoy told me, it had become clear that Willingford Hall's financial problems were so severe that Sir Thomas would soon be forced to sell off his farms one by one. In a matter of seconds, I'd convinced Lovejoy that I was as serious about Willingford Hall as I had ever been, and he'd promised to show my offer to Sir Thomas immediately. He added that given the possibility of 'competitive bids,' I'd better come to close the deal as fast as possible. I left London for Lechlade that evening."

I found my voice after a couple of tries. "Did Mr. Norton know you wanted to start a stable here?"

"Norton?" His lordship frowned. "I don't see how he could have . . . oh, Lord! Vanter must have told him about my offer so the two of them could get their bids in while Sir Thomas was still sick."

"The hounds," muttered Goodwin.

"Precisely," said his lordship. "But what puzzles me is that the two of them seem to have been interested only in competitive bids, not horses. So why your question, Harry?"

"Just that when Mr. Norton . . . caught me, he told me that he was going to buy Chandace Grange and found a stable there that promoted haute école. And he wanted me to become his groom."

"I'll be damned," said his lordship. "He thought you'd undercut your father by accepting?"

I took a deep breath. "He knew he could make me accept it. He had records and papers that proved I was a girl, not a lad—"

"—Records?" said Lord Sandford, laughing. "He couldn't believe his own eyes?"

As I stared at him, speechless, I remembered the sudden snap I'd felt when our eyes had met, the day he'd ridden Errant on the bridle paths and been mistaken for me. *Don't worry,* he'd said as we'd parted. *I'll tell nobody.*

At the time, smarting from his suggestion that I might be meeting with 'bad company' when I was riding out, I had misunderstood him. So he'd known! And probably Lady Sylvia had known as well, judging from the looks she was exchanging with the Goodwins.

"The real question," said his lordship, "is how Norton made your being a girl a matter for blackmail."

"That's easy, sir," I said, gradually recovering my voice. "He said Sir Thomas would dismiss my father if it were found out his Head Groom had kept the truth from him."

"Good heavens!" said Lady Sylvia. "Did you think that true?"

Knowing what I knew now about Sir Thomas's pride, I could hardly say no, but my silence hovered in the air until Errant began to paw the grass. As Lord Sandford frowned at him, I looked at Lady Sylvia. "Almost everything that Mr. Norton told me was false. I'd rather not explain all of it, if you don't mind."

Lord Sandford turned back to me. "So far as I'm concerned, the only thing you need to explain is why a horse as beautifully trained as this one hasn't been taught to stand."

I blushed as Errant dug up another tuft. "I thought it was just a part of the way he was."

Lady Sylvia laughed. "And I suppose you thought it was inborn patience that made Atlas and Goodwin's team stand for minutes at a time?"

We all laughed at that, and Lord Sandford took the horses' reins from me, gesturing towards the gate. "Dust Atlas off and saddle him up, why don't you, Harry? You can show us the way back through Chandace Grange."

It was an order like Hugh's, and I took it in the same spirit, pausing only to give Mrs. Goodwin a hug before I ran off. As I saddled Atlas, I heard the Goodwins' voices rise in astonishment, but I could catch no words. I kept my face neutral as I joined them, but I couldn't help noticing that Goodwin looked as if somebody had given him a hogshead of ale, and that Mrs. Goodwin was smiling through tears.

"Off we go, Harry!" said Lord Sandford, looking a little embarrassed, and we trotted down to the fork and up the lane towards Chandace Grange.

As we neared the view at the top of the rise, Lady Sylvia urged Sebilla beside Errant. "This is the spot I was telling you about," she said. "Isn't it beautiful?"

Lord Sandford, who had clearly been thinking of something else, pulled Errant up and gazed at it. "Lovely! The essence of Old England." He shook his head. "The way its traditions linger drives me to distraction, but . . . here it is."

If only it weren't so damn beautiful.

I hadn't realized I'd spoken aloud, but Lord Sandford and Lady Sylvia both looked at me with sympathetic surprise.

"It's hard to think of it as anything else," said Lady Sylvia. "But when I look at this, I remember my father's estate, which is being swallowed up by London. It's right. It's just. How can it not be, when it gives homes to thousands of families instead of only one and fifty tenants? But all its old loveliness is covered by row houses, now."

"There has to be an alternative, by God," said Lord Sandford. "If there isn't, I'm going to invent one. Like your hospital, it'll be a gamble, but it's worth the risk."

I looked at Lady Sylvia. "Your hospital?"

"The Baineses and I are going to turn Chandace Grange into a hospital. We'll lease the farm from Sandy, here—" she nodded to Lord Sandford "—and gradually we'll build up a place that provides inexpensive professional help to people with problems like influenza, minor injuries, childbirth."

Childbirth. What a difference such a place would have made to my mother . . . I stopped, suddenly asking myself, *Which mother?* And answering, *Both.*

"It's a terrific undertaking," said Lord Sandford. "It and the stable are a substantial part of the alternative. And the Goodwins seem to be open to all sorts of ideas for dividing their farm equitably amongst its present tenants."

"The Goodwins!" I began—but he went on.

"The problem," he said, "is the bungalows, which will change the nature of the place entirely. The work has stopped on the place now, which makes the time ripe to make an offer on the Haskins farm. Unfortunately, Norton left it to his kid, and it seems cruel to deal with him and his mother right now."

His kid. "The Haskins Farm belongs to Cyril now?"

"That little brat you gave a ride to?" asked Lady Sylvia.

"Yes, but he's not all brat." I told them about Cyril's lessons on Atlas, and the promise he'd kept about the catapult.

"Hm," said Lord Sandford. "With his father and those minions of his out of the way, maybe he'd be a decent kid if he had a pony to help him along. I have a good, solid Welsh cross coming with the rest, probably next week. Let's see if we can at least strike up a friendship with the boy and his mum, leaving talk about the farm until later."

"Ripping!" I said. "Only—wait! You said the Welsh cross was coming with 'the rest.' How many horses will that be?"

"Ten," he said, smiling. "Two Viennese mares I'm hoping Errant will take a fancy to, two ponies, and six exquisitely-bred youngsters nobody has had time to train. With estates closing and the number of motors rising, it has been easy to find good horses. Not to mention, good grooms."

I felt a sudden chill. "My father . . . ?"

The two of them laughed. "Harry," said his lordship, "Ned Green has a reputation famous throughout England. Every lad I've convinced to work in my stable has said he would be honored to work under him." He tapped Errant's shoulder to stop him from pawing the lane before looking at me again. "And I'm sure that once the original shock has worn off, none of them will object to working with a rider as fine as *Harriet* Green."

I looked once more at the vista, thinking of Hugh and feeling Lady Sylvia's eyes watch me. Finally, I heard myself say, "Thank you, my lord. I'm honored by your offer, and I'll be happy to work in the stable as much as I can. But this morning I decided to attend the Lechlade School, and—"

"Whoop!" shouted Lady Sylvia, sending Sebilla into a little pirouette of surprise. "Harry, that's wonderful! Joseph and Lucinda Baines will be dancing in the streets, and Richard will play the pipes!"

She checked Sebilla's prancing and looked at me more seriously. "Among other things, the Lechlade School may soften the shock you'll feel when it becomes generally known you're a girl. Bright stable boys are generally accepted by other men, whereas women . . . well, the wretched class system isn't the only one that represses without meaning to be unjust. Think of Sir Thomas's reaction to my riding astride, or of his disapproval of my driving—and that's only the beginning. Still, if you can face down a murderer, I daresay you can deal with a little masculine disapproval."

"I should say so," said Lord Sandford with a respectful glance that made me blush. "Too bad you weren't with me when I tried facing down the Olympic Committee. You should have *seen* their horror when I suggested that women should compete in future Equestrian Events."

"Outmoded Victorian idiots," muttered Lady Sylvia.

"Exactly!" his lordship agreed. "But as I say, there are alternatives— and in a few years, I'm willing to bet Willingford Hall will have established itself as a venue for dressage meets in which women and men can compete on equal footing."

"You mean . . . you mean . . ." I stammered, ". . . Errant and I could . . . ?"

His lordship gave me a smile that somehow reminded me of Hugh's. "I'll look forward to seeing you best all the others, m'lass. Between now and then, go to the Lechlade School, maybe even to Oxford or London. I'll join Richard on the pipes, and the stable can, as the Americans say, work around the rest." He touched Errant with his heel, and the three of us rode down the rise together.

Epilogue

21 April 1919

On Easter Monday, I worked Errant on lead changes for a half hour, and he did them so beautifully that Lord Sandford said I should reward him with a good trot and canter on the bridle paths. I had many things to do, but the day was glorious, with leaves beginning to burst out and a breeze that seemed to pull the sunlight out of the air.

So I nodded, waved to my father—who had been watching us with a couple of the new lads—and headed to the Dell, planning to ride to the vista Hugh had loved. As we neared the Dell, Errant shortened his stride just enough to remind me that although full spring and the flurry of events made it feel as if it had been months since he'd been cruelly hit by a stone from Mr. Norton's catapult, it had in fact been only six weeks.

Errant and I had both learned a great deal from Lord Sandford in those weeks, I reflected. But outside the manège, my education had been . . . well, extensive. Mrs. Baines had taken me to a barber who had tamed my self-cut hair into what she called "a bob." She'd also taught me how to manage skirts, wear women's shoes, and iron blouses.

Lady Sylvia had expunged "sir" and "ma'am" from my vocabulary and taught me how to carry myself like an independent woman instead of a stable boy or a servant. Doctor Baines had shown me plant and animal cells through his microscope and given me fascinating scientific articles to discuss with him. Richard had insisted that I visit him for an hour each day to talk over the newspapers he received.

My father and I had moved back into the Head Groom's cottage. No longer freed from domestic chores by the servants' hall, I'd dredged up the cooking skills I'd learned from Mum, Father had gone to market with Lord Sandford's kitchen boy, and, to my gratified surprise, we'd more or less shared whatever dusting, sweeping, and washing up needed to be done.

The true tale of my birth still lay between us, with unspoken regrets on his side and equally unspoken reproaches on mine. Keeping up the cottage, however, made us lose some of the frozen distance that had grown between us since Mum's death, and so for the moment, I let the past rest.

I felt a little adrift in the stream of all these new things. What I learned frequently made me see that life outside the whole wretched system was short on certainties I'd always taken for granted. But my old fears of being found out, and even the nightmares that had haunted my sleep, gradually faded away, and I was looking forward to tomorrow's beginning of term with only a little trepidation.

Errant brought me back to the present by snorting at a few lambs, and, laughing, I turned onto the North Road. Suddenly, his ears shot forward, and I halted him in surprise, for a motor had stopped on the far side of the bridge, and a lanky man was leaning against it. For a moment, all my old fears clustered around me, but the clatter of hoofbeats made him turn towards us and limp forward with a smile.

"Tim!" I shouted joyously. "I didn't know you were back!"

"Got in late last night," he said, walking towards us as we crossed the bridge. "Your father told me you'd be riding this way, so thought I'd stop by and pass on greetings from Sir Thomas—not to mention Mrs. Middleton and Mr. Parks."

I stared at him. "They're with him in Bournemouth?"

Tim nodded. "Sir Thomas has leased a house he likes there, and he says the sea air has been good for his cough. It's probably more relief from financial troubles and the shock of the murders, but he's looking better than he has for years, and he has made friends in circumstances similar to his own, so he plans to stay there permanently."

He glanced up at me. "You're thinking of Hugh."

"I'm always thinking of Hugh," I said. "But he'd approve, don't you think?"

"Absolutely. The stable has its old hum, not to mention its great plans. And Sandford is slowly working on the kinds of land divisions Hugh wanted to do. It's complicated, legally speaking—Lovejoy is tearing his hair, but I think he's enjoying the challenge."

"And you?" I said, looking at him closely. "You look . . . radiant!"

"The absence of pain can have that effect," he said, with the smile I remembered from the days before the trenches. "The doctor Baines referred me to worked miracles."

"So soon you'll be interviewing likely lads to work under you as police chief?"

"I'm not sure," he said. "The Council wants to hire somebody to do investigative work for them, at roughly double the salary and four times the challenge of police work. They insisted that I meet with them as soon as I got home."

"You mean they want to make you a detective?"

"I'll tell you as soon as I find out myself," he said. "Which should be at eleven o'clock today. In the meantime, I wanted to be sure to catch you before you start at the Lechlade School, because I might be of use to you."

I frowned. "With lessons?"

"No, no! With transportation. That was so complicated in my day that some nights Charlie Goodwin had to stay in town. But now, with the Farrington Farm becoming the Goodwin Farm, and my moving with my parents into the Goodwin's old cottage behind the stable—"

"—You'll get awfully wet. They're still replacing its roof."

"I'm promised it will keep us dry by the end of the week. And Lord Sandford hopes I'll buy it."

"Buy it! Is that possible?"

"He's determined to *make* it possible. That's one of the details Lovejoy is tearing his hair about. But the point is, soon I'll be living near you and the Rushdales, and I'll have a motor. So unless there's an emergency, I should be able to drive you to my old school on my way to work, leaving Rushdale to collect you at the end of the day. If you approve, of course."

"Approve! That would be ripping!" I caught myself. "Can I still say that?"

"Harry the Brave, you can save the world a lot of foolish prevarication by saying anything you want. Within reason, of course. Or even beyond it, come to think of it. Listen to Lady Sylvia sometime when she's angry—she picked up an admirable 'masculine' vocabulary at the Front."

I thought of arguing that an earl's daughter could use language in a way a girl of indeterminate status could not. Instead, I found myself saying, "Were you disappointed?"

"Disappointed? At what?"

"At my being . . . not masculine."

"Relieved, is closer to the mark," he said, briefly laying his hand on my knee. "It was getting harder and harder not to notice." He stepped back as Errant began to paw the cobblestones. "Off with you, now! I'll see you tomorrow morning at half-past six."

I'd planned to ride up the path to the vista at a trot, but after we'd turned at the fork, I urged Errant into a hand gallop up the rise. He expressed his approval with an enormous buck—and instead of checking him, I let out a whoop that made the workers in the field turn and laugh.

Acknowledgments

I owe many thanks to my family, which has read drafts of this book many times. My daughters, Meg Staloff and Kate O'Connell, have been through this before, and have been uniformly encouraging. My son-in-law Jason Staloff has proofread every chapter and guided me through the computerized labyrinth of preparing it for the press. My sister Diana Banat has read at least two versions, always supportively. Arthur and Lynda Copeland read early drafts and made me clear up many inconsistencies. Their granddaughter, Katrina Schmitt, provided essential pointers about dressage and horse personalities. Everybody has been most patient with my periods of distraction and frustration.

My debt is great to the fellow writers whose comments grace its pages: Janis Bellow-Freedman, Melanie Finn, Beth Kanell, Liza Ketchum, Reeve Lindbergh, and Scudder Parker.

Many thanks are also due to Stephen McArthur of Rootstock Publishing, who declared himself hooked on the manuscript after reading its first forty pages; to Rickey Gard Diamond, my intrepid editor; and to Samantha Kolber and Marisa Keller, who have guided me through the publication process. Many thanks to Timothy Jay Newcomb for the map of Willingford Hall. Nancy Libby deserves my deep gratitude for her patience and the beautiful painting on the cover.

About the Author

Laura C. Stevenson is the award-winning author of four novels for young adults and two for adults, as well as the author of a monograph on Elizabethan literature and society, several articles on the Golden Age of Children's Literature, and three essays on deafness. She was trained as a historian at the University of Michigan and Yale University, and she taught writing and humanities at Marlboro College from 1986 to 2013. She lives in her family's old summer house in Vermont.

 **Also Available from Rootstock Publishing:**

The Atomic Bomb on My Back by Taniguchi Sumiteru

Pauli Murray's Revolutionary Life by Simki Kuznick

Blue Desert by Celia Jeffries

China in Another Time: A Personal Story by Claire Malcolm Lintilhac

Collecting Courage: Anti-Black Racism in the Charitable Sector
Edited by Nneka Allen, Camila Vital Nunes Pereira, & Nicole Salmon

An Everyday Cult by Gerette Buglion

Fly with A Murder of Crows: A Memoir by Tuvia Feldman

Horodno Burning: A Novel by Michael Freed-Thall

I Could Hardly Keep from Laughing by Don Hooper & Bill Mares

The Inland Sea: A Mystery by Sam Clark

Intent to Commit by Bernie Lambek

Junkyard at No Town by J.C. Myers

The Language of Liberty: A Citizen's Vocabulary by Edwin C. Hagenstein

A Lawyer's Life to Live by Kimberly B. Cheney

Lifting Stones: Poems by Doug Stanfield

The Lost Grip: Poems by Eva Zimet

Lucy Dancer Story and Illustrations by Eva Zimet

Nobody Hitchhikes Anymore by Ed Griffin-Nolan

Preaching Happiness: Creating a Just and Joyful World by Ginny Sassaman

Red Scare in the Green Mountains: Vermont in the McCarthy Era 1946-1960 by Rick Winston

Safe as Lightning: Poems by Scudder H. Parker

Street of Storytellers by Doug Wilhelm

Tales of Bialystok: A Jewish Journey from Czarist Russia to America by Charles Zachariah Goldberg

To the Man in the Red Suit: Poems by Christina Fulton

Uncivil Liberties: A Novel by Bernie Lambek

Venice Beach: A Novel by William Mark Habeeb

The Violin Family by Melissa Perley; Illustrated by Fiona Lee Maclean

Walking Home: Trail Stories by Celia Ryker

Wave of the Day: Collected Poems by Mary Elizabeth Winn

Whole Worlds Could Pass Away: Collected Stories by Rickey Gard Diamond

You Have a Hammer: Building Grant Proposals for Social Change by Barbara Floersch

CPSIA information can be obtained
at www.ICGtesting.com
Printed in the USA
BVHW080813160122
625815BV00001B/5

9 781578 690794